W9-BOD-116

Hill of Secrets

MICHAL HARTSTEIN

Copyright © 2013 by Michal Hartstein
All rights reserved
ISBN: 150057788X
ISBN-13: 978-1500577889

DEDICATION

To my husband and my son

ACKNOWLEDGMENTS

I would like to thank my parents, Adina and Asher Kruk, for their support, and to my dear friend, Orit Reuven, for her patience and understanding. I would like also to thank Yuval Gilad and Yael Shachnay, who helped me editing the book.

CHAPTER 1

Monday, 5.18.2009

A month before Meir Danilowitz got up in the middle of the night to shoot his entire family and then himself to death, I divorced my husband. My name is Hadas Levinger; I am thirty-three years old and am a detective with the Israeli Police. Although, if you ask my mother, she would better define this situation as, "a successful lawyer who decided to throw her career in the trash to become a cop."

After a year serving on the force, during which I did not take one day off, I decided to use all the vacation days I had left to go to London and forget the gloomy reality of my life. Did I ask too much? Some museums, some theater, lots of much needed serenity. I had to relax and distance myself. I just needed to get away—from my stressful, all-consuming job, from Alon, my uncompromising commander, from my somewhat overinvolved family, but mostly from Yinon, the man I loved and had not stopped loving for the last seven years.

I was perusing the email I'd been sent from the travel agency, comparing the different deals. Everything was too expensive for a police officer, but I knew I had to run away. I fantasized about losing myself among the bizarre shops and street artists in Covent Garden, about napping on a bench in the shade of

Kensington Gardens, but then my cell phone rang.

It was Alon.

I was sure he had a problem with the Vaserano indictment that I had brought to him the day before.

"Good morning," I said pleasantly, hoping to set a positive tone.

"Levinger." He ignored the niceties, as he usually does, and got straight to the point. "Drop whatever you're doing and go to Harduf Hanechalim 6 in Givaat Shmuel."

"Alon—" I paused for a moment, fearing that every word I said might be interpreted as disrespect. "You remember I'm on vacation, right?"

"Are you at home?"

"Yes."

"Are you going anywhere?"

"Yes."

"Where?"

"London."

"When?"

"I don't have a ticket yet…"

"Great. So get down here as quickly as possible—the vacation's off."

I rummaged through my closet and managed to find some sort of appropriate attire—something that I wouldn't have to answer to my mother about later on. Alon refused to tell me what this was about, but the urgency in his voice made me worry that I may be filmed by the news that day, and the last thing I needed was a lecture from my mother about the way I looked and how dare I go on television like that.

I think I'm pretty quick, even compared to men. During the whole of my five-year marriage, Yinon never had to wait for me (I, on the other hand, sometimes waited ages while he finished getting ready), but I apparently wasn't quick enough for Alon, who kept calling me every five minutes.

On his third call, I was already starting my battered old Fiat.

"Levinger," Alon said, "how's it going?"

"I'm on my way, but I'm out of gas."

"You're not out of anything; you probably still have a quarter of a tank and you're just stressing out. You only have to get to Givaat Shmuel."

"The yellow light's been on for two days now."

"Why do you always leave everything to the last minute?" he huffed.

"Well, I didn't think my car would be leaving the driveway during the next two weeks…" I tried to retort.

"Okay, but make it quick. You can even go to the competition," he joked, and I knew he wasn't angry. When the Dor family son was born forty- three years earlier, they didn't imagine that his name would be the name of a chain of gas stations.

Thirty-five minutes after Alon's first phone call, I arrived at the address that he had dictated to me six times in the last half hour. It was a small alley perpendicular to new Givaat Shmuel's main street, about 200 meters from the building my sister lives in. Despite this, I was not familiar with the street. I only ever came to Givaat Shmuel to visit my sister. It wasn't exactly the place for shopping or leisure.

In the last couple of years, Givaat Shmuel had become a stronghold of the middle class Religious Zionist public. About two-thirds of my classmates from the religious high school I attended had moved to this neighborhood in the past decade, and that alone was reason enough to steer clear of the place. This was not the best location for misanthropes; you needed social resilience of the kind that I have not yet managed to acquire.

Outside, two police cars had been parked with some fanfare, and the people of the neighborhood had begun to gather around the building. Even before I understood the magnitude of the event, I knew it was a matter of minutes before our dear friends from the media would arrive at the scene.

It was also clear to Alon, and once he saw me arrive, he nearly dragged me into his car, which was parked on the curb near the building's entrance.

"Levinger," he said with a serious tone, "I'm giving you an opportunity here."

I felt like this was the investigation that would finally establish my place in the unit.

"I was deliberating about who to give this case to, and I chose you, despite the vacation I know you're cancelling because of me."

I smiled.

"No need to smile; actually, the other investigators are pretty busy right now."

My smile vanished.

"But not only because of that. As far as I recall, you're the only detective in the department with a religious background."

"Ephraim and Asher are religious."

"Ephraim and Asher are buried in other investigations."

"Why would you need a religious background?"

"I have a feeling we need someone familiar with the neighborhood and the community. Doesn't your brother live around here?"

"My sister... don't tell me you want me to involve her in the investigation?"

"Of course not, but I'm sure she could help you get closer to the community."

"Religious Zionists—knitted yarmulke wearers—are not like Haredi Jews. It's not a closed community. I don't think I'll be needing that sort of help."

"Maybe we should continue to the crime scene?" He changed the subject.

"Maybe we should."

"Before we go up, I must warn you it's a very rough scene. One of the roughest I've ever seen, and I'm sure the worst you'll have seen." I was already nervous so I didn't stop him.

Alon took a deep breath and continued. "This morning, a few minutes before nine o'clock, a call was received by the 100 police hotline. A woman named Aviva Levin called and said she couldn't reach her daughter, Hannah, or her son-in-law, Meir. Hannah was supposed to meet her mother at eight o'clock, and when she didn't arrive, she tried to call her son-in-law's cell phone, to no avail. She called the granddaughter's kindergarten and the grandson's school and discovered that they were both absent that morning. She called Meir's workplace and heard that he missed a very important meeting scheduled for eight-thirty that morning. By that point, she was really panicked."

"Wait," I stopped him. "She didn't call Hannah's workplace?"

"I'm happy to see you're paying attention. Hannah hasn't worked these last few years, since their second child was born."

"How many kids do they have?"

"They had three kids." Alon used the past tense and I realized this was not going to be simple.

"I don't exactly remember their names, but the oldest was a boy, in second grade, their second, a girl, probably recently turned five and the baby girl was four months old."

My jaw dropped. Alon ignored it and went on. "While we requested Mrs. Levin to keep trying to reach them, we sent a patrol car to the family's house. Because we were unable to locate any of them, and since no one answered the officers' knocks at the door, they broke in and found the entire family dead."

"Wow," I blurted out, horrified, even though I had already realized where this story was going. "Do we know the cause of death?"

"Apparently, gunshot wounds from a pistol belonging to the father."

I looked away. How could someone kill a four-month-old baby?

"Hadas, it's a rough scene, but there's no choice. If you want to be in charge of this investigation, you have to see it before it's disturbed."

I nodded and we exited the car. I saw that there were now even more curious bystanders surrounding the building. People still had no idea why there were two police cars parked below the building.

We went up to the fourth floor, to Apartment 14. A police officer was standing at the door, keeping passersby from entering. Alon waved his badge and we entered the apartment.

The first thing I saw was the body of seven-and-a-half-year-old Ariel, lying between the living room and the dining room. In the dining room, two shocked policemen were sitting with distressed looks splashed across their faces. In the carefully designed living room, on a pastel-colored sofa, lay the father. The gun, from which the shots were apparently fired, lay between the sofa and the coffee table.

I approached the gun and carefully picked it up. The barrel was covered by a makeshift silencer made of mineral wool, which was probably why no one heard anything.

We continued to the bedrooms, down the hall to Galit's room. The door was closed. Apparently, the police officers couldn't bear the sight. On the door was a colorful poster: "Happy 5th Birthday Galit!" I opened the door. I couldn't have imagined a more painful contrast than that of the childish, pink room and the tiny little girl lying at the foot of the bed. By the way the body lay, I conjectured that she'd woken up and sat up before she was shot. A gaping red hole scarred her small body, and in her hand was still a (presumably brand new) Bratz doll. The doll and the girl were in a pool of blood.

"Do you want to take a break?" Alon asked me. I guess the worst was yet to come; I still hadn't seen baby Noa's body.

"No, it's okay," I breathed heavily. "I want to survey the scene and get out of here as soon as possible."

We continued down the hall and reached the parents' bedroom.

On the double bed was the body of Hannah, the mother. I looked at her. She was a very beautiful woman. Even the bullet hole staining her forehead didn't tarnish her classic look of loveliness: long hair, now caked with blood; high cheekbones; and plump, colorless lips. Even though she had given birth just four months before, her body was apparently back to its previous shape, and it seemed as if she was lying on the side of the bed where she slept every night, her lower half covered.

"Did anyone cover her?" I ask Alon.

"No, the patrol officers didn't touch anything."

At the edge of the room, right next to the bed and nearby Hannah's body, stood a small crib. I approached it with great angst. Even though I already knew what I would find in there, I wished that maybe they had all been wrong—maybe the baby had survived. My stomach churned and my face twisted at the horrifying sight carving its way into my eyes. In the crib was another dead body: the tiny, pale corpse of a baby lying in a small pool of blood.

I accidentally touched the mobile attached to the crib, and it began turning and playing the tune of a well-known nursery rhyme. The sight of the tiny, lifeless baby with four stuffed animals revolving above it to the sound of *Twinkle Twinkle Little Star* was unbearable. I struggled with the mobile to shut it off, but couldn't stop it.

I stood above Noa's little body for several more seconds. I turned to Alon with tears in my eyes.

"I have to leave now," I said, choking back tears. I had to get some air.

I ran outside, to the hallway and elevator. I went out to the building's parking lot and again noticed the gathering of curious neighbors, mostly senior citizens and young mothers. Also, there was the broadcast van of one of the news channels. I know I couldn't be seen like this, but I couldn't help it. I hid behind two columns and puked my guts out. When I tried to lift myself up, dripping tears and vomit, I was so dizzy from the gruesome sights that I nearly fell over. Alon caught me.

*H"*ere." He handed me a cold bottle of water. I gulped it down.

"Thank you," I said, almost whispering. "I'm sorry about how I reacted, but it's just horrifying".

"Take it easy. One of the patrol officers didn't even make it as far as the parking lot."

"Don't tell me he threw up at the scene!" I was appalled by the thought that the crime scene had been tainted by the vomit of one of the officers.

"No." He smiled, happy to see me keeping my focus even in my emotional state. "He made it to the elevator."

"Ugh." I made a face.

"Luckily for us, the building was cleaned today."

Alon gave me a few more minutes to calm down. The forensics team had just arrived, so he approached them and escorted them up to the scene. He came back about ten minutes later.

"I'm guessing the guys from forensics didn't throw up."

"They've seen a lot, but I know this is one of the roughest scenes I've ever seen—I'm sure they're not indifferent to it either." Alon was quiet for a few seconds before regaining his official tone. "So… what do you say, Levinger?"

“I want to go back up."

"Are you sure?"

"Yes," I lied.

We went back up to the apartment. Now, all the patrol officers were sitting in the hallway and Alon instructed two of them to go down and help control the crowd gathering around the building.

I entered the apartment again, and even though I knew what I was about to see, the scene was still hard to stomach. However, I knew I had to examine the scene carefully if I wanted to head this investigation properly.

"So what do you think?"

"The apartment was locked from the inside when the cops broke in?"

"Correct."

"Okay." I took a deep breath. "Let me go through the bedrooms again."

Now that I was already aware of what I'd be seeing, the surprise factor disappeared. This didn't make it much easier, though. I noted that all of the windows were shut in a way that is usually possible only from inside the apartment, which reinforced the suspicion that the killer didn't escape via a window and the assumption that the killer carefully planned the murder and made sure that the sound of the gunshots, which was lessened by the makeshift silencer, wouldn't reach the neighboring apartments. This time, I lingered longer around each body, occasionally consulting with the forensics team and making some requests about gunpowder residue and fingerprints, mainly from the doors and the windows around the whole apartment.

When I finally reached the final bedroom, even though I already knew what I'd see, I couldn't look into the crib. The sight of that baby was etched in my memory, and I also knew that the forensics team would photograph it from every possible angle.

I looked at the mother's dead body. A strange sensation came over me. I returned to the hall, but shortly after, turned around, reentered the bedroom and took a good look at Hannah's peaceful, lifeless face.

I knew what was bothering me.

It was Hanni Levin from my grade at school.

Hanni Levin and I studied at the religious high school for girls in Ramat Gan. Actually, in my day, the high school was still a mixed sex school and not just for girls. We were in the second to last class that still allowed boys. Unfortunately, in the process of becoming more religious—or more Haredi, I should say—Religious Zionist fervor also swept over my school, causing the school to lose its unique character as one of the few religious high schools that taught both boys and girls in the same educational institution.

Now, my connection to the religious public and especially to my former classmates was weak, but as far as I knew, it was a good move on their part. The rate of those leaving the religious life (*Yetzia Besheela*) in the mixed grades was much higher than that of girls who studied in single sex schools.

To be honest, I never really left religion; I was simply never truly religious. My parents raised me on the heritage of the Hapoe'l Hamizrachi (Eastern Worker) movement, on values of religion and labor. But they stressed the fact that I should develop the ability to think independently. I always considered myself a relatively intelligent person and couldn't understand how so many other people, some with no less IQ than mine, blindly followed religious rulings completely detached from reality.

Many religious people cut corners here and there and said, with a little smirk, "That's not what God meant." This is exactly the point I argued, which my family members refused to listen to. I claimed that God (if He even exists, but that's a different story altogether) didn't mean any word or interpretation written in all of the Halacha books, which are all entirely created by men, and, if I say so myself, in many cases, were not His best work.

In my case, the fact that I studied in the same class with boys didn't have any effect on the fact that I eventually went astray. When I was a student in high school, my only friends were girls. We were a group of five girls: Dganit, Tamar, Anat, Inbal and myself. We separated ourselves socially, especially from the boys' class.

While all the others from our grade met every Friday night on the street corner across from the local Bnei Akivah chapter, flirting and hanging out, we met at one of our houses to fantasize about the day we would also have the courage to sit on the street corner with all the cool boys and girls. Don't get me wrong, the meetings on the street across from Bnei Akivah were not especially glamorous affairs. Not dance parties full of alcohol and cigarette smoke like secular youth, just a get-together of all the guys and girls. Everyone was dressed in accordance with the Bnei Akivah dress code: boys in tailored pants and a white shirt and the girls in skirts no higher than the knee and long sleeved blouses.

Not really Sodom and Gomorrah. The most risqué it could

get was if someone invited a girl for a walk around the nearby synagogue, which led to much speculation, the most extreme of which was that they kissed. This was, more or less, the farthest we dared to go.

The fact that we avoided social contact with our male classmates didn't stem from religious modesty, but from chronic shyness. We very much wanted to talk to them, but we couldn't. Almost every Friday, we would plan to go to the street corner and we almost always ended up in one of the girls' houses. On the few occasions we reached the street corner, we understood why we never came. No one took the slightest notice of us. Nothing was done maliciously. Everyone always greeted us nicely and even chatted with us a bit about the recent history exam or the latest gossip about the civics teacher, but after a few minutes of polite chit chat, we were left alone on the street corner.

The couch at home was much more comfortable. There, we could also talk freely, that is, gossip about all of the grade hotshots. At some stage we were dubbed "The Convent." I think I invented that nickname, but I might be mistaken.

Once we finished high school, we parted ways, although we still tried to meet up on Fridays. This became more difficult with time. Dganit and I went to the army, while Tamar, Inbal and Anat did civil service.

The first one who officially left the convent was Anat. During her civil service, she met Motti, and by the age of twenty she was a married woman. I was happy for my friend, but there was also a little pinch in my heart. I knew the age of The Convent was over.

Hanni Levin, on the other hand, spent almost every Friday night on the street corner and was always surrounded by boys. She was a true beauty. None of The Convent girls were ugly—we were all fairly normal girls, nice looking, even pretty—but no one was as beautiful as Hanni. The word about her spread as far as the Malabes branch. In fact, we all called her "Pretty Hanni." Not that there was an ugly Hanni, but that’s just how she was known.

Hanni had blonde hair—*naturally* blonde hair (in religious society, teenagers don't normally dye their hair)—and huge blue eyes. Although it was not acceptable for us to wear revealing clothing, Hanni knew how to show off an amazing sculpted body within the appropriate boundaries. Years after we finished high school, I ran into her at the grocery store. She was with her son, who was rather small then, and she was much less beautiful than I remembered. Everything was still in place: the hair, the eyes, even the body, but there was something a bit more fatigued about her.

In the store, as in all of the years we studied together, Hanni made a point of ignoring me. I looked at her passing through the aisles of fruit and vegetables, occasionally scolding her little boy who was running all around the shop. There were moments when our eyes almost met, but she kept from looking in my direction. I had a feeling this was not accidental. In high school, the little attention I did receive from the cool kids came from the fact that I was a very good student and someone always needed some favor from me.

Hanni didn't need me. She was an excellent student in her own right. Actually, she was younger than all of us because she skipped the first grade. I think she was just jealous of me. She was good, but I was a little bit better than she was and didn't fuss over my grades too much. The few times she gave me any notice was after math tests. She always compared her score with mine, which were usually the same.

In our math midterm in the 12th grade, I finished first (as I usually did) and was waiting outside for Tamar, who studied for five study units along with me. A few more students came out after me and about five minutes before the test ended, Hanni came out as well. As usual, she approached me to compare results. All of our answers were the same except for one main, very complicated question which was worth fifteen points. Hanni was alarmed and rushed to compare her answer with the others that had come out of the class by then. Most of the students got an answer similar to hers. No one got mine.

"Don't worry," she said, with a smile she couldn't hide, "Eighty-five's also a good score." She tried to console me.

A week later, we came to school for a physics lesson that would prepare us for the final test. To our surprise, the math tests were already checked and ready to be returned to us. I was the only one who scored 100. Hanni got ninety (the teacher gave her five points out of fifteen for the question that rest of the class failed to answer, apart from me). I will never forget the cold, hard glare she gave me, as if I stole ten points from her. As if I was guilty for the fact that only I managed to answer the question correctly.

The other students got grades ranging from thirty to eighty-five. Hanni wouldn't accept the respectable second place; she went to school management and demanded they cancel the "faulty" question.

"It's impossible that only one student could solve it, apparently by chance," she lectured. In the end, everyone was awarded an extra 5 points (except for me because I couldn't score over 100) and the teacher agreed to give her a 100 as her final grade.

I hadn't seen her since we graduated from high school (apart from that time at the grocery store). She did a year of service while I, as an officer, served in the army for almost four years. Occasionally, when I met with my Convent friends, we would talk about her, just as we talked about the rest of our classmates. That was how I learned that right after her year of service she started law school at Bar-Ilan University. There, she also excelled and made sure that her successes were well publicized (the news of them reached me, so there you go).

At the age of twenty-three, after four years in the army and a year of travelling in South America and the United States, I began law school at Tel-Aviv University. Hanni was already at the height of her internship.

Now, Hanni was lying still on the bed. The bullet hole disfigured her forehead and her light hair was streaked with the blood that had flowed from her skull. Although we weren't friends, it was painful for me to see her like this. I recalled her smiling, confident and exuberant image, and my heart cringed.

I knew she had married a guy named Meir, who was one of the more sought after bachelors (with a winning combination of good looks and a wealthy family) in Petach Tikva. What brought this Meir, who was now lying lifeless on the leather couch in their living room, to shoot his wife and three kids and then take his own life? Or maybe our presumption was wrong. Maybe the killer was on the loose?

Who had put an end to this ideal family?

A killer from outside the family was an interesting, and even possible theory—maybe even a professional? Someone able to do a job like this quietly and leave the apartment with no uncovered tracks? But why would a professional do something like this? What could the Danilowitz family have done to anyone?

The gun that was probably used to commit the murder was found in the living room near Meir's body, which was why he was the main suspect, but Ariel's body was also found not far from the weapon. Maybe Ariel found his daddy's gun and thought it was a toy? It was a bizarre scenario, but not something completely detached from reality that hadn't happened before.

That same day, I crossed little Ariel off the list of potential suspects because the bullet that killed him entered his body from the back. The thought that this infant child probably ran for his life horrified me. How could someone shoot a child in the back?

There were no signs of forced entry. The door was, as we already knew, locked from inside, and the apartment's windows were shut tightly and securely. The balcony that was used as a laundry room was the only place where a potential intruder could have escaped from the scene, but no footprints were found to indicate someone had come in or out of the laundry room. The only prints found on the gun were Meir's, and there was gunpowder residue on his hands. Solid evidence, but the kind that is possible to fake.

Seemingly, there was no other option besides Meir, the father. According to the analysis of the scene, we estimated that Meir first shot his wife while she slept. Then he shot baby Noa; they were both killed in their sleep, so we assumed they were the first killed. Seven-year-old Ariel tried to escape and was shot in the back, and the body of five-year-old Galit was found shot dead at the foot of her bed. Apparently, she woke up, but the shooter caught her seconds after she left her bed. The body of Meir, the father, was found on the sofa. Meir was shot in the head at point blank range. The gun was lying on the floor and I assumed that, if Meir had killed himself, the gun's thrust cause it to fly from his hand.

The apartment was locked from the inside. There were no signs of forced entry. There were no visible signs on Meir to suggest a struggle with a potential killer. This was not the first time, and, unfortunately, wouldn't be the last, that a family member had committed such a horrifying act, but in spite of all the evidence, the thought of a father doing something like this was hard to stomach. Within me, I hoped that we would find an external killer (though I knew the chances of that were nonexistent), not that this would reduce the severity of the event, but it would remove the horrible thought that a father could do this to his own children.

Alon swore to me that he'd had no idea I knew Hanni from high school. "A chilling coincidence," was how he put it. Because I was never close with Hanni, I saw no reason to disqualify myself from the investigation. Alon thought so as well.

We decided not to ignore the option of a killer who escaped from the scene. Despite the miniscule chance of this, we assumed that if this was an escaped murderer, it had to be a skilled professional. Meir left no suicide note or explanation for this insane act, so we took the family's computer to be examined. We hoped to find a lead that would shed some light and maybe clarify the reasoning for this. Maybe we would find a motive for another killer?

A little before noon, we received word that Hanni's and Meir's parents had been notified. Hanni's mother wanted to come to the scene, but her husband and the police officers finally convinced her to relinquish the unbearable experience. Immediately after the families had been updated about the scale of this horror, we issued a press release. Alon wanted my inauguration to be complete, so I had to deal with the news reporters. I went down to the street, where the broadcast vans of all the Israeli news channels and two or three foreign press vans now stood.

I can imagine that some cops enjoy the limelight, especially those with flawless complexions or a blessed lack of personal awareness. I, unfortunately, was not blessed with either of these characteristics, nor did I have a personal makeup artist. I stood before the herd of vultures, praying that the cameras weren't seeing the new pimple that had sprouted on my chin or the dark circles that this week had sprouted under my eyes.

Again and again, I had to describe the gruesome scene, while attempting to be as gentle as possible. Apart from describing the bare facts (five family members dead) I added no detail. Of course, this didn't appease their insatiable hunger. I heard a barrage of questions, some relevant, most not: "When was the murder committed?" "How was it no one heard anything?" "Was this done by a professional hit man?" "A serial killer?" "Are the rumors about involvement with the Mob true?"

I never understood why reporters ask questions, knowing they weren't going to receive an answer. They may do it only to get their question heard. The fact that the question was asked was enough to generate a headline with an array of speculations, provocations, conspiracies and assumptions surrounding it.

When I got back to the office, I went over the details of the investigation again and again. It's a little hard to admit, but the longer you stare at them, the easier it is to see the gruesome images.

A short while after sitting down in my dark, little office, Amos from the computer lab called me. "Almost all of the data has been erased from the computer," he said, "including the internet search history."

"Can anything be restored?"

"Of course it can be restored," he chuckled. Amos was a computing genius who had turned down dozens of lucrative job offers from dozens of high-tech companies, preferring to work for next to nothing for the police. "It's just a question of time and a bit of luck," he explained.

"Take your time."

The fact that somebody went through the trouble of deleting all data from the computer showed meticulous planning. This was not a spontaneous murder. This was no act of insanity, but a calculated, cold-blooded murder. Someone tried to hide something before killing them all.

I was exhausted. I knew there was a lot of work ahead of me in the next few days, so I decided to go home earlier than would be expected on the first day of an investigation (about seven o'clock in the evening).

I stopped at Alon's office before I left.

"Leaving already?"

"I have to get a bit of rest; I don't have too much information to work with, anyway."

"It's not every day you see a scene like that," Alon nodded with understanding.

"I need a key to the scene," I said. A police locksmith had changed the locks of the apartment, which was now a crime scene. Alon handed me a key.

"The entry code downstairs is #2795."

"I'm going to go over there tomorrow morning."

"Do you want me to send someone there?"

"If I need anyone I'll contact you."

"No problem, I should be in the office all day tomorrow. If not, you can call my cell."

When I got home, I was too tired to cook anything for myself.

When we were married, Yinon would sometimes surprise me and cook me a pampering dinner, especially when I was working at Lipkin, Danieli and Co., the law firm, and had just come home from a non-stop work marathon.

Now, divorced and alone, I settled for a microwave pizza and half a carton of ice cream. Shira, my sister, was always appalled by my eating habits, even more so by the fact that I never gained an ounce.

The images from the scene kept running through my brain. I couldn't fall asleep. I took the best sleeping pill I could think of: I watched *Ferris Bueller's Day Off* for the 534th time (more or less), the well-known and beloved movie that had become a cult favorite of Yinon's and mine. Yinon and I had what you might call "cultural perversions," like listening religiously to Professor Karasso's shows on the radio on Friday afternoons, thus lowering the average age of his listeners to about sixty-five.

We never missed a public screening of *The Rocky Horror Picture Show* (always making sure to come equipped with newspapers, rice and candles) and our favorite movies were the teen movies of the eighties: *Can't Buy Me Love*, *The Breakfast Cl*ub, *Sixteen Candles, Pretty in Pink* and, most of all, *Ferris Bueller's Day Off*, a movie that always made us laugh and relaxed us, even though we knew all the lines by heart. The movie quickly succeeded in helping me forget my rough day and before Ferris Bueller got back home from a day of pure pleasure, I'd sunk into a deep sleep.

CHAPTER 2

Tuesday, 5.19.2009

The following day at the Danilowitz apartment, I was already better prepared to face the horror. Although the bodies had been transferred the day before to the Abu Kabir Forensic Institute to be autopsied, the blood stains and the marks made by the forensic team that remained in the apartment were terrible scars of the horrendous crime that had taken place there. Alon updated me that the funerals of the wife and children were to take place that day at the Yarkon Cemetery at four o'clock. Meir's parents, who understood the delicate situation, announced that they would not be coming to the funeral of their grandchildren and daughter-in-law.

I began surveying the apartment. One of the things that caught my attention was the fact that the apartment seemed very neat and organized, as if Hanni knew someone was coming to visit. I may be a bit overly sensitive to this because my house is always in chaos, and when someone comes over, I simply shove everything in a senseless jumble into closets and cupboards to create the illusion of a perfectly organized apartment. Despite the shocking crime which took place there, everything was, surprisingly, in its place.

I went into the kitchen and poured myself a glass of water. The kitchen was carefully decorated and trendy. White cupboards, red countertop, a silver table with red chairs to match. The housewares were lined up in the cupboards like an Ikea showroom. I opened the fridge, which was stocked full of plastic containers filled with cooked vegetables, rice and chicken left over from Shabbat, fresh fruit and vegetables, dairy products and yogurts. It was Tuesday. For the Danilowitz family, time stopped on Monday morning. This was a Sunday fridge, after a Shabbat full of meals.

I moved on to the living room. The marks where little Ariel's body had lain on the floor, and Meir's body on the sofa, sullied the stylish décor. Light leather couches, a heavy wooden table and a sideboard to match. A large LCD television and trendy spot lighting. A standard Israeli living room. The complete opposite of my living room, which had two worn-out sofas (a result of failing to educate the dog, who wreaked havoc on them), a glass-top table that I'd purchased for an exaggerated price on Herzl Street in Tel-Aviv (I was positive that I finally acquired some taste until my mother and sister saw it and nearly cried laughing) and a 32-inch television, not a flat screen.

It's true that an LCD TV is no longer a status symbol in our world, but in Meir and Hanni's apartment, everything exuded the air of petit bourgeois luxury. I'm not a big expert on home décor—I assume I could be tricked quite easily as to the true value of a couch or a chair—but I had no doubt that quite a bit of time and money had been invested in Meir and Hanni's apartment. No giant chandeliers or polished marble, but precise, clean decorating, where everything matched and, no less importantly, had its place. For example, the leather couches in the living room matched the leather seat covers on the heavy chairs in the dining room. The children's rooms were designed and fully equipped. Ariel's room was themed around race cars, including a bed in the shape of a giant car, and Galit's was pink and princess-themed.

Meir and Hanni's bedroom was spacious. In its center was a huge double bed; heavy wooden armoires matched the big closet against the wall. On the wall across from the bed was another large LCD television. Even the bathrooms, which were spotlessly clean, were tastefully decorated, with light wood cabinets and embellished china. I thought to myself that if someone had to survey my bathroom, I would die of shame, if my mother hadn't already killed me for the way I was so criminally neglecting myself. Broken and missing china, a decrepit shelf instead of a cabinet, not to mention scum and lime scale in every corner.

I opened the closets, which were packed with clothes, all neatly folded. I once again thought of my own closet; if one shirt was folded in there, it was accidental. My closet looked full, but only because I avoided tidying it.

In the study stood a state-of-the-art treadmill, folded up against the wall, and on the wall across from it was another LCD television. Under the window stood a desk, where once stood the computer that had been transferred to Amos's lab. In the room was a large cabinet, part of which was in a honeycomb formation and held picture albums, a few ring binders, a full Bible with interpretations and a few albums and reading books gathering dust on the top shelves.

I pulled out one of the picture albums. On its cover was inscribed, in large letters, "Holland—August 2008." The ultimate family vacation: a pregnant Hanni with her arms around her two older children with interchanging views in the background. Occasionally, Meir was also in the picture, or replaced Hanni to be photographed with his two kids.

I put the album back in its place and selected the one that I guessed was Hanni and Meir's wedding album. I was not mistaken.

According to the invitation stapled to the album, Meir and Hanni were married in a lavish wedding on December 28th, 2000 at one of Tel-Aviv's luxury hotels. Hanni could not have looked more regal than in the glamorous, slinky dress she was wearing. Meir was beaming with joy. He was right by her side in all of the photos, holding on to her like a child who had been given the most delicious lollipop in the candy store.

This couple was once happy and in love. What happened here? What caused this dream to be shattered? I took the photo album and placed it near the doorway. I wanted to scan some of the pictures so I would have pictures of the people close to the couple.

Above the album shelf was a black binder with no writing on it. I pulled the binder out and sat at the table. In it were erratically-filed pay stubs, employment agreements, insurance notices and policies, with no logical order or chronology. I knew Hanni had not worked for a number of years, so I didn't look for any contracts or pay stubs bearing her name.

I tried to organize Meir's paperwork a bit. It became clear to me that Meir worked for Discount Bank. I found a number of pay stubs from recent months. I continued perusing the binder and discovered that he had worked for a different company before working at Discount Bank. I was amazed by the difference in pay between the two work places. Meir was a graduate of the Department of Economics and Business Management at Bar Ilan University. At Discount Bank, he was most recently employed in a managerial role as an economist in the financial department and enjoyed a handsome gross salary of about 15,000 Shekels. At Fiberlight, his pay had been more than double that. There, Meir had been employed as a financial officer and was paid 40,000 Shekels a month. I stared at the number in shock. That was my salary for three months (plus overtime).

Was Meir finding it difficult to adjust to his new status? From a financial officer with an enormous salary, he had become a lowly employee with a salary that was meager in comparison to the fat paychecks he had from the Fiberlight company.

At three-thirty, I was at the Yarkon Cemetery. There were already some friends and relatives there and, of course, many camera crews. The family didn't know me yet, so I refrained from getting any closer.

Cemeteries always put me in a gothic mood. I have a tendency to get lost between the graves, looking for familiar surnames, calculating the deceased's age, wondering about double graves, especially those which only one person is buried in. Who says life is over at eighty? My mother's father died when he was seventy-five years old. My grandmother was seventy then and was still waiting to be buried next to him.

Children's graves are the most terrible. I passed by a triple grave, smiling to myself that someone was probably buried there with his wife and his lover, but my smile was erased when I discovered that it was the grave of two parents and their child who all died in a car accident. A chill went down my spine, and I remembered that I had come to a funeral no less difficult. I hurried toward the gathering area. The funeral had begun.

It was a tough burial. Even I, who was no relation to them, couldn't stop the tears when Ariel, Galit and Noa's tiny bodies were laid to rest.

Hanni's parents refused to leave the fresh graves, which allowed the news photographers to get a good gallery of pictures to illustrate the horror. The presence of the media was so maddening to me. Why must they push themselves into such an intimate and difficult moment? Did the public have to see the three little bodies laid to rest? You don't need too much imagination to be appalled by this, much less a photo. The funeral ended at six-thirty, an hour and a half before Meir was to be buried.

I went to my car and waited there for an hour. I made lists of who I wanted to talk to and left a voicemail for Riki, the admin assistant at the station house, to bring in some of the neighbors whom the patrol officers questioned. Hanni's parents went to their house to sit *Shiva* [mourn] along with Hanni's three brothers. I decided it would be inappropriate to question them during the Shiva. In spite of my secret hopes to find an external killer and clear Meir of guilt, I knew that the chances were slim. The investigation focused on the question why?—not who?

From the cemetery, I drove to the station house. Most of the offices were already empty. I turned on the light. My current office bore no resemblance to the parquet floor, rich wood furniture and the lithographs of Nachum Guttman and Chagall that I had left behind in the office at Lipkin, Danieli and Co. Mine, like most offices in the station, had a sort of unionized look which included crooked floors with obsolete tiles, plaster peeling off the walls and old-fashioned metal furniture. The wall was decorated with two giant maps, one of Gush Dan and one of the State of Israel. The room was small but was meant for two investigators. The second investigator who was sharing the room with me, Roei, was almost always on undercover activity, so really, the space was almost entirely mine.

I set the photo albums and binders that I had taken from Hanni and Meir's apartment on Roei's desk. He wasn't meant to be coming to the office during the next two weeks anyway, and my desk couldn't hold another pin without it getting lost.

Alon was just on his way out and explained that since the basic assumption was that Meir was the killer, he saw no reason to allot more investigators to the case. There was a great deal of excitement and public frenzy, but it would pass, he predicted. There was no public urgency to solve this case, and he didn't think that a killer was walking among us. The objective was to understand why Meir committed the murder and close the case as soon as possible. Riki reported that she managed to contact three neighbors and would try to track a few more down. She told them all to come to the station Thursday afternoon.

I had missed watching the news that day, so I went online to the news websites, which were flooded with the story of the case and background stories of a beautiful, perfect family, of shock. The news sites had more resources than the police, and they had already managed to research and publish stories about the Danilowitz family, Galit's friends from kindergarten and Ariel's classmates, and to speak to Meir's co-workers and, of course, to the neighbors.

No one anticipated this.

No one knew anything.

No one heard anything.

That is why this came as such a shock.

I tried to take these stories on television and on the internet with a pinch of salt. They were pressed for time and they had to deliver the goods.

It was impossible for everyone to know nothing.

CHAPTER 3

Wednesday, 5.20.2009

The next morning, I contacted Discount Bank and reached Danit Yaacobi-Live, Meir's direct manager. We agreed to meet at her office. She was eager to talk to me and assist.

When I entered her office about an hour after we spoke on the phone, the turmoil was evident on her face. She was around forty years old, she was quite good-looking and very well kept. Her hair was in a carefully blow-dried bob and her face was very finely made up. She was dressed in a feminine, restrained business suit. She tried to assume a cool, strictly business facade, but failed to hide the quaver in her voice when we began talking.

I sat down across from her and refused her offer of a glass of water. I wanted to get started.

She began working at Discount Bank about nine years earlier. She was an accountant, and after finishing her residency, she decided to work in the convenient environment of a bank. A year after she started working at the bank, Meir, who had just finished his studies in university, joined her team.

"What did he study?" I interrupted her.

"Economics and business management."

"Where?"

"As I recall, he graduated from Bar-Ilan."

"And you were his manager?"

"At that time, we were more or less the same rank," she continued the story, "although, I was a certified accountant and had already worked here close to a year, but I also had small children and worked part-time. You probably know how it is."

"How what is?"

"Being a mom in a big institution."

"Not really."

"Oh, sorry. I assumed you have kids."

"I don't."

"Then, when you do have them…"

I didn't want to go there. I had more important things to clear up with her, so I didn't tell her that I wouldn't be having any. What good would it do right now? I simply nodded and she went on.

"Anyway, we worked together for about two years. When I was on maternity leave with my little girl, Meir moved to a startup company."

"Fiberlight?"

"I think so."

"Do you remember when that was?"

"It was early 2004. I remember that I came back to work at the beginning of March 2004 and he was already gone."

"What do you remember about him at that time? Were you surprised that he left for Fiberlight?"

"Actually, I was," she stopped herself for a minute, getting her thoughts together and realizing that this was not the time or place to keep anything inside. "Meir was not the most talented economist on the team. If I had to choose someone to be a financial officer for a startup company, I'd have chosen someone else."

"Like yourself, for instance?" I teased her, wanting to see her reaction.

"Not me, actually." She smiled and gave me an amused look. She was much more intelligent than I had wanted to admit. "I wasn't looking for jobs of that sort because they don't leave you too much time for family."

"So who would you have offered the job to?"

"I don't remember names and it's not important, but Meir wasn't at the top of my list."

"Was he that ill-equipped for it?"

"He was actually very diligent and hardworking; that's probably why he impressed the guys from Fiberlight."

"They knew him before he started working there?"

"Yes." She smiled again. "The Fiberlight guys were clients of the bank."

"And it's acceptable to move to a client like that?"

"It happens."

"Can you tell me a little bit about Fiberlight?"

"I don't remember too much." She typed something on the computer. "Fiberlight was a startup company that dealt with amplifiers for optical communications."

"Do you have an idea of what that means?"

"Not really." She smiled. "I know finance, not technology."

"And Meir knew technology?"

"More than me, that's for sure. That company raised about fifteen million dollars by the end of 2002."

"So, Meir worked on the case for a year and then transferred to the company?"

"More or less."

"To your astonishment."

"I can't say I was astonished—Meir sucked up to them endlessly."

"Do you know what his pay was at Fiberlight?"

"Yes." She smiled. "Three times what he made at the bank at that time."

"How do you know?"

"All of the company's financial data was open to us."

"Were you all jealous?"

"I'd be lying if I said we weren't."

"But you said you didn't want the job."

"The job, no, but I wouldn't object to making almost 40,000

shekels a month."

"What did you think of that salary?"

"That it was outrageous."

"Because Meir didn't have the experience and knowledge?"

"Not only that."

"Then why?"

"Because it was a startup company that hadn't sold as much as a screw."

"Then how did they make the decision to pay such sums to the management?"

"I've no idea; they probably assumed you have to pay for good management."

"But Meir wasn't such good management, you said."

"Not especially, seeing as he and the rest of the management couldn't save the company from collapsing."

"Did they run out of money?"

"Not as far as I remember."

"Then why was it closed?"

"The shareholders realized there was no point in watching all of their money get guzzled up, so they went for voluntary liquidation."

"When was this?"

"About three years ago?"

"How long did Meir work there?"

"Around two and a half years."

"And then what happened? How did he resume his job at Discount Bank?"

"After the company shut down, Meir tried his luck for a few months, unsuccessfully, until he saw my manager at the wedding of a shared relative, and a vacancy had just arisen here."

"And, just like that, he agreed to return to a junior position for a third of the salary?"

"I guess he didn't have too many options. He had a wife and two little kids to provide for."

"Then he probably felt humiliated?"

"He didn't say anything to me, but I can imagine that was the situation. He returned to more or less the same position, while all of the others were promoted or left."

"And you became his manager."

"That's right."

"How did he accept having a woman for a manager?"

"He didn't even hint that it bothered him," she said with an amused gaze.

"But…?"

"But my intuition told me that it bothered him immensely."

"How did you sense that?"

"He was too eager to please me, tried too hard to be good… there was something fake about his behavior."

"So you weren't surprised that he got up one morning and shot his entire family."

"I didn't say that."

"So what do you think of what he did?"

"Did he really do it? In the news, they keep saying that the police aren't confirming Meir is the killer, but he's the main suspect."

"I'm sure you understand I can't tell you more than you know."

She smiled and I continued.

"What do you think? Was he capable of killing his entire family and committing suicide?"

"I'm not an expert in psychology, but he seemed like a completely normal person."

"What kind of father did he seem like?"

"Completely standard."

"And as a husband?"

"I didn't know his wife too well, but there was a sense that she was managing him."

"What do you mean?"

"He was a little scared of her."

"Can you give me an example?"

"There were all sorts of examples, but I particularly

remember that about six months ago, his wife was near the end of her pregnancy. It was December and there was a lot of pressure here because it was the end of the year, but it didn't stop her from harassing him left and right."

"Still… a very pregnant woman…"

"As far as I know, she didn't work, not during the pregnancy and not before it, and she wasn't on bed rest. I think she could have been a bit more sensitive."

"Why? Was he facing termination?"

"No, but he was still the sole provider in the house."

"So his absences hurt his job?"

"No, he would come in at crazy hours and on Fridays to make up hours and work."

"A real dedicated employee."

"And a bit of a slow one," she added sweetly.

After the meeting at the bank, I decided to go see my sister, Shira, who lived in Givaat Shmuel. My sister lived not far from the Danilowitz's house. Shira was not a friend of the family, but she knew them from temple and from the playground. My sister was an occupational therapist, and worked with children in her house. She told me to come over at two o'clock, after she'd finished with her patients, and promised me a meal and a talk.

The fact that both of us were born to the same pair of parents was some sort of medical miracle. There was no similarity between us—external or internal. She was a well-groomed, and slightly chubby (though very beautiful, in my opinion), while I was neglected and skinny. She had always been a *balabusta* [a great homemaker]. She cooked amazingly, managed a house and three kids, while I managed to burn as little as scrambled eggs and, apart from dogs, I knew I would never raise any living creature besides myself. I went to study a "cold" trade like law, and she, who was always a caregiver, studied occupational therapy.

I have no idea what she saw in me, but she always cared for me and loved me. I loved her too, but I was always haunted by the unpleasant feeling that I didn't repay her for all the things she did for me.

"Hadasi, sorry I didn't get around to making something for you, but I have schnitzel and spaghetti from yesterday."

I chuckled to myself. I didn't want her to know what I usually had for lunch, if I had anything at all; yesterday's schnitzel and spaghetti sounded like a feast to me.

The meal was served and I gobbled it up like a starving child.

"Be careful you don't swallow the fork," Shira joked.

"Stop cooking so well," I said with my mouth full.

"Mom says Evyatar's thing seems very serious to her this time."

Evyatar, our youngest brother, had been dating a girl for six months already, a record for our sought-after, pretty boy brother.

"Great," I said and sipped from the cool Coke glass. "Maybe she'll finally get off my back for a little while."

I put the glass on the table and flopped down, full up to my throat, on Shira's couch.

About a month before Meir Danilowitz got up before dawn and shot his entire family, and then himself, dead, I divorced my husband.

Divorce is a messy business, even if it's consensual and even if no kids are involved. For someone who didn't even want to get married, divorce took a pretty heavy toll on me. I felt as if I had failed at one of the best things I had in my life: my partnership with Yinon.

I met Yinon, my ex-husband, at Tel-Aviv University. I was halfway through my third year of law school and he was halfway through his third year studying mechanical engineering.

We met in the library of the Faculty of Medicine. Neither of us had any reason to be there except for silence. It was the quietest library on campus. In the entrance to the library stood a giant fish tank with an especially communicative fish. The fish would get real close to the observers and really make contact with them. Each time I was there, I marveled at the smart fish.

"That fish is something," Yinon smiled at me when he first noticed me, standing and playing with the fish. I smiled.

"Are you a student here? I've never seen you." I felt like he'd caught me red-handed.

"I'm not a student here exactly; I discovered this library two weeks ago and it's just so quiet."

"It's okay, I don't study here either. I'm in mechanical engineering, but I come here to study."

"Great library."

"There's also a really good cafeteria here."

"I'm just taking a break," I smiled shyly.

That's more or less how our story began. At the beginning of our fourth year, we moved in together and about a year and a half later we were married. Personally, getting married wasn't very important to me. Yinon and my mother pressured me. I was almost twenty-eight, Yinon was twenty-nine, and I didn't have a firm opinion on the marital institution, so I agreed to it, although I had a very firm stance about children, an opinion I didn't bother hiding from anyone, especially Yinon.

From a young age, I knew I didn't want children. In a country like ours, with demographic threats and religious fanaticism, I definitely qualify as an excellent candidate for the psych ward, but, somehow, I managed to grow up in Israel and not in a northern European country, and without the urgent need to duplicate myself several times.

Yinon, as well as my mother, thought that I would eventually change my mind, which was why marriage was so important to them. I had no problem with getting married because I didn't feel as if I was deceiving anyone. A few months into our relationship, I told him I still didn't see myself as a mother. At the time, the subject was no more than an anecdote. We were still deep into our studies and Yinon wasn't even thinking of starting a family. When Yinon started talking about marriage right after we finished school, I initiated slightly "heavier" conversations about the subject with him. I explained to him that I just didn't want children and that he should take that into account when deciding to tie his life to mine. Yinon believed, or wanted to believe, that we were in the same place in our lives.

But we weren't.

Compared to me, he was one of the calmest, most peaceful people I knew. This trait of his managed to calm me down even in very stressful moments in life. He always knew when to stop, sit down and enjoy the view, and not just the race. He was always good at listening and being a shoulder to cry on. Not just for me, but for everyone who knew him. I always told him that if he wasn't an engineer, he should have been a psychologist. Or any kind of therapist. He had an ability to give that very few people possess. I knew he could be a great father someday.

I, on the other hand, never dreamed of being a mother. I don't even recall playing with dolls, though my mother claims I simply don't remember. When the girls in my class began getting engaged and married, I wasn't jealous, I didn't see marriage as my life's purpose, much less children. Shira was a year-and-a-half older than me and got married when she was twenty-two; I was still in the army at that age.

About three years later, her eldest daughter was born. Nurit was (and still is) an adorable, lovely little girl. I enjoyed holding and cuddling her, but mostly I liked the fact that it was all I had to do. I saw my exhausted sister and mostly felt sorry for her. I hadn't met Yinon yet, meaning I didn't even have a boyfriend, but I didn't think I should be pitied—the supposedly lonely one. It should rather be my sister, who, at least in my opinion, had no life.

About two years later, Shira was pregnant for the second time and my sister, Ayala, who was more than four years younger than me, got married. People were careful around me. Everybody thought I was in an emotional state with Shira already having a second child and my younger sister getting married, while I wasn't showing any signs of progress. At some point, I stopped trying to explain myself. No one believed me. It's hard for people to believe that some people don't see starting a family as their utmost priority. I was longing for love and I had boyfriends here and there, but bringing children into the world seemed like an insane act to me.

I couldn't understand how sane people, with no background as nurses, could be interested in chaining their life to that of tiny creatures (cute as they may be), in the most beautiful time of their lives, when they're young and full of energy. I must be very extreme in my thought processes, because most of the parents I know don't take care of their children twenty-four hours a day, but I also saw no point in bringing a child into the world if someone else would be taking care of it. The world was on the verge of overpopulation as it was, so I saw no reason to add another child to this negative trend.

When I got married, Shira already had two kids and Ayala was in her second pregnancy. Although my parents (especially my mother) knew I was not interested in having children, they hoped the fact that I was getting married was the first step toward a change in attitude. Yinon thought so as well.

We were happy together, but Yinon's biological clock didn't stop ticking, and we knew that at some point this story might explode. After I received my license to practice law, I continued to work at the office where I interned. It was a successful commercial office and I produced excellent work. I didn't have small children to run to every day at four; nothing got in the way of my professional development.

About three years after I began working as a lawyer, something changed. I was tired and unhappy. Allegedly, I had nothing to complain about: I had an excellent position with high pay, the bosses and clients were all pleased, but I felt like I was lacking something. Yinon didn't like to see his wife in agony, but secretly he was happy because he hoped the desire to have kids was awakening inside me.

I went through a very confusing time and Yinon managed to confuse me even more. He kept hinting that it was time to change, time to become a family. I was in a bad place and was wondering if this was how I was supposed to feel in order to want to become a mother. Was this the yearning for a child? A sense of confusion and unease?

We decided that the best way to understand what I wanted was to get away. In February 2008, we packed ourselves up and left for two months for New Zealand. It was an amazing vacation. I guess you have to travel to the other ends of the Earth to really get away. The spectacular views and endless serenity were a neat bonus. I finally had some peace and quiet.

When the vacation was over, I knew exactly what I wanted, or more accurately what I didn't want: I didn't want to continue working for Lipkin, Danieli and Co. Unfortunately for Yinon, I still didn't want to be a mother. I realized that my lack of satisfaction didn't stem from my family situation, but from the choices I had made in my professional life. Yinon was convinced that, upon our return, we would start working on expanding the family unit, but instead I enrolled myself in the selection process for the police.

I have always loved spy novels and movies. I always dreamed of being a police officer, but the stigma about it stopped me from following my heart. I was an honor roll student in high school and university, I could work wherever I wanted, and when I first voiced my aspirations of working in the Police Investigation Department, my mother was appalled. In her eyes, people who went to work for the police were those that couldn't find a profitable job.

Actually, I quite quickly discovered that there were all kinds of people in the police, including those who could work wherever they wanted, but chose to work at a place that would challenge them professionally.

The more my professional life blossomed, the more my personal life withered. Yinon realized that I had not changed my mind on the issue that mattered most to him. He was already thirty-three, we had been married for over four years, and he didn't see any reason to keep on waiting. People around me began to suspect we had fertility problems. The thought that I simply didn't want kids never crossed their minds.

In August 2008, we celebrated Yinon's thirty-third birthday with friends of his, a couple. We invited them over to our house and they were charmed by our "bachelor pad." They were more or less our age, with two kids and another on the way. It had just been a month since I joined the police.

"You were so brave to leave the office and transfer to the police," Revital said after she finished updating us on all of the exams she was going through and how hard it was to be pregnant with two little ones in the house.

"I owed it to myself," I explained.

"I imagine in the police it'll be easier for you to get pregnant. Still, a government job…"

I stared at her in shock as she continued. "Excuse me for butting in like this, but, personally, I don't think it's anything to be ashamed of," she added, caressing her round belly. "I had a hard time getting pregnant, too, and Ido's a result of treatment. I remember it was so difficult for me, not just the treatments, but also how I was treated in my work place—that's what it's like in private companies."

"Why do you think I'm having treatment?"

Revital blushed and Ronen, her husband, lowered his eyes in embarrassment. "Sorry, I was just sure that… you've been married for four years, you're over thirty… I was sure—"

"We're not trying to get pregnant," I announced.

"Really?" Ronen seemed shocked.

"Yes, really," I answered decisively.

"You're already thirty, aren't you?"

"I'm thirty-two."

"That's starting to get a little tight. Aren't you scared?"

"Of what?" I played dumb.

"That you'll be too old."

"That's not going to be a problem because I just don't want kids."

Revital and Ronen looked at me in astonishment and then turned their gaze to Yinon, who, in turn, looked down in embarrassment.

"You're not serious?" Ronen was part-asking, part-telling.

"I'm totally serious."

"What sort of thing is not wanting kids? It's the most natural thing in the world."

"So…I'm a freak of nature," I joked. I don't think I managed to make anyone else laugh, especially not Yinon.

"And if you change your mind in ten years, you won't be able to get pregnant then." Revital explained the facts of life to me.

"I'd rather regret not having them than having them and regretting it. Besides, these days, women in their fifties are getting pregnant."

"And you want to be a mother at the age of a grandmother?" Ronen protested.

"Right now, I don't want to be a mother at all, so it doesn't concern me."

"I don't know any parent who regrets having children," Ronen said decidedly.

"That's what you think," I smiled. "I constantly meet parents who never stop complaining how their lives ended when they became parents."

"That's just whining in a moment of weakness." Revital continued to stroke her belly, as though trying to protect her unborn baby from my blasphemous words. "There's no greater happiness than watching your baby grow and develop."

"If you ask me, most people lie to others and, most of all, to themselves about the joy of parenting. If parenting's so satisfying and amazing, why do people bother having children and then ask other people to take care of them? I'm always amazed by people at the office—men and women who worked until eight o'clock every night, or even later. They barely see their kids. Where's the great joy in that?"

I knew I was touching a painful subject, because both Ronen and Revital were mechanical engineers, like Yinon, and they both worked jobs that required endless working hours.

"If everyone talked like you, the human race would become extinct." Ronen said, obviously pleased with himself.

"If the human race is ever in danger of extinction, come back to me and I'll consider donating my uterus," I smiled.

"Don't you want to leave someone to follow you? Children are a type of perpetuation." Revital was curious.

"I don't think I'm interested in what happens after I die."

"And who'll take care of you when you're old?" Ronen once again tried to undermine me.

"I have a great insurance plan. I really hope you're not having kids so someone will take care of you. Insurance is far cheaper and more efficient. Children aren't an insurance policy… maybe they'll live in another country, disown you, or simply not be interested in nursing."

"I had children simply because they bring me joy," Revital declared.

"I can't argue with that," I smiled. "I don't think they'd make me happy, which is why I'm not taking the risk and taking that kind of burden on myself."

"Children are not a burden," Ronen said decisively.

Revital rolled her eyes at him. "For you they're not! Because you almost never help me!"

I was glad Revital was beginning to side with me, but one look at Yinon made it clear that I had gone too far, that it was his birthday, and I was not supposed to make his friends fight.

"I think that people should have kids only if they make them happy," I said to Revital. "All the other reasons are irrelevant. I think that a lot of people, especially here in Israel, have kids because that's what everybody does and nobody wants to be the odd person out."

An hour later, the conversation between the men and the women parted. Yinon chatted with Ronen and I talked with Revital.

"You're very brave," she said in a low voice.

"Really? I've always wanted to be a police officer."

"No, I'm talking about the kids thing. I see parents every day who shouldn't have done it, who didn't think it through. You have the courage to think and do what you really want."

"Thanks," I answered shyly. She moved me.

Out of the corner of my eye, I saw that Ronen was talking to Yinon heatedly. I was dying to know what he was saying.

"What did Ronen say to you?" I asked after they left.

"He said that if he was in my place, he'd separate from you."

I opened my eyes wide in amazement. Where did this guy get the nerve to say something like this to my husband?

"What did you say?"

"I didn't say anything."

"Really?"

"I wouldn't."

"Yinon, you've known almost from the start of our relationship that I don't want kids."

"I hoped you'd change your mind."

"But I haven't."

"That's a problem."

"It's *your* problem, I haven't changed anything."

"I don't know if we can stay together."

I started tearing up. "Because of what Ronen said?"

"Of course not." He stroked my cheeks. "I don't know if I can go on waiting."

Four months later, we separated and four months after that, we were divorced.

"Mom's worried about you." Shira tried to soften me up. The person who took my divorce the hardest was my mother.

"I'm a big girl."

"Mom is Mom. I'd tell you that someday you'll understand, but I don't want to enrage you." Shira smiled. She was definitely the only one in the family who managed to comprehend me.

I finished eating and Shira washed the dishes while I began questioning her.

"I know them." She thought for a second and then corrected herself. "I *knew* them, mainly from the synagogue. I don't think I ever once spoke to them."

"What did they seem like to you?"

"It's just an impression from their appearance—I don't really know them."

"Any impression will help me right now." I knew my sister would talk to me in the most direct way.

"She seemed like a real bitch." Shira blushed. "I hate to say that about someone who's dead, but it's the truth."

"Can you be more specific?"

"Her son—I think his name was Ariel—was only a month older than my Noam, but Noam was born in December, so they didn't start the first grade together."

"So they were in kindergarten together?"

"Not the same exact one, but in the same cluster. I sometimes saw her coming in... always looking very nice, always standing around and sharing secrets with other mothers. I remember there was some story about a teacher's aide in the afternoon daycare who she managed to get kicked out."

"Do you remember her name?"

"No, not at all, she was an aide in another kindergarten—I wasn't familiar with the staff there—I only knew there was an aide there that she made sure was replaced."

"Do you know what the story was?"

"Not too much. I only know that some parents claimed it was much ado about nothing."

I recalled the riot Hanni caused when I was the only one in the class who scored 100 in the math midterm.

"So why do you think she was a bitch? Because she was good looking?"

Shira smiled and wiped her wet hands on her worn T-shirt. "Maybe I'm jealous, but most mothers, especially working ones, don't have too much time to get their hair and nails done every week. We don't go down to pick up the kids from kindergarten dressed like something out of a fashion magazine."

"She dressed like in the magazines?"

"I may be exaggerating, but she was dressed nicer than me."

"So she had time—that doesn't make her a bad person."

"Not at all." Shira made a face and said, "Look, do you want me to be politically correct or honest?"

"Honest!"

"Then let me explain something to you about the lives of some of the women in Givaat Shmuel: New Givaat Shmuel is mostly populated by Religious Zionist families. These are usually young couples. Nearly all of them are people from a mid-level or even high socioeconomic class. There are quite a few women, like Hanni for instance, who can afford not to work. Excuse me for criticizing, but I think there's something extremely atrophied in that. They sit around all morning in the new shopping mall, walk around the stores and busy themselves mostly with gossip. The latest trend is to have at least four children, and that's—more or less—their excuse for not doing anything but shop for clothes and gossip."

"Hanni only had three kids."

"She didn't manage another one." Shira said with a wicked smile. "That's another thing that drives me crazy! I've no idea why they're so hung up on having so many kids, when, in many cases, I get the sense that they don't have any particular interest in parenting. They see parenting as some kind of unpleasant chore, which is especially amazing in light of the fact that they don't work."

"Maybe they work from home, like you?"

"Believe me, I'd know. Hanni knew I'm an occupational therapist."

"How do you know?"

"Her eldest son, the one who's—*was*—a month older than Noam, needed therapy. I don't know exactly what the problem was, but he had difficulties, and my friend, whose son was in Ariel's kindergarten, recommended me."

"And did she contact you?"

"You think?"

"Why not?"

"Hell would freeze over before she'd send her son to be treated by me. The last thing she'd want is for her son to become the talk of the synagogue."

"She didn't trust you to be discreet?"

"Apparently not. She was probably used to the standards she knew from up close."

"You mean daily gossip."

"Exactly."

"Do you have that friend's phone number?"

"Sure, but if you want, you can come to story time with me, I bet we'll meet a few more common acquaintances."

I was happy for the opportunity, so we went together to pick up the kids and go to the library.

On our way to the library, we picked up little Eran from daycare and Noam from school. Nurit, Shira's elder daughter, went to do her homework with a friend. I was amazed to discover that the classes in school were separated by gender.

"Since when do Religious Zionists study in separate classes in elementary school?" When we were in grade school, we studied in mixed classes; when I was in high school, our school was turned into a girls' only high school, but I didn't think this Haredi direction had reached the lower grades. Why would eight-year-old kids need to be separated?

"We were really against it," Shira defended herself, "but it was already a given fact and it's very hard to fight against an existing situation."

The shift toward Haredi orthodox practices in the Religious Zionist sector was very disappointing, and even scary to me. Although I was not a mother, if I had kids, I believe it would be important to me that they be educated in co-ed systems. I remembered a case of sexual molestation in a Yeshiva, a story that wasn't covered by the media because it was kept under wraps. A number of seventeen-year-old boys molested a gentle boy of thirteen. The case was closed because the parents of the boy who was allegedly molested were persuaded to withdraw their complaint, and the boy was transferred to a different Yeshiva.

I was shocked by this story, but Alon had not been at all

surprised. He told me that there were a lot of cases like this in Yeshivas, especially Haredi ones. Teenagers at the height of their sexual awakening are forcefully separated from girls, and this was sometimes the result.

While we waited at the school gate, I noticed the obituaries posted at the entrance. Little Ariel had studied here, and the shock was still very recent. Noam, my sister's son, was almost the last one to exit the school's doors, accompanied by Udi, his best friend. Shira had always been the most popular girl in class. Unlike me, for instance, she never missed the social gathering on the street corner across from Bnei Akivah on Friday nights. She always had tons of girlfriends, and many boyfriends, and she was always up to date with the fashions. I was sure that her son, and Udi, being the school's number one geeks wasn't making her too proud. She claimed that it amused her, but I'm sure that, deep down, she was waiting for the day when he'd become a little more like her and a little less like her husband, Moshe. Udi and Noam, bespectacled and daydreaming, slowly approached us while arguing with one another about which Bakugan had greater powers.

"Noam and Udi, we're going to miss story time," Shira tried to hurry them up unsuccessfully.

We arrived about fifteen minutes before story time started. I studied the audience. In the middle of the library, the librarian arranged tiny chairs for the children and benches for the parents. Like the school, the library's doors also displayed obituary notices, this time for Hanni and the two deceased girls. No mention of father Meir. We arrived exactly as the rest of the parents began gathering: mainly mothers, some dressed in worn-out sweatshirts or casual jeans like my sister; some had probably just got back from their office jobs, dressed in tailored clothes; some with kerchiefs over their hair, most without. I noticed two dads with their children, and was excited to discover that there were also some fathers watching their children.

"Don't get too excited," Shira cooled me down. "It's their

day of the week. On every other day, their wives take care of the kids."

Some of the kids were now seated on the tiny chairs. Noam and Udi claimed the two central seats. More children ran around the library, while the parents all stood in groups, talking heatedly, and the topic was, of course, the Danilowitz family. The shock was fresh, and the community refused to believe the story and the tragic outcome. I tried to listen to what they were saying, but the talkative medley ceased when I neared. Some of them recognized me from the news.

The librarian tried to seat the parents on the benches. The actress that had come to perform gave the librarian an impatient glare and the librarian raised her voice.

"Dear parents, like you, I'm shocked from recent events in the neighborhood, but we must begin story time."

The actress approached one of the mothers, a beautiful blonde woman who had completely ignored the librarian's plea for quiet.

"Is this one yours?" She pointed to the girl with the blonde pigtails who sat on the chair before her.

"Yes," she nodded.

"Have you ever thought about trying her out for television?"

The mother looked at her, amazed. "Not really; although I've been told a number of times that she could be a model."

"I'm casting a TV show for the educational network right now, so come to me at the end of the activity and give me your phone number, okay?"

The mother nodded in awe and went silent.

Now, story time was able to begin.

Just as the actress started, my phone rang. It was Alon. The actress gave me an angry look and I silenced the phone.

When the actress was finished, I asked all the parents to stay seated.

"Hello, everyone. My name is Hadas Levinger and, as some of you apparently know from the news broadcast from two days ago, I'm investigating the Danilowitz family case."

I was careful not to say "murder" or "suicide" because all the kids had their innocent eyes on me.

"And, if anyone doesn't know, I'm also Shira Landau's sister." Shira nodded and smiled to everyone in embarrassment.

"In the next couple of days, we'll be contacting some of you as part of the investigation process. There's nothing to worry about, we simply want to bring this difficult affair to an end. If there's anyone here who's able to assist the investigation and knows the family, I'll leave my phone number and e-mail with the librarian. I'd like to emphasize that there's no other branch investigating this case, so if someone approaches you claiming otherwise, I'd like to hear about it." I approached Ziva, the librarian, and wrote down my e-mail address and my phone number.

The blonde mother approached the actress with a note. "This is my phone number." The actress gave her a curious look. "About the show you mentioned before," she explained.

"Oh…" The actress smiled heartily and thanked the proud mother with a cheery smile. As soon as the mother had left the library, she threw the note into the trash can behind her. I smiled to her and she returned a knowing smile.

The library emptied and I noticed Shira was talking to a young girl who was holding a chubby baby in her arms.

"Hadasi," Shira called, "this is Renana. She's the friend I told you about earlier."

"I wouldn't say friend," Renana smiled. "I'm a friend of your sister's. Hanni was an acquaintance of mine."

"Are you willing to talk to me?"

"Now?"

"If it's possible," I answered, staring at the pinkish baby.

Shira reached out her hands to the baby. "I'll watch him till you're done."

"He'll need to eat in a little while," Renana tried to deter Shira.

"I'll cope," Shira smiled. If there was one thing nobody doubted, it was my sister's parenting skills. That apple couldn't have fallen farther from the other apple—me—in our case.

We walked toward Renana's house. She lived in one of the ground-level houses on the outskirts of the neighborhood, not far from my sister's and the house of the late Danilowitz family. Everything was so close.

Shira was given a short briefing on handling the baby, an explanation that was completely unnecessary as far as Shira was concerned, and Renana and I went to the workroom on the top floor, while Shira took all the kids down to the games room in the basement.

We closed the door and I took out my recording device. Renana stared at it.

"Renana, I understand this is a little difficult and probably out of the ordinary, but you need to understand that the conversation between us is, in fact, a police interrogation. Anything you say will be recorded and entered in the investigation file. At this point, I don't think we're going to reach a trial situation, but if there's a trial, we may have to summon you to give a testimony based on this interrogation."

Renana went on staring at me. "I didn't know it was this official."

"It can be more official."

"What do you mean?"

"I intend to make a list of people I'm interested in questioning, and I assume that, as someone who knew the deceased well, I would summon you to come talk to me in the station anyway. I think this way it's more pleasant for you." Despite my not-so-hidden threat, I tried to sound compassionate and Renana assented and sat down beside me.

I switched on the recording device and we started talking. First, I asked her, for protocol, to identify herself.

"I understand you know my sister, Shira."

"Yes," she smiled, "our daughters are in the same class."

"And how long have you known each other?"

"Wow, more or less since we became mothers."

"So, about ten years?"

"Something like that. Your sister moved here when Nurit was two months old."

"And how did you meet Hanni Danilowitz?"

"My second son was in class with Ariel, her son."

"Meaning they were in the same classes throughout all of their years."

"Right. Noam, your sister's son, was born in the same year, but your sister chose to keep him in kindergarten for another year."

"Yes, I know."

"If you ask me, it wouldn't have hurt Ariel to stay another year in kindergarten."

"What do you mean?"

"Noam wasn't in the exact same kindergarten as Ariel and Idan, my son. So Shira doesn't know exactly what went on there. Ariel was a very difficult child. A beautiful boy, smart too, but with no boundaries and, to my understanding, he had learning and attention problems."

"How did you understand that?"

"First of all, she told me."

"Who is ‘she’?"

"Hanni. She knew I took my son to an occupational therapist, so she asked me if I knew anyone."

"So you recommended my sister?"

"Of course, I'll have you know, your sister’s amazing." As if I wasn't aware.

"I understand she didn't go to my sister in the end."

"Of course not," Renana chuckled. "People of Hanni's kind don't air their dirty laundry inside the neighborhood."

"So she went to someone else?"

"I’ve no idea, but her kid needed therapy, that's for sure."

"Why do you say that?"

"When they were still in kindergarten, her son misbehaved all the time. In one of his fits he threw food at the aide so she took his plate away and he didn't eat. When Hanni found out that her son hadn't eaten that day, she made sure to rile up some of the parents and that aide was kicked out of the kindergarten."

"Well, she did withhold food from the child—"

"She didn't do anything that any other parent wouldn't have done. It'd do him no harm to miss one meal. Instead of dealing with the real problem, she turned the heat in the wrong direction. I watched her child several times, especially at Idan's birthday parties. He was just reckless and disobedient. Couldn't sit still for longer than two minutes."

"And what did you think of Hanni?"

"The truth? Just the truth? I couldn't stand her."

"Why?"

"I think there was a lot of evil in her." Renana paused for a moment and decided to rephrase her answer. "You know what, not evil—miserliness."

"What do you mean?"

"Maybe I'm just pretending, but I got the feeling that she was very, very jealous of me."

"Why?"

"I know her husband was a pretty successful economist, but I also know that he was fired from some start-up company and went to work for a bank."

I didn't confirm her statement, although it was surprisingly accurate.

"I assume he earned a pretty good salary at the bank, but I don't think he made as much as my husband does, even when he was with the start-up."

"What does your husband do?"

"My husband owns a business, importing children's clothing."

"Not a bad business in Israel." I thought about all those families with at least four children.

"*Baruch Hashem* [Thank God]," Renana smiled. "It was my father-in-law's business. He retired around five years ago, and since the business came into my husband's hands, it's virtually doubled and even tripled itself. My husband has a sense for business," she said, eyes sparkling.

"That's great," I encouraged her.

"Anyway," she got back on track, "Hanni and Meir maybe had means, but not like ours. I'm not trying to brag—I'm just stating the facts. They lived in a very nice apartment, but it's hard for me to believe that they could afford a private home here in Givaat Shmuel."

"How do you know they were even interested in a house like yours?"

"I know it for a fact because the house next door to us was put up for sale and they expressed an interest. She even came to me to ask how much our house cost because she was astounded by the price they demanded."

"Are the prices here high?"

"Very. When we came here, the prices were pretty high, but today, they're insane!"

"So she wanted a house like yours… what else?"

"Almost two years ago, my husband and I celebrated our tenth wedding anniversary and he bought me a black Mitsubishi Outland." I had no idea what she was referring to, I assumed it was the tank parked in front of the house. "I remember she saw me getting out of the car and asked me if I wasn't scared of driving such a big vehicle. I told her I was getting used to it and excitedly told her about the big anniversary surprise. She had this frozen smile, very non-appreciative, but I ignored it. She asked me why I need such a large car for three children, so I told her we were expecting a fourth."

"And how did she react?"

"She wasn't too happy for me, but she forced out the phoniest smile she could muster. The funny thing was that about two months later, she also had a Mitsubishi Outland. Not a new one, but a similar model."

I couldn't hide my smile. Renana smiled back. "This isn't the only story."

"What else?"

"That summer, two years ago, a little after I got the new car, we went on a family vacation to Holland, an amazing organized trip for families. When we returned, Hanni had heard about the trip and said she thought there was no point in taking little kids abroad, that in the long term it had no value. But one year later…" She shrugged.

"Hanni also took the trip?" I recalled the photo album from Holland that was sitting in my office.

"Yes," Renana giggled. "The following summer they went to the same resort that we stayed in."

"So you were a real role model for her?"

"Not really."

"What do you mean?"

"She only cared about my material things. We never sat down for an in-depth conversation, she never asked my advice about the kids. I really don't like to judge mothers, but I wasn't a fan of her parenting style."

"What do you mean?"

"Like Hanni, I also don't work. My husband, *Baruch Hashem*, earns enough money for me to stay home. I know women like you who have a career look at me accusingly, as if I'm a danger to the feminist revolution, but I love being a mother and I'm very good at it. I simply enjoy raising them and watching them grow. I think Hanni wasn't like this. She didn't go out to work, but didn't really nurture her children either. For instance, I'm not sure why her children needed after-school daycare.

"Believe me, I can afford it for my kids, but I see no reason for them to stay in kindergarten and at school until the afternoon if I'm at home and not working. If I didn't have learning disabilities myself, I'd even consider homeschooling, but I know I wouldn't be able to teach them. But Hanni was mostly occupied with finding after school arrangements for Ariel and her little girl, whose name I don't remember. I remember she tried to use us, too, a couple of times, but I couldn't deal with her son, who had no boundaries whatsoever, and I can understand why—she didn't make any effort to educate him. She tried to be fair and suggested that Idan come to her house in return, but I didn't need any favors and I admit

I was a little apprehensive about sending Idan over to their house."

"Why?"

"I didn't trust her to watch them properly."

"Did you know Meir?"

"Not really. A little, from synagogue and maybe a bit from school."

"And how did he seem to you?"

"I must admit that I had no opinion about him. He was like air next to her."

"Meaning?"

"I don't remember him speaking, not once."

"Really?"

"Maybe because I barely saw him. He worked a lot and usually looked tired."

"Did you ever see him lose it, raise his voice, hit someone?"

"Not at all. He seemed pretty gentle to me, a lot of times I wondered what he was doing with Hanni, but I assumed that opposites attract."

"He was Hanni's opposite?"

"It's hard for me to say because I didn't know him; actually, I didn't know her too well, either, but I certainly knew her better than him. She was always very talkative and the main event, while he was very quiet. I remember one occasion at the kindergarten… I think it was Ariel's birthday, so they were both there. She was arguing about something with the kindergarten teacher and he was trying to calm her down. I didn't hear any of the argument, but I remember that he said something to her about the fact that it was their son's celebration and they shouldn't ruin it."

"Can you imagine him committing a murder?"

"So it really was him?"

"I didn't say that," I smiled. You would have to be a complete moron not to understand. "We're examining possible directions."

"Listen, I understood from the news that it's him, but it's

really, really hard for me to believe. He always seemed like such a gentle, calm guy. I can't understand what could cause him to do such a thing."

The apartment door had been locked from inside, but maybe it was still someone from outside? Someone who came in through the door, locked it and went out the window...?

"Can you maybe think of anyone who was at odds with the Danilowitz family? Anyone who could have possibly wanted them dead?"

"Absolutely not," Renana rolled her eyes. "I'm not saying everyone in the neighborhood loves one another, but no feud would ever reach this level."

That's what she thinks, I thought to myself. So many murders have occurred linked to feuds about nothing.

Renana provided me with the class contact sheet and marked for me the mothers who were connected to Hanni.

When I left her house, I checked my phone, which had been on vibrate ever since the session in the library. I always forget to turn the ringer back on. Two missed calls from my mother and three more from Alon.

Alon hates to leave messages and he never texts. This time he acted differently.

"Levinger." I heard the irritation in his voice. "Where are you? Why does it take a phone call from the dead woman's parents for me to hear you still haven't questioned them? I'm turning off my phone because we're going to a wedding tonight and I won't be able to hear anything anyway, but contact them—and me—urgently tomorrow morning."

I parted from Shira and Renana and rushed to my car.

On the way, I heard a familiar voice shouting in my direction.

"Gunger!" I turned toward the voice. It was Tamar, my friend from the Convent. How could I forget that a substantial number of my classmates from high school were now residents of this neighborhood? "Gunger" was the nickname given to me in high school, a sort of twist on Levinger, my surname. I don't remember who came up with it, but it just caught on and they hadn't bothered to say my real name for years.

I approached Tamar to discover that she was pregnant again. The last time we spoke, she'd had two kids.

"Gunger, wow! I haven't seen you in so long!"

I embraced her warmly, with love. Despite the years that had passed, I would always have a warm spot for her in my heart. All throughout high school, we sat next to one another. Of all of the Convent's members, she was the one closest to me. We were both excellent students and Tamar, who had better learning skills than me, went on to medical school after her civil service. I idolized her because she was a doctor and a devoted mother. She managed to get it all in: a career and a family, too.

I'm always in awe of people who manage to do so much. I really, truly admire these active people, like Tamar. Even when we were in high school, she was all about activities and friends. I, on the other hand, sought peace and quiet, to be alone for a bit. I loved my family and enjoyed social gatherings, but I also had to be by myself from time to time. I had fun by myself. I considered myself a great person to pass the time with. I didn't get bored.

"Congratulations," I point to her growing belly. "This is your third, isn't it?"

Tamar smiled. "The fourth."

I definitely could not keep up with the factory pace.

"I didn't know." I made an embarrassed face.

"It's okay." Tamar gave a big smile. "It's not like I call you every morning."

"So, what are you having?"

"I have three boys at home and finally a girl as well." Tamar gently caressed her round belly.

"That's great." I was happy for her. "Do you still work at Tel-Hashomer?"

"No," she smiled. "Now I'm a family physician for Maccabi."

"Very nice." I was deeply impressed.

"Convenient hours."

"How's Yossi?" I asked after her husband.

"Yonni," she corrected me. "He's just fine, works at the same place."

I couldn't remember where he worked, but I wouldn't show my ignorance by asking.

"What about you?" she asked carefully. "I heard you left the office you were working in." I saw she was struggling with the question, so I completed it for her:

"And I also left Yinon."

She made a sad face. "That's a shame; I was sure you were such a good couple."

"We were a very good couple." I smiled a comforting smile, as if Tamar was the one who got divorced and I had to cheer her up.

"So why?"

"Because. It didn't work out."

"So what are you doing here? Did you come to visit your sister?"

"That, and I'm also working here."

"Really?" she looked around in amazement, as if searching for the nearest law firm.

"Where?"

"You really don't know?"

"Know what?"

"You haven't seen the news?"

"We don't have a TV."

"Really?"

"Yes."

"Because of a religious thing?" I asked, curious. I didn't understand how it was possible to raise three kids without the ultimate babysitter.

"Because of an educational thing," she said proudly.

"Very nice. Did you know I became a police officer?"

"Really?" She was shocked and began to link all the details. "Since when?"

"Almost a year."

"So you must have something to do with the Danilowitz

family investigation."

"I'm investigating the case."

"Wow, that can't be easy."

"No, not really."

"Just horrible."

"Did you know them?"

"Barely," she said. "We live on the other side of the neighborhood, so we don't attend the same synagogue."

"And school? Kindergartens?"

"Our kids aren't the same ages; I've never actually seen the husband, except the pictures in the newspaper."

"And her?"

"She'd hang around the mall a lot, so I'd see her every once in a while, but we weren't in touch."

I saw Tamar couldn't be a source for me. "How are the rest of the Convent?" I asked, preferring not to get into confidential details of the investigation. "Are you in touch with anyone?"

"Anat lives nearby, so we meet up every once in a while. I haven't spoken with Inbal in months and I talk to Dganit occasionally."

"How are they?"

"Okay."

We stood in awkward silence. I felt a bit sad. At one point in our lives, we couldn't stop talking. We'd meet, chatter endlessly and call one another the second we got home. I missed that a little. I didn't have too many girlfriends. I know a lot of friendships dissolve over the years, especially with the arrival of children, but it doesn't have to be like that. Yinon, for instance, has quite a few friends, including childhood friends. The main difference is that Yinon's friends are secular, like him. Between my childhood and flaws within myself, friends are a deep chasm that's very difficult to bridge.

"Listen, I have to run to the office, but we've got to meet up sometime, the whole Convent."

"Dganit is out of the country now—"

"So, when she gets back." I knew this wouldn't happen. It

never did.

"Excellent, we'll be in touch."

"Sure." I checked to see I had her current number and rushed to my car.

Half an hour later, I was already sitting at my desk, sifting through all the pieces of paper to find Aviva and Shimon Levin's phone number. Aviva's sister answered my call. I heard a commotion at her end; it was eight o'clock in the evening and I assumed the house was packed with people who had come to console the family for the *Shiva.*

Aviva couldn't come to the phone and Shimon took the call.

"Mr. Levin?" I asked hesitantly.

"Speaking."

"Hello, sir, this is Hadas Levinger from Israeli Police."

"Hello, Hadas."

"First of all, allow me to express my condolences for the horrible tragedy that has befallen you."

"Thank you," he said in a whisper and I could hear the tears choke up his throat.

"I'm responsible for the investigation of the murder of your daughter and grandchildren."

"I know."

"I understand you were expecting me to come see you?"

"That's right."

"I'd like to apologize for that. Since the leads in the case are pretty clear, I didn't see the need to bother you during the *Shiva.* I thought it would be rude of me."

"It's okay," he said calmly.

"If it's still possible, I can come over tomorrow."

"Morning would be the most convenient time," he said. "Most people come from afternoon on."

"I'll be there at nine."

"That's fine."

I had a hard time understanding why Alon was so stressed in the message he left me.

CHAPTER 4

Thursday, 5.21.2009

The following day, everything became clear. Hanni Levin had, apparently, inherited her temper from her mother. I arrived at the grieving home at nine-thirty in the morning, hoping there would be no visitors there.

Despite the early hour, the house was packed and the door was open; I entered the living room. About a year earlier, my grandfather had passed away at the age of ninety-two. He had been very ill to the point that he no longer recognizes anyone, so his *Shiva* was some kind of a pleasant social gathering. A lot of memories came up and there was quite a bit of laughter. There is a very fundamental difference between the *Shiva* of a ninety-year-old elderly man—who passes away at a ripe old age, when all of his descendants are ready to part from him—and the *Shiva* of a young girl like Hanni and her three little children. In fact, no one sat *Shiva* for Ariel, Galit and little Noa because all the people who could sit *Shiva* for them were no longer alive.

Although we were in high school together, I never got to visit Hanni's parents' home. As far as I recalled, it was the same apartment they had lived in when we were in high school: a spacious, well-kept apartment in the heart of Ramat Gan. Hanni's father, Shimon Levin, sat in the center of the living room. He was a tall, handsome man who had worked for years as an engineer in the Israeli Aerospace industry and had retired with a comfortable pension plan three years earlier. Since then he had worked as an engineering consultant for a number of companies. Next to him, with red eyes, sat his wife, Aviva Levin. Despite the heavy grief that was evident in her face, her hair and clothes were immaculate. Beneath the carefully-styled hair and designer clothes, she was a heavy set, not overly attractive woman. Hanni got her beauty from her father.

I went straight to Aviva, who glared at me angrily.

"Aviva, Shimon, allow me to express my condolences."

"Thank you very much," Shimon said, almost in a whisper.

"I'm Hadas Levinger from the central unit. I'm in charge of the investigation—"

"We know who you are." Aviva cut me off with an impatient tone.

"I think it'll be best if we go to the study." Shimon decided to avoid an unpleasant scene in front of all the guests.

The two lifted themselves off the stools they were sitting on and turned toward one of the inner rooms. Dozens of eyes followed me.

The study was decorated with heavy wooden shelves. Dozens of holy books, Babylonian Talmud, Shulchan Aruch, a full bible of Daat Mikra, the Rambam's *Guide for the Perplexed* and more books I wasn't familiar with. In the corner of the room stood three crates of light refreshments for the *Shiva:* soft drinks and bags of cookies, store-bought cakes and plastic disposable tableware.

Shimon sat down on a chair close to the desk and Aviva and I sat across from him on the couch. The room had the familiar and beloved scent of the study in my parents' house, and I suddenly felt closer to Hanni. We had the same starting point, but destiny swept each of us to a completely different place.

"Listen," Aviva said in a reproving voice, "it just doesn't seem reasonable to me that I'm here sitting *Shiva* for my daughter and three grandchildren and I have to call the police and call you over."

I realized there was no reason to argue and decided simply to apologize. "I apologize, Mrs. Levin. As you know, the main and only suspect at this moment is your late son-in-law. There's no danger to the public here, so I thought there was no point in bothering you during the *Shiva*."

"You thought wrong," Aviva retorted angrily.

"Aviva, stop." Shimon laid his hand on his wife's shoulder and tried to calm her. "There were no bad intentions here."

Aviva ignored her husband's attempts to appease her and went on with her attack. "Didn't you go to school with my Hanni?"

"I was in her grade."

"And you don't think there's a problem with the fact that you're investigating my daughter's murder?"

"If there was any conflict of interest, I would not have been assigned this case." I replied in an authoritative tone. "Hanni and I weren't friends in high school." I remembered I was in a grieving home and immediately added "… for the simple reason that we didn't study in the same class. And since we finished high school…" I rolled my eyes to remember, "…fifteen years ago, as I recall, and I wasn't in touch with your daughter, there's no reason why I shouldn't investigate this case."

"That's perfectly fine with us," Shimon said in a quivering voice. "The most important thing is that we understand why this tragedy happened to us."

I looked into Shimon's sad, blue eyes.

I smiled a doleful smile and said, "We just placed a gag order on the case because of the minute chance that the murder was committed by a killer who fled the scene. According to all of the signs and evidence we've gathered, it appears that your son-in-law, Meir, shot all of the members of his family and then put an end to his life."

Aviva wept and Shimon sat down next to her and hugged her. I took his place on the chair.

"I know there's a lot of public interest in this story, but our goal in the investigation is, first of all, to ensure that there isn't a killer on the loose and to find the motive for Meir's actions as best we can. It's clear to all of us that there's no suitable motive for the murder of a wife and three small children, but maybe understanding the motives that caused Meir to commit this horrible act will help you in your grief."

"The journalists are like vultures," Aviva said, and Shimon went on comforting his sobbing wife.

"I know," I said in a sympathetic voice, "and right now there's a gag order on the case, but if we do solve it there may be no choice but to reveal some or all of its details."

Aviva went on weeping and Shimon hugged her warmly. After a few moments of tense silence, I got up from the chair. "I don't want to disturb you. After you finish the *Shiva,* I'll call you down to the station for questioning."

"Question us now!" Aviva took me by surprise. I thought she wasn't able to speak.

"Are you sure?"

Shimon asked to speak with his wife in private. About three minutes later they came back into the room with two additional chairs.

"Yes, we're ready for questioning," Aviva said.

"There's an extra chair here." They looked at me, not understanding.

"The questioning is one-on-one," I explained, and took the recording device out of my bag.

"You're recording us?"

"Despite the circumstances, you must realize this is a police investigation."

"We understand," Shimon said to prevent his wife from initiating another pointless argument.

Aviva wanted to be first, so Shimon went back to the guests and mourners in the living room.

"Tell me a little bit about your daughter."

"Since you knew her way back in high school, you probably remember that she was always a very good girl. The prettiest, the smartest, the most popular." Yes, I remember... "She was actually a year younger than you, since she skipped a grade. When she was in the first grade, she already knew how to read and write, so her teacher thought there was no reason for her to be bored. Nowadays, a lot of kids know how to read and write in kindergarten, but, back then, Hanni was different."

She wet her mouth and went on. "She was generally a special child. Everyone loved her so much." Of course, I didn't correct her mistake. "After high school, she did a year of civil service and then started law school. She was on the Dean's list every year and all the firms chased her to intern for them."

"When did she meet Meir?"

"They met years before they started dating. You must know what it's like with teenagers in Bnei Akivah—everyone knows everyone. I think they first met when she was still in high school."

"And nothing happened?"

"No, as far as I know."

"So when did they become a couple?"

"In Hanni's final year of university, she met up with Meir, who was just starting to study economics. Since they knew one another, they started talking and then dating."

"How long was it before they were married?"

"It took them about a year and a half."

"Which is a while in your circles."

"Don't forget Hanni was very young—she skipped a grade." Aviva didn't miss a single opportunity to mention this.

And also did only one year of civil service, I thought to myself.

"They weren't in any rush," Aviva continued. "Also, Meir had just started studying and Hanni was very busy with her internship and the bar exams."

"When did they get married?"

"December 28th, 2000." Aviva closed her eyes and fondly reminisced. "It was an amazing wedding—the seventh candle of Chanuka, at the Dan Panorama Hotel in Tel-Aviv."

"Sounds very impressive."

"It was amazing." She blew her nose.

"What kind a couple were Meir and Hanni?"

"They were an amazing couple."

"They didn't have any crises during the first year? The second year?"

"Not at all," she answered decisively. "Everything was just fine. Hanni received her license two or three months before they were married and at first she was the breadwinner, until Meir finished his degree and started working at the bank. A little while after he started working at the bank, Ariel, their eldest was born."

"And Hanni continued to work?"

"Yes, his salary wasn't enough to sustain a family, so she continued to work."

"She didn't go on working because she wanted to fulfil herself career wise?"

"You can have a career when you're forty," Aviva snorted in disdain. "Hanni already had a degree. She knew what's important and what needs to be done."

What needs to be done, I thought to myself. I wondered if Hanni really wanted to have kids instead of a career. Was she really willing to put off her self-fulfillment until she was forty?

"What do you mean, 'she knew'? Was someone pressuring her?"

"Not at all, no." Aviva disregarded me with a wave of the hand. "It completely came from her; she wanted to raise children without the troubles of work and only when Meir got the job in that startup…" Aviva was trying to remember the name.

"Fiberlight?"

"Yes, at Fiberlight, as far as I remember, I didn't concern myself with his job too much. He got an excellent job with a salary that matched his skills and allowed Hanni to stop working. She was pregnant for the second time and it was just right in all respects."

"And what happened when he was fired from Fiberlight?"

"He wasn't fired," Aviva corrected me, careful not to tarnish the son-in-law who had murdered her daughter and grandchildren three days earlier. "The company fell apart."

"And wasn't it difficult for them? A family of four with no income."

"I wasn't worried for them. If he managed to get that job at Feriblight—"

"Fiberlight."

"Whatever the name was. Meir could find a job that was just as good and they had enough savings from when he was working. He also got excellent compensation."

"How do you know?"

"My daughter told me everything."

Apparently not everything, if one morning her husband gets up and kills her and her children, I thought to myself.

"But in the end, he didn't find another executive position, but returned to his old job at the bank."

"Right."

Aviva made a disappointed face. "In my opinion, he didn't look hard enough. Maybe he hoped he'd get some offers and when a few months passed and he didn't get any big offers, he just went back to work at the bank."

"I understand you weren't happy with that choice?"

"Not really." Aviva tried to scrape an imaginary stain off the table that stood beside us. "He was able to get much more, position wise and salary wise."

"And now they had two children."

"Right."

"And he was still the sole provider?"

"Yes."

"But in the past, that hadn't been enough to raise one child."

"First of all, he wasn't a junior bank clerk anymore; the bank took into consideration the seniority that he had accumulated. Besides, Hanni always believed it was just a matter of time before he got a new executive position."

"And how did they manage? Financially, I mean, a couple with two kids, but half the salary?"

"It wasn't half the salary." Aviva waved me off again with the same dismissive flick of the wrist.

"Frankly, it was even less than half the salary."

"Really?" She was surprised.

"Yes."

"Listen, they managed, cut back a little..." I thought about the big car and the vacation abroad "...and, also... " Aviva paused, uncertain whether to share, but realizing this wasn't the place to hide, "...they also got some help from their parents." Aviva made an embarrassed face. "There's no shame in it; a lot of couples get help from their parents occasionally."

"So you assisted them financially?"

"As much as we could. We live a pretty good life, but we're pensioners."

"And Meir's parents?"

"Meir's parents are very wealthy people; I assume they helped a little more."

"Hanni didn't share this with you?"

"No."

I felt there was no point of continuing the conversation at that point, so I told her she could call Shimon in. I had the feeling that she wasn't telling the whole truth, but I decided not to push her into a corner. The woman was still sitting *Shiva* for her daughter and three grandchildren. Like many other people, Aviva was in denial. Her daughter was the most perfect, and her son-in-law was the most talented, and they all lived happily ever after until the moment Meir decided to kill them all.

I always hated this hypocrisy. I didn't understand why it was important to people to hide the flaws, the mistakes, the pain, and put up a false front that everything's okay. I learned in my job that, even in the hardest moments, people will hide things and lie—even if there's no good reason to do so, except for the will not to be seen as a failure by others. The most interesting and pleasant people I'd ever met were those who never tried to embellish their reality. My sister, Shira, was like that. Yinon, too. I, also, always tried to be honest with myself and not cover up and try to embellish reality, not to myself and certainly not to others.

The door of the room was hesitantly opened and I jumped in alarm.

"Oh, I didn't mean to frighten you," Shimon said softly.

"No, it's okay." I smiled and gestured to him to sit in the chair across from me. "What can you tell me about your son-in-law?"

"He was a good guy."

"Was there something in his behavior that could be an indication for such an insane act?"

"What do you mean?"

"Sudden rage, verbal or physical abuse, threats of any kind?"

"Not at all." Shimon shook his head. "If anything, the opposite."

"The opposite?"

"He was a very quiet man." I thought of all the serial killers who were outstanding citizens on the outside.

"There weren't any signs of distressing behavior?"

"Not that I noticed."

"Obsessive behavior?"

"What do you mean?"

"Like an obsession for cleanliness, quiet, order?"

"No."

"Excuse my forward question, but do you know of any infidelity or disloyalty by either one of them?"

"I've already heard these vicious rumors." Some internet sites had published assertions that little Noa was not Meir's daughter. "And I'm telling you there's no chance." He sounded very convincing.

"How can you be sure?"

"I know my daughter."

"So maybe it was Meir?"

"Even if Meir had someone on the side, what reason in the

world would he have to kill his wife and kids because of it, and then kill himself?"

He was right. "Can you make any comment on why Meir did what he apparently did?"

"I really can't. Believe me, it's killing me."

"Maybe money issues?"

"They had problems with money?"

"I understood from Aviva that you helped them out."

"No more than we help our other children."

"And still, Meir had a very good job and he was forced to transfer to a far less rewarding job."

"Still, it was a job with a handsome salary, as far as I know."

"So you don't think there were money worries here?"

"It's hard for me to believe. After all, you know who Meir's parents are."

"I haven't met them yet."

"Meir's father's a very successful food importer and his mother's the daughter of a very wealthy family. She has dozens of properties in Tel-Aviv and Haifa. I can't imagine a situation where their son would want for anything."

I decided that I should meet Meir's parents as soon as possible. I said goodbye to Shimon and Aviva and promised to update them when things became a bit clearer.

I wanted to call Riki at the station to get the Danilowitz family's phone number. I had left my cell phone in the car and now discovered fifteen missed calls from my mother. If this wasn't my mother, I'd fear something terrible happened in my family.

"Where are you?" my mother shoots the second she answers the call.

"Working."

"Then why aren't you with your phone?"

"I left it in the car."

"What do you have a mobile phone for? If there's an emergency, you can't be reached!"

"There's an emergency?"

"Sort of." (This meant, "No.")

"Where are you?"

"On the way to work."

"Physically, where are you now?"

"Ramat Gan."

"Great." She breathed a sigh of relief. "Can you go to our house and see if I switched the iron off? I'm with your father on the way to Be'er Sheva. He has an appointment there with the income tax department, so I decided to go with him to visit Aunt Henia from Tkuma. She's in hospital in Soroka. You remember, she had her surgery a week ago—"

"Okay," I cut her off. I didn't have time to hear Aunt Henia's complete medical history. "I'll send you a text message after I check."

"But go now, it's very dangerous."

"Okay, okay," I answered impatiently and made a U-turn to get to my parents' house.

Lately, I'd been getting quite a few of these calls and texts from my mother. If I wasn't worried about her, I'd be annoyed with her constantly rushing me to her house to check that the gas/oven/iron/boiler was shut off. They always were.

She never did this to my sisters, because they had kids. Evyatar got the calls sometimes, mostly when I was unavailable.

The iron was, of course, not even plugged in. I went to the refrigerator and pulled out a box of cubed watermelon. How simple to buy a watermelon, cut it up and put it in the fridge. How come I never did that?

I sat down in the study and stared at the library. The room was surprisingly similar to the study at the Levin house, where I had sat a few minutes earlier. I stared at the holy books and the different albums. Suddenly my photo album from high school caught my eye. I began leafing through it and saw that most of the pictures were of me with my Convent friends. I looked at the image of sixteen-year-old me. I hadn't changed much. Apart from the religious-girl clothes and the zits, I'd stayed exactly the same. Not only externally.

Toward the end of the album, I stopped and froze. There was a picture there of Hanni and me, standing side by side at the high school graduation ceremony. The only reason that brought fate to put us in the same picture together was the fact that we'd had similar last names and were called after one another to receive our diplomas. Maybe Hanni's mother also had this picture of Hanni smiling with a wide grin, with me standing next to her forcing a smile. Maybe she'd also perused her daughter's albums, as many grieving families do, and seen this picture and felt a tinge of sadness. Two girls graduated high school side by side, and fifteen years later one was investigating the murder of the other one. I felt sorry for her.

I took the picture and closed the album, even more determined to find out what happened to Hanni.

I remembered that I hadn't yet called Riki to get the Danilowitz family's phone number. Meir's sister picked up the phone and called her father.

"Natan Danilowitz?" I asked carefully.

"Who's asking?"

"Hadas Levinger from the central unit, Israel Police."

"Hello, Hadas," he said and loudly moaned.

"Hello, Sir, first of all, allow me to express my condolences for your tremendous loss."

"Thank you."

"I was just with your in-laws, asking them some questions. I wanted to know if I could possibly come to see you as well."

"Could it wait until after the *Shiva*?" His voice was shaking. I didn't know if he was angry or sad.

"It's your choice."

"Then we'd rather leave it until Monday."

"When do you want me to come?"

"We can come to you," he answered courteously and surprised me. I'd sensed he was angry, but now I realized he was just deep in his grief.

I thought for a moment. I'd prefer to see the Danilowitz's

home. "I'll come to you."

"We finish the *Shiva* on Monday, so you can come Monday afternoon."

"No problem." I hung up quickly. It was difficult for him, and I didn't want to pester a person in such deep grief.

The whole way to the station, I thought about the conversations I had earlier with Hanni's parents. I had pretty good intuition about people. Hanni's mother seemed as if she had something to hide, while her father was open and matter of fact.

I still didn't have a lead as to Meir's horrible motive, if it really was him. I got the impression that the couple were having financial problems that had pushed Meir to the edge. It wouldn't be the first time a person committed suicide because of financial pressures. To kill off your entire family as well, because of financial pressures, is a bit more unusual, though not unknown.

But since Meir's parents were very wealthy, my line of thought began to waver. I was not a mother, but I assumed that a parent would do anything for their children, even when they're adults. It was hard for me to believe that Meir's parents had allowed him to fall upon hard times.

I didn't know if there were infidelities in their marriage, but DNA samples had proven Meir's paternity of all of the children.

What could be the story here? By the way Hanni's body was placed, there were no signs of struggle, meaning this wasn't a fight that got out of control, though they may have fought earlier and Meir couldn't calm down.

I got to the office, and on the desk, waiting for me, were the Danilowitz's bank statements, printouts of data that I had requested from the Office of Internal Affairs and the Income Tax Department, and all of the numbers called in the last six months from all of the landlines and cell phones belonging to the couple.

According to the bank statements, Hanni and Meir were up

to their neck in debt: some accounts with an 150,000 shekels overdraft, loans as high as 600,000 shekels, and a mortgage of 1,400,000 shekels.

Assuming the worth of the apartment they were living in was about a million and a half shekels, even if they sold their apartment to cover their debt, they would still be left with a negative balance. There was good reason to talk to the branch manager to understand the issue of their debt.

I looked over the analysis of the printout of their phone calls. The landline in their house was hardly ever used. Most of the calls were made using their cellular phones, specifically Hanni's. Most of the calls were to the number belonging to Hanni's mother. After this were many calls to the number of a user called Iris Green, as well as calls to Meir's number. Meir's cell phone was not as active as Hanni's, and most of his calls were to Hanni.

I called Iris Green's number and was asked to type in a secret code. She was probably out of the country.

"You have people here to be interrogated," Riki informed me on the phone; I went to the reception desk.

A young religious man accompanied by his pretty wife were there waiting for me, also the neighbors from the apartment above. Riki had contacted some friends and neighbors from the building and the neighboring building. Some had been questioned immediately after the bodies were discovered. I sat with each of them separately in the interrogation room. Amazingly, none of the neighbors heard the gunshots. The killer made sure to shut all the windows tight, and had wrapped the gun in a piece of mineral wool to dull the sound of the shots.

Mineral wool was a material used for insulation used mainly by building contractors. The fact that Meir, allegedly, equipped himself with a piece of mineral wool raised the assumption that the murder was premeditated. The friends and neighbors testified that Hanni and Meir were the model family. Hanni was very involved in the community life of the neighborhood, Meir and the kids came to synagogue every Shabbat and participated in many of the events organized by the synagogue committee. Their shock at this story was evident in their faces.

At eight o'clock, after hours of the same questions and answers, I took a short coffee break, and when I returned, the last neighbor of the day was waiting for me.

She was Orit Sagiv, the neighbor from the next building whose apartment overlooked the balcony of the Danilowitz apartment. She sat with her legs crossed on the interrogation chair, her foot moving impatiently, holding a plastic cup of water given to her by Riki.

"Hello," I said and quickly sat down. "Sorry about the delay. I had to breathe for a minute. I've been interrogating for hours."

Orit rolled her eyes. I saw my excuses didn't especially interest her, but, like most civilians, she chose not to yell at me, especially in a police station, no less.

I explained to her that the conversation between us was to be recorded and asked her to state, for protocol, her identifying details.

"My name is Orit Sagiv, thirty-eight, from Givaat Shmuel."

"Where do you work?"

"For Teva."

"How do you know the Danilowitz family?"

"I've known Meir since he was a kid." She surprised me. I'd thought she was just a neighbor.

"How exactly?"

"His sister, Michal, is a childhood friend of mine from Petach Tikva."

"And what can you tell me about Meir?"

"Not too much. He was a cute kid. As a teenager, he was quite popular. He was very good-looking and his family's pretty rich, so he stood out at Bnei Akivah."

"Do you remember an aggressive or violent boy?"

"Not really, but I have to admit I didn't know him. Michal

was my friend in high school and then we parted ways. I met her accidentally a few years ago, just when Meir and Hanni moved across from us. She came to a housewarming and told me that her brother was moving in right across from me."

"Do you remember when this was?"

"Chanuka of 2003."

"How do you remember?"

"I was pregnant with my third daughter. Hanni was also pregnant with her second."

"So you were on maternity leave together."

Orit snorted in contempt. "Hanni didn't need maternity leave. She didn't work."

"So you raised your daughters together?" I corrected myself.

"Not really. We never really gelled."

"Why?"

"Listen." She sipped the last drop of water from the plastic cup. "I'm an honest person, and I don't like hypocrisy or falseness. I can tell you that, just now, my sister-in-law, my husband's sister, left her home and husband for another man. There's no normal person who isn't shocked by a young woman taking two little girls and wrecking their home, but I just told her to her face what everyone's thinking and too afraid to say. Hanni wasn't my sister-in-law and I really didn't care for her and her family, so she never heard what I thought about her, but I think she saw that I couldn't really stand her."

"How would she see that?"

"I didn't initiate any social relationship with them, even though I actually knew her husband from childhood."

"Did she have many social connections?"

"She was pretty popular in the neighborhood."

"What does popular mean?"

"She'd sit a lot in the coffee shops in the mall, or gossip with moms in the park while her kids were going wild."

"Her kids were wild?"

"Mostly the big one. No boundaries, that one."

"And was the little girl friends with your daughter?"

"They were in the same kindergarten, really a sweet girl, it's a shame."

"Then why couldn't you stand her?"

"Put it this way..." She took a deep breath and continued. "Whatever I think of Sharon, my sister-in-law, I think even she was a better mother than Hanni."

"But Hanni was a full-time mom."

"Even worse. My sister-in-law, for example, is a lawyer, and she still finds the time to devote to her girls. Hanni sat at home all day, or in cafés, to be exact. I don't think I'm perfect, but once I get home, I'm fully with my kids, or at least I try to be. Any working mom knows how difficult it is to juggle everything, and sometimes it's impossible. I, personally, work mainly because for the money, but also for interest. But if I worked only, maybe, part time, which is impossible in my field—if I didn't work, like Hanni, for instance, I don't know if I'd leave my kids in afternoon daycare. If all my mornings were free, I'd use them to do errands and socializing so I'd have all the time in the world with the kids."

"And Hanni wasn't like that?"

"I don't think so. I'd often see her walking around in the mall in the afternoon, and when she was with her children she didn't seem too attentive to them. I'll never forget how—about two years ago—my daughter and her daughter played together in the sand box in the playground. I sat near them and watched them and she was sitting at the other end of the playground chatting with her friends, not even bothered. How can you sit like that, not even knowing where your three-year-old is? It drove me crazy. At some point, I wanted to go home and I didn't want to leave the little girl by herself so I took her to her mother. She turned on me and immediately attacked me, saying she didn't ask me to babysit. I asked her how she could let such a small child play unattended and she yelled at me that I couldn't educate her and teach her how to be a mother."

"What else do you remember about her?"

"The playground... in September or October. In August of

the same year, we went for a vacation, to a country house in the north with friends. I don't remember the name of the place, but it was very nice, if a bit simple. In the afternoon, we sat on the lawn and had a barbecue with our friends. It was very quiet and nice until we suddenly heard shouting from one of the houses nearby. A woman was yelling—screaming, really—at her husband."

"What?" I was curious.

"Something along the lines of, 'What kind of a dump did you bring us to? The one time I ask you to take care of something and we end up in this dump!' The man was trying to calm her down and tell her this was what he'd been able to get in their price range. It was a site that included a number of country houses—some of them made of wood, which were newer, and some made of stone, which were quite old. The whole site wasn't very luxurious, but in August everything's insanely expensive and it was a vacation for the kids, so it was more important to us that there would be a lawn, a pool and nearby attractions than a fancy room.

"The woman went on screaming and then Meir came out of their cabin and walked toward Reception. He came back a few minutes later and we understood that he'd tried to switch to a fancier one, but they were all booked. A few minutes later, Meir, Hanni, and both their kids came out of the cabin in bathing suits, and only then did Hanni notice me. I think she was embarrassed because she realized that we'd heard her; she walked away quickly and didn't stop near us."

"Did you ever hear her shout like that at home, in Givaat Shmuel?"

"Not as clearly as in the cabin. They always kept their windows shut, as if they were trying to keep all of the shouting inside. I heard her numerous times, reprimanding her husband and yelling at him and the kids, but because the windows were shut, I couldn't clearly hear what the yelling was about."

"Can you tell me how it's possible that none of the other neighbors heard the shouting you're describing?"

"I've no idea. You have to understand that our study overlooks their balcony directly, so I guess I had the best spot. When we were in the country, there were no other people from the neighborhood there, and the windows were also open, unlike their house."

She went silent. I sensed she had something else to tell.

"Is there anything else you want to tell me?"

"Uh…" she began stuttering. "I'm not sure… I could be wrong."

"Tell me what you think you know. My job is to check the facts."

"When we were in the north, I think I also heard her hit her son. I don't know if it was a one-time thing, or something that happened regularly. I only came across it there, so maybe there she didn't hide it as well."

"What did you hear?"

"When she was yelling at Meir and he went out, her boy was crying and getting a little wild so she screamed at him and I heard hitting sounds. After that the boy was only crying. When they went out, his eyes were red and she was tugging him forcefully. It was only when she noticed us that I got the feeling that she toned her behavior down."

"And you didn't hear or see her hitting her kids at home?"

"Of course not. If I was certain this was an ongoing thing you can be sure I'd have made a complaint to the police. Unfortunately, she wasn't much different from parents who smack their kids now and then, but would never do it in public, surely not anywhere anyone knows them, and surely not in a neighborhood like Givaat Shmuel where every little thing immediately turns to neighborhood gossip. There in the north, she thought she was alone, so she allowed herself to be a little less cautious."

"Did you hear the gunshots this Monday?"

"No, but the windows were shut as usual, and, from what I understand, the shots were fired when we were sleeping."

"What do you think about what happened? You've known

Meir since childhood. Does he seem like someone who's able to get up one morning, kill his entire family and shoot himself?"

"My degree's in chemistry, not psychology, but I have to say I was shocked. Specifically because I've known Meir since childhood. He was a super-normal guy, even a little bit of a nerd. If anything, of the two of them, she was the violent one. Not that, God forbid, I think she was capable of committing murder, but he was kind of 'whipped.' Like, during that vacation, we saw them at breakfast in the dining room a few times. She gave him the runaround. I remember I joked with my husband that I should act a little more like Hanni, then maybe he'd appreciate me."

"Sounds like you had a pretty robust opinion of her."

"Don't get me wrong, I have a life and Hanni was definitely not part of it, but I admit that after that incident in the north and that episode in the playground, I was intrigued by the woman. Seeing a person so self-involved—that's not something you see every day."

When Orit's interrogation was over, I was exhausted. The station was almost empty, a calm quiet enveloping it. I made myself a cup of coffee and treated myself to a chocolate bar from the vending machine near the entrance.

I sat down in my quiet office and looked despondently at the permanent mess covering my table. I took out the picture of Hanni and me that I found in the photo album; Hanni's beaming smile compared to my forced smile. It was interesting that I didn't remember us going up together to receive our diplomas. Frankly, I didn't remember too many details from high school, which were not exactly the best years of my life.

I was far from being a social creature. I was never invited to parties that I knew were being held here and there in the houses of my classmates. There were also these gatherings at Hanni's house, which I never got to be a part of. My social world consisted of my Convent friends, and even they were a bit more social than I was.

I was an excellent student, but this fact didn't make me

teacher's pet. I was what a religious high school would call a "rebellious student." My only rebellion was my stern refusal to go to morning prayers and the fact that, throughout all my high school years, I continually argued with my Bible study teachers. I recalled "marital relations" class in junior year, when our teacher, a young woman who'd been married not long before, explained *Halachot Nidda* [rules concerning women's menstruation] to us with glimmering eyes, while stressing how beautiful the Jewish religion is and how it respects the woman.

I couldn't keep quiet. I asked the young teacher, who was no more than five years my elder, how she could possibly say that the Jewish religion respects the Jewish woman when we women didn't even have the right to testify. I was a good student, but I had numerous examples I could use to prove to her that the Jewish religion is anything but equal and respecting. My young teacher was left speechless. Her reaction was the same as the reaction of any religious Jew who is proven wrong and shown that he's mistaken in his beliefs. She claimed I was taking things out of context and that I must look at the big picture. To this day, I can't understand this answer. The fact that, for instance, a woman can't testify, is very specific and doesn't belong to any big picture.

And so, despite having the highest scores in the grade, each semester I was somehow passed over when diplomas were given out. When excellent students were sent on a delegation to England, they didn't even bother to offer it to me (Hanni went, of course); when excellent students were sent to a ceremony at the president's house, I wasn't there. The only time the school wanted to honor me was when they wanted to send me to a national math competition. They knew they would have a better chance of succeeding if they sent me. I, of course, declined the honor. I didn't like the fact that they were reminded of my abilities only when they could be used to benefit the school.

By my senior year, my rebelliousness had reached its peak. I sternly refused to attend the lectures they organized about civil service. When my homeroom teacher asked me why I wouldn't go, I told her I'd go to these lectures if they also gave us lectures about military service.

I graduated high school with excellent grades, except for bible studies, not because I didn't know the curriculum, but because the teacher didn't like my answers. I was the ideal candidate to receive the award for excellence at the graduation ceremony. Hanni received it.

Maybe that's the reason for my sour smile? Was I jealous of Hanni? I imagine I was.

I remember my mother was very disappointed that I didn't get the award, although I fully deserved it. Throughout my whole life, I managed to disappoint her so many times because of my stubborn opinions and "inappropriate" behavior, as she called it. If there was one action where I succeed in bringing her some joy, it was my scholarly achievements. She was eventually compensated by my diplomas of excellence in the army and at university, but to this day, she never forgot that I should have gotten that award at my high school graduation—and didn't.

I didn't recall if I was disappointed myself or for her, but I was left with a bitter taste in my mouth from that ceremony, where Hanni was crowned the best student and I was left behind, with a pathetic smile and an ordinary diploma.

CHAPTER 5

Friday, 5.22.2009

I wanted to meet Ariel's teacher at his school. Batya Gantz had a free hour every Friday morning. She waited for me in the principal's room and looked like everything I remembered from an elementary school teacher: she had short, graying hair, wore ill-fitting and outdated clothes, and wore strange silver jewelry, most of it the craftwork of amateur artists. She gestured for me to take the chair on the other side of the table. On her arm was a bracelet fashioned out of a fork. Even her tone of voice was that of a teacher. When she spoke, she only showed her bottom teeth.

The lady in front of me had got lost somewhere in the eighties. She introduced herself as the homeroom teacher of second grade number one, one of the boys' classes. She had been teaching at the school since it was founded, and before that she had taught in a school in Petach Tikva.

"I have no words to express to you how shocked I am by this whole story," she said, and blew her nose. "I couldn't sleep for two days. I'm just exhausted right now. I've been a teacher for thirty years and I've never gone through such a horrifying ordeal."

I told her that if it was difficult for her, we could meet when she'd calmed down, but she wanted to proceed with the questioning, and wanted to help as much as she could.

"Arieli was a beautiful boy," Batya said lovingly. "He had big, intelligent eyes." Batya broke down in tears again and I nudged the pack of tissues in her direction.

"Was he a good student?"

Batya smiled timidly. It was obvious that she was finding it difficult to speak ill of the dead. "He was very smart, but he didn't reach his full potential."

"Why?"

"I'm no expert, but I do have thirty years of teaching experience. I think the boy had an undiagnosed attention deficit disorder."

"Can you expand?"

"May I know how this is relevant to the investigation?"

It was still unclear to me, too, but I wanted to get to know the late Danilowitz family as well as I could.

"Mrs. Gantz, I ask the questions here," I said and smiled to soften her up, and she went on.

"The boy had obvious difficulty sitting down in class. His notebooks were a mess. He had a hard time reading, and he was way behind everyone in math."

"Maybe he wasn't smart enough?"

"I think he was very smart. When I sat with him alone and explained it to him, I saw that his comprehension was excellent, even above average, but his attention disorder got in the way of his ability to advance."

"Was he diagnosed as suffering from attention deficit disorder?"

"No. Well, I never saw such a diagnosis."

"So how do you know he had such a problem?"

"Formally, I don't know, but I do have years of experience and I've had dozens, if not hundreds, of cases in which I knew before the parents did and actually guided them until they sought the appropriate treatment."

"And what did you recommend to Ariel's parents?"

"I told them what I told you, that he was a smart boy, but his difficulty was getting in the way of his development. I explained that there was no reason to be afraid of diagnosis and treatment."

"What treatment?"

"In Ariel's case, and from my experience, the only effective therapy could have been medicinal."

"Ritalin?"

"Yes, Ritalin. Or Concerta, whatever the doctor prescribes. I, of course, don't hand out prescriptions, but I often bring it up with the parents so they can go to the doctor with an open mind. I think there's a lot of ignorance about this subject. Someone hears a child experiences side-effects because of Ritalin and immediately they talk about the medicine as if it's poison."

"Did you mention Ritalin to Meir and Hanni as well?"

"To Hanni. Meir didn't come to the parent-teacher meetings," Batya corrected me.

"I have a feeling she didn't like your advice."

"To say the least. I don't remember such an outburst of rage from a parent."

"What did she say?"

Batya chuckled. "She said she wasn't going to drug her child so it would be easier for me in the classroom."

"Why are you laughing?"

"Because it's a pretty common line from parents, when they don't understand two fundamental things: the first is that I'm only with the child for part of each day, while they have to deal with a restless child during most of the day, and the second is that the medical treatment is for the good of the child and not the good of the teacher."

"And there's no other treatment that doesn't involve medication?"

"There's an option to give the child a wide range of

treatments that increase the attention span and decrease the need for medicine, but that only works when the disorder's not very severe to begin with, and when the parents are prepared and willing to invest a lot of themselves. Medical therapy requires the parent to give the child a pill and a glass of water. Alternative therapy requires many hours of treatment at the expense of the parents' and the child's free time."

"Was Ariel treated?"

"I've seen so many children and parents that I can categorize them quite easily. I'm rarely surprised. Ariel was the type of kid whose parents think pampering with brands constitutes good parenting. They replace parental giving with shopping. Don't get me wrong, I don't object to gifts and all sorts of treats. But you see some children who have no value for money and are busy morning until night with the next toy he wants to get. I can also understand where this stems from. Many parents work in a very pressurized job, they barely see the kids and the gifts are the parents' way of expressing their love and mainly quieting their conscience. Two weeks ago, I had to do some tests at Asuta hospital in Ramat Hachayal. Have you ever been there?"

"No."

"Right across from Asuta is the big, beautiful building of a high-tech company, I think it's Comverse. Below it are a few cafés and restaurants, and right in the center is a toy store. It's not a residential area, not a shopping center, there are no schools or kindergartens there. A toy store in the heart of a high-tech area. On second thoughts, I realized that whoever put the store there was a genius. He put it right where he could get the most loyal, potential customers: guilt-ridden high-tech workers."

"Excuse me for stopping you," I took advantage of a short break in Batya's flow of words, "but Meir and Hanni weren't high-tech workers. Meir may have worked very hard, but Hanni was a full-time mother."

Batya smiled. "The fact that a woman doesn't go out to work doesn't automatically make her a full-time mom. I see this happening quite a lot as well. Non-working mothers, who think new shoes are more important than playing with the child one-on-one. Even here, I think the purchase comes from a place of guilt. They understand they're doing something wrong and try to make it up to the kids with gifts and new clothes."

"So you think Ariel didn't get the appropriate care from his parents?"

"Listen," Batya fidgeted with one of the giant rings that graced her chubby fingers, "I don't think they were bad parents. They definitely loved their kids. The parents saw that the toys helped the boy fit in, because a child who has toys is a popular child, and they thought they'd found a solution, but there's no real magic solution to attention deficit disorder. The only solution is treatment."

"Medication."

"Medication, or para-medicinal. It all depends on the child. I recommended to Hanni that she go see a neurologist and seek options for occupational therapy treatments that the HMO covers."

I was reminded of Renana, my friend's sister who told me Hanni asked her about an occupational therapist. Perhaps Hanni didn't completely ignore the teacher's advice.

"Are you sure Ariel didn't get treatment at any point?"

"It's really hard for me to say. I have a feeling that he did, especially lately. He'd calmed down a little bit, was more introverted and less impulsive."

"Is that a result of occupational therapy?"

"Occupational therapy usually improves the child's graphic abilities and not the attention span. I guess Ariel had started taking Ritalin in the last couple of months."

As I exited the school, I thought about what the teacher told me. I wasn't an expert in this field at all, but I also had the feeling that medications like Ritalin are a convenient solution for teachers. Up to today, when I saw a child being unruly, I was simply happy that it wasn't my child and it only strengthened my decision not to bring a child into this world, but could I be so judgmental toward people who choose to give their child Ritalin?

"Hadas?" A masculine voice jolted me from my thoughts.

It was Yuval Eidelman, who was in the Amishav branch of Bnei Akivah. Yuval was one of the more popular boys in the branch. Unlike me, he never missed a meeting "on the street corner" each Friday night. He was tall and handsome, and half of the girls in the branch were in love with him. When we were sixteen, he'd hardly noticed my existence, so I was surprised that he even knew my name. Unlike my close girlfriends, who called me "Gunger," people less close to me called me by my first name.

The years—how can I put this gently—hadn't been kind to Yuval. He was still tall, but had also grown sideways a bit. His hair had thinned and his bald head shone between the few hairs gracing his head.

"You haven't changed at all!" he enthused.

I had changed. In high school my face was covered with dozens of zits, and I had the constant appearance of a waif. I was always very thin, and religious girls' skirts never suited me. Fifteen years later, I still didn't know how to dress, but my zits had gone and my figure was maintained, so now I looked a bit less neglected in jeans.

"Neither have you," I lied.

Yuval gently stroked his belly. Maybe he noticed the sarcasm in my voice? He looked me over from head to toe.

"Do you have kids in this school?"

"I don't have any kids."

"Really?" He was surprised. "I was sure I heard you got married." I was surprised that rumors of my marriage reached Mr. Eidelman.

"I'm already divorced."

"You don't say?" He made a surprised and impressed face, as if he was at this very moment looking at the queen of Tel Aviv nightlife, taking a short break from a line of trance parties to stop by the Naftali Heritage Elementary School in Givaat Shmuel. "So what are you doing here, then?"

"You really don't know?" Did no one see me on television?

"No." He scratched the top of his head and I was suddenly flashing back to the last visit I took with my nephews to the monkey zoo.

"I'm investigating the Danilowitz family case."

"Oh," he nodded, in recognition. "An appalling story, just horrible." I nodded. "Are you a police officer?" He looked at me, surprised. "I thought you were a lawyer." How the hell did he know I studied law?

"I'm still a lawyer. I joined the police about a year ago." I understood it would be rude not to ask him what he does for a living. "Where do you work?" I asked without much interest.

"I'm still at Amdox." He said "still" as if I was meant to know that.

"Are you an engineer?" I tried my luck.

"No." He was surprised that I didn't know all about his résumé. "I studied economics and business management. I'm in the financial department."

"Sounds interesting," I lied. "Are you married?"

"Of course." *What an idiotic question!* "I married Hila Erlich from the Achdut branch," he said this as if I was supposed to know Miss Hila Erlich from the Achdut branch.

"Am I supposed to know her?"

"She's Oren's sister."

"Oren Erlich?" I was struck. Oren was Yuval's best friend. They both ruled the branch, tall and beautiful, no one challenged their reign. I remember on one of the rare Saturdays when I bothered showing up at the branch, right after the evening prayer. The girls of the branch had agreed to meet later in Orda Square for pizza and ice cream. I was going, and was asked to pass the message to the boys' circle. "Who decided that?" Oren asked in a belittling tone. "*You*?" He almost spat. It was inconceivable that everyone would go out because of me to Orda Square, the nearly permanent hangout of the popular clique every Saturday night.

"Today, we're not just best friends, we're brothers by law." Yuval was amused by his own joke.

"I assume you have kids here?"

"Right." He smiled proudly. "I brought my second born in late because he had a hearing test."

"How many kids do you have?"

"Three and another one on the way." Yuval was right on the "four kids" trend.

"Nice," I lied again.

"Are you in touch with anyone?" Yuval was curious to discover if he could expand his gossip circle.

"Not really. I ran into Tamar here, two days ago."

"Tamar?" He furrowed his brow.

"Tamar Golan." He still stared at me with a dumbfounded look. "She was in my class. She's a doctor now."

"Oh! Tamar Shlezinger."

"Yeah, she lives not far from here. Are you in touch with her?"

"Not really. Givaat Shmuel has gotten really big." Despite all the years that had passed, the cliques were still maintained.

"Did you know the Danilowitz family?"

"We were in touch."

"Really? How did you know them?"

"You know… synagogue, running into each other at the playground, at the mall."

"And what were they like?"

"A lovely couple. I can't understand what came over him."

"Did you know him?" I hoped that maybe, finally, here was someone who also knew Meir and not only Hanni.

"We weren't close friends, but we occasionally talked, no heart-to-hearts, just small talk."

"And what was your impression of him?"

"Nice guy, maybe a bit introverted, but very positive."

"Violent?"

"Not in the least, maybe even the opposite - too gentle."

"And did you know Hanni?"

"Hanni was a branch member with us," he reminded me. “Amazing girl, beautiful, a great mom." Apparently the opinions about Hanni's parenting skills weren't unanimous. "You know, she was a lawyer too, but she put her career on hold to be a full-time mom."

I had the feeling he was chiding me for the fact that I was still not fulfilling my demographic designation. "So she was a good mother?"

"Great. I'd see her a lot in the playground and her kids were always dressed like out of a magazine." Yuval was of Shira's opinion, that Hanni and her children were magazine material, though Shira had made it sound like a negative thing, while Yuval saw it as an advantage.

"Did you ever talk to her? Did she tell you if something was bothering her?"

"I didn't talk to her as much. Maybe my wife could help you." I took out a small notepad and wrote down a phone number for Hila Eidelman (formerly Erlich).

I gave Yuval my business card, in case he heard something interesting and wanted to share it with me.

"We may be having an Amishav branch reunion. I'll email you the details," he said, waving the card I handed him.

"Excellent." I smiled an artificial smile. I'd rather watch paint dry on a wall than meet up with this gossipy bunch.

Yuval felt, for some reason, that this accidental meeting has made us friends and he came nearer to me and whispered, "Excuse me for interfering, but, in your shoes, I'd go with a sperm bank. There are even religious girls our age, now, who’ve given up on finding a husband, and had a kid by themselves before their biological clock runs out."

Yuval misinterpreted my silence. He probably thought his words touched me, so he lightly patted my shoulder and said, "I hope I was of help to you," and ran out to his car, which was blocking the entrance gate to the school.

CHAPTER 6

Saturday, 5.23.2009

Ever since I could remember, in our family, Shira was considered the successful child and I was the black sheep. Although we had two more siblings—Ayala, who was four years younger than me and Evyatar, who was six years younger than me—comparisons were always made between the two of us. The difference between the classic model for a good kid and what I grew up to become and what Shira grew up to become, is a chasm. We were both academic and I even studied an established profession like law, but, as you know, I eventually did nothing practical with my degree, and if you asked my mother, she'd say I threw away a degree that cost me tens of thousands of shekels just to become "a cop."

She told me this only before I joined the police. After the deed was done, she made sure not to belittle it to my face, but only behind my back. Shira, who was born a year and a half before me, was an occupational therapist, a profession that fitted her like a glove.

My parents had taken special care not to talk about the childlessness issue with me. Those conversations never ended well and here, too, Shira fulfilled for them everything they expected from their offspring. Shira had three adorable, beautiful and well-brought up children.

But, beyond the dry facts of career and children, Shira was simply a model daughter, always remembered to send flowers on Mother's Day (in all our names), call every aunt and uncle to wish them a happy new year at Rosh Hashanah, when our grandfather was sick, she ran around the hospitals with my mother. When someone wasn't feeling well, she always took an interest and cared for them. And on top of all this, she also ran her household single-handedly.

I lived alone, and my apartment looked like a disaster area. Shira's house was always impeccably neat, especially given that she had three children. She always claimed she had no choice because patients came to her house and she felt obligated, but that was Shira's way of making me feel comfortable with the fact that I couldn't organize myself. Because of the mess, and because I could hardly cook an egg, I didn't entertain my family at my house too often. My mother and Shira covered for me by claiming that it was impossible to get to my house by foot on Shabbat, and that my house wasn't really Kosher, but those were just excuses, because they could come on a weekday and I could buy plastic tableware. The real reason was that nobody wanted to come to my house to eat frozen processed food heated up in the microwave, when they could go to Shira's for a luxurious meal.

That weekend, Shira invited my parents to spend the Sabbath at her house. The whole family was supposed to go to a hotel to celebrate Shavuot the next weekend, but a sudden ant infestation had forced my parents into exile (until the smell of the extermination passed). Since I had no religious qualms about driving on Shabbat, I joined them for lunch. Evyatar, our younger brother, had gone to spend Shabbat with a friend of his in Karnei Shomron. Ayala, our third sister lived in Ramat Gan, like my parents. But this time she passed, as she was early into her third pregnancy and didn't have the energy.

I arrived at Shira's relatively early. My dad was lying on the lazy-boy, the weekend papers scattered around him, his head lolling, his mouth agape, snoring steadily. My mother, who, after thirty-seven years of marriage had become completely indifferent to the symphonies produced by my father as he slept, lay comfortably on the couch, reading a book.

"*Shabbat Shalom*," I smiled at her. She lifted her eyes from the book and gave me a warm smile.

"*Shabbat Shalom* to you, too… you're a little early."

"I wanted to play with the kids a bit."

"They went to the playground with Moshe."

"Where's Shira?"

"Resting in her room."

"Is she asleep?"

"I don't know, maybe."

I tiptoed to Shira and Moshe's bedroom and peeked inside. Shira was lying on the bed, reading a book. She sensed someone was looking at her and looked up.

"*Shabbat Shalom!*" She smiled at me and lifted herself from her lair.

"*Shabbat Shalom*. Where are the kids?" I asked quickly.

"What? I'm not good enough?" She pretended to be insulted. I leaned toward her and gave her a warm hug. Although I will never be like Shira, she never gave me the impression that she thought she was better than me.

"I just miss them. This week when I was at your house, we didn't get to play that much. I was busy with my investigation and they didn't get the attention they deserve."

"Wow, what an aunt!" She pinched me on the cheek. "Moshe went out with them about thirty minutes ago. He's probably at the playground."

"Which one?" In the park at the heart of the new neighborhood were a number of playgrounds.

"Probably the nearest one, though sometimes he takes them on a longer walk."

The playground was packed with children. After a few rounds, I saw that Moshe and the kids weren't there.

It was pretty hot and I'd forgotten to take a bottle of water. I decided to wait where I was and hope Moshe would come to this playground, rather than walk around and risk dehydration.

I sat down on one of the benches near a young woman holding a plastic bowl, snacking on apple slices from it. Her young husband was chasing an active toddler of about two. Although I'm no longer a part of the Religious Zionist public, I can still differentiate pretty clearly between its sub-sectors. The young couple I was gazing at was of the religious-observant-spiritual variety. The man was wearing a large, white, knitted yarmulke. Like most of the men in the playground, he was also wearing a white shirt, but his was a bit less buttoned down and shabby.

His wife's head was swathed in a blue fabric head wrap so none of her hair was showing. She wore a loose dress that matched her headgear, of the kind that were worn by secular girls who had come back from travelling the Far East, but she was also wearing a white shirt underneath it with sleeves down to her elbows. They were both wearing Source sandals, which I assume they also used for more challenging hikes than going down to the playground on Saturday morning.

There's a higher chance of coming across this kind of couple in community settlements, mostly more remote settlements and settlements deep inside the occupied territories. The infamous Hilltop Youth gives them a bad name, because most of them do have nationalistic right wing tendencies, but most of them, if not all, are law abiding citizens who pay their taxes and serve in the army, have high environmental awareness and connect to nature and anything natural, which is why they escaped the cities.

Most of the people in the playground were Religious Zionist, Modern Orthodox and Religious-lite. The external differences between them were familiar mainly to those who knew these terms. They all wore knitted skullcaps, almost all the men were wearing white, button-down shirts and tailored pants, and all the women wore dresses intended mainly for Shabbat or celebrations. No one wore jeans on Shabbat, though there's no prohibition to in the Halacha. T-shirts were worn only if they were really beautiful and embellished.

The differences between their world views, most of them to do with lifestyle and amount of deeds to commit, were reflected in small nuances like the size of the skull cap and its color, the length of the sleeve or skirt, and the type of head wrap (the vast majority of the neighborhood's women didn't cover their hair, but even a religious-lite woman wouldn't dare enter a synagogue with a bare head).

I was out of place in the playground in my jeans and my tight T-shirt. There were a good number of secular families in the neighborhood, but they probably chose to go out of the neighborhood on Saturdays or at least not to visit the playground during the hours when the religious public "overtook" it. I stared at the passersby and they ignored me, or pretended to. Just like in high school, I was of no interest to anyone here, as usual, finding it hard to fit in, except now I had no desire to be a part of the crowd. These people, who I once was a part of, intrigued me. On the one hand, they were completely integrated in the life of secular society. Everybody worked as doctors, as lawyers, as engineers and such, and went out to the movies and Kosher restaurants in the main entertainment centers, but on the other hand, they lived in a community that was mostly expressed on Sabbaths and holidays.

Since they were immobile on Shabbat and holidays, they met at the synagogue or the neighborhood playground and had no way to escape being part of the community, unless they chose to shut themselves in their house every Sabbath. Because everyone knew one another, there was social pressure to at least appear to be a united and perfect family unit. The children and parents were all dressed in Shabbat clothes and looked nice. I hadn't had "Shabbat clothes" for years. I had two or three dresses that were a bit fancier, but not particularly modest, so they couldn't be considered "Shabbat clothes." A second glance at some of the women made it clear to me that I was a bit hard on myself in regard to modesty. Many women, of the Religious-lite variety, wore the shortest skirts. They sat in groups on the benches and let the men watch the kids.

I remembered the visit I made to the library earlier that week: during the week, it seemed that the mothers carried most of the parenting load, and on the Sabbath, the dads took the reins. The couple next to me wasn't playing or talking to anyone. The other people who sat at some distance from where I were sitting talking heatedly among themselves, I assumed about the Danilowitz family. It had only been five days since Meir shot his family and killed himself; it was a hot and powerful story. I wished I was sitting closer to them. Maybe I could have overheard things that they wouldn't tell me in an interview situation. On the other hand, I knew that if they were to discover who I was, the conversations would not be free in my presence.

Out of the corner of my eye, I noticed that a couple with a stroller had stopped by the couple of "Spiritualists" next to me. The man was embracing the young man warmly. I looked at the couple again and recognized them. They were Anat, my Convent friend, and Motti, her husband, who were apparently attached to their latest offspring.

"Anat?" I half called, half asked.

Anat turned her head in my direction and happily called out, "Gunger!" She approached me and I got up from the bench in her honor and we hugged happily.

"What are you doing here? Don't tell me you're working on the investigation right now..." I realized that she had already spoken to Tamar.

"No, not at all," I smiled. "I'm looking for my sister's husband and my nephews."

"I think I saw them in the playground near my house."

"How do you know them?"

"This is Givaat Shmuel," she laughed. "Everyone knows everyone."

"What are you doing here?"

"We're on our way to the second weekend family meal, at Tamar's."

Motti approached me, pushing a stroller with a toddler of about two or three years inside it.

"*Shabbat Shalom.*" He smiled at me. I hadn't seen him in years and he'd aged considerably. His hair had thinned and grayed and tiny wrinkles carved his face near his eyes. He was always a kind and quiet guy. Anat was one of the first in our grade to get married. We were only twenty years old, and a year later she was already a mother. Back then, the Convent gang, who were all single except for Anat, went on meeting, and Reut, Anat's eldest daughter, belonged to all of us—our pet baby.

"*Shabbat Shalom.*" I looked at the toddler, who was incredibly cute, but couldn't have been our Reuti. "Where's Reut? And the rest of the kids?" I had no idea how many children Motti and Anat had produced since Reut, and I didn't want to make a faux pas.

"Reut is off at the Bat Mitzva Shabbat of her best friend in Nir Etzyion. Elad and Eyal went straight there after synagogue with Haggai and Neriya."

By the way I was looking at her, she understood that I had no idea who she was talking about and added, "Elad and Eyal, my boys, are in the same classes as Haggai and Neriya, Tamar's boys. And this is Smadari, our little one." She bent down and wet-wiped the girl's face, which was covered with chocolate.

"How old is she now?" I asked, as if I remembered that she had four kids.

"Two-and-a-half." She straightened up and examined my svelte figure, as if searching for stretch marks. "I assume you're still into the 'no kids' thing?"

"Still into it." I smiled a satisfied smile. Anat could never understand me, but has since given up trying.

"I was sorry to hear you and Yinon broke up."

"Yeah, so was I."

I knew she had a lot to say to me, especially about the reason for my separation, but Motti and Avner interrupted us. Tamar and Yoni were waiting for them and they were anxious to go.

"Maybe you could join us?" Anit offered.

"My sister's waiting for me."

"So go up and tell her."

"Some other time," I evaded and, to my relief, Motti and Avner were too much in a hurry to try and prevent Anat from insisting.

After the group walked away, I spotted Noam, Shira's other son, running toward me. In the distance behind him, Moshe was slowly approaching, holding Eran.

"Aunt Hadas!" he yelled joyfully and hugged me. "Did you come to visit us again?"

"Yes," I smiled and he sat by me and updated me on all his latest news, and especially about the big fight he just had with Udi Reichman and Yuvi Blich.

Within a few minutes, Moshe sat down at my side, dripping with sweat. He put Eran down and announced to him that he would walk the rest of the way alone.

"Shira insists that he doesn't sit in a stroller anymore," he explained to me, "but what can I do when he's so lazy?" I had no doubt that if Shira thought Eran should walk, then Eran would walk.

"Where's Nurit?" I asked after my eldest niece.

"She's at her friend's house next door."

"How time flies," I said and Moshe smiled.

"What are you doing here?"

"Waiting for you."

"Been waiting long?"

"No, it's okay, I ran into Anat Kaufman."

"Who?"

"Oh, sorry, Anat Malitz."

"I saw her."

"I know, she told me."

"How do you know her?"

"We went to school together."

"Nice, I see half your branch moved here," he sighed, got up and called Eran and Noam.

Twenty meters later he was carrying Eran again and we all went up to their house.

"Shira, could you maybe sit down for a second?" I scolded Shira, who was running around the table, which was laden with food.

"Here, here, I'm sitting!" she said, sat by Eran and helped him to eat the fish that Moshe cut into tiny pieces for him.

"Apparently, you were right."

"Of course I was right," she smiled. "May I know what about?"

"There really is a four-child trend."

She laughed and my mother, herself a mother of four, asked what we were talking about.

"Shira told me this week that there's a new trend of having four children."

"Then you're four children off-trend." My dad couldn't help himself.

I gave him a fake smile and went on. "This week, I ran into three friends from high school and they all have four children or three with a fourth on the way."

"Who did you meet?"

"Just now I met Anat Kaufman and she has four kids. On Wednesday I met Tamar Golan and she's pregnant with her fourth, and yesterday I saw Yuval Eidelman, and his wife is in her fourth pregnancy."

"Yuval Eidelman went to school with you?" Shira asked.

"No, he was in the branch with me."

"Really?" Shira was surprised. "I didn't know."

"Do you know him?"

"A little bit, from synagogue. I'm not particularly fond of him."

"Why?"

"He's full of hot air," she said and I laughed.

"Can you explain to me what the 'four child trend' is?" My

mother interrupted us.

"I explained to Hadas this week," Shira took the reins, "that, lately, there's been a sort of trend to have four children. Once it was three and now it's four. It's sort of a status symbol."

"So that's why you're not having another child? Because everybody else does?" my mother inquired.

"I'll have a child only when I want another child, and it's very possible that I won't want another child. I feel, and I might be wrong," she paused, even though it was clear to all of us that Shira was hardly ever wrong, "that there's some sort of peer pressure to have four kids, as if four kids say something about how good a parent you are, as if the fact that whoever has more kids is a better, more dedicated parent, or maybe it shows something about how well-off they are."

"I think you're overreacting," my mother stopped her. "We had four children because it's what we always wanted."

"And, really, when we were kids, the fashion was three kids, which, in my opinion, is one kid more than most parents are able to raise properly. You and dad didn't have a fourth child because that's what everyone was doing, but because it's what you wanted."

"So you think anyone who has four kids is actually unfit to do so because having a fourth child, because of social pressure, is an injustice toward the child?"

"No need to get carried away. Even among those people who had a fourth child for the wrong reasons, most are good, fit parents."

"Then, what are you saying?"

"Look, mother, maybe I'm generalizing, but I'm a mother and I also work with children and I see children and parents every day and I see very few parents who really have parenting in their soul. Most are good parents, but I'm not convinced that they'd have had children if it weren't so customary in this country."

"So our Hadas is actually right, all along, by refusing to become a mother?" My mother was stunned by Shira.

"I admire Hadas." Shira amazed me. "Unlike so many others, she really thought about what it means to be a parent before getting into it and realizing that it wasn't for her. I wish more parents thought that way."

"Like Meir Danilowitz, for instance." Moshe threw in his two cents' worth.

"For instance," Shira agreed with him, "I can't understand a person who could shoot his own children, no matter for what reason. The fact that he killed himself afterwards doesn't change the simple and regrettable fact that this man should not have been a father."

There was silence all around the table. Shira broke it by turning to me. "Hadasi, what do you think, you chose not to have children and you're investigating this case. Do you think Meir should have had children?"

I was silent. I thought over what I was allowed and not allowed to say, even though I had no doubt that no one at the table would get me in trouble.

"Shira, you shouldn't put her on the spot like that - she can't talk about it." My father scolded Shira.

"It's okay, Dad," I assuaged him. "I can talk as long as I don't reveal any confidential details."

"So, what do you think?" My mother was curious.

"Objectively, there's no doubt that an act like Meir's is a testament to the fact that the man shouldn't have had children—if he really did this, but since I'm investigating the case, I have a feeling that maybe Hanni shouldn't have had children either."

"Where do you get that from?" My mother was surprised. Shira's gaze told me I had said exactly what she was thinking.

"Almost everyone I talk to tells me about a woman whose kids were hardly the center of her universe."

"How do you come to that conclusion?" My mother was intrigued.

"For example, I understand that her children were enrolled in afternoon daycare, even though she wasn't working."

"And that means she was a bad mother?" Shira cried out. "I hate that judgmental attitude! I can imagine Renana told you that." I didn't confirm her suspicion, though Shira was dead right.

"I really don't understand why someone who doesn't work needs to put her kids in afternoon daycare," my mother thought out loud.

"May I remind you that my kids are also in daycare," Shira was angry, "so maybe I'm also an unfit mother?" We all shuddered at the thought.

"But you work." My mother immediately defended her.

"I don't work every day and often not in the afternoon. I just use that time to take care of all sorts of errands and tasks and also, God forbid, to rest sometimes."

"But Hanni didn't work at all." I tried to make my point.

"How do you know what she did every day? Maybe she was writing a book, maybe she studied something, or maybe she volunteered somewhere?"

I doubted Hanni did volunteer work, but Shira's words embarrassed me. I always tried to not be too judgmental and I felt like I'd judged Hanni without really knowing her.

"Don't get me wrong," Shira addressed me. "I also sensed that Hanni wasn't exactly mother of the year, but it really annoys me that mothers are judged on the amount of time they spend with their children rather than the quality of those minutes."

"Quantity leads to quality," my mother noted. "Personally, I don't understand why all these 'career women' have kids." My mother emphasized "career women" with small finger gestures. "Being a mother is seeing the kids a little over half an hour in the evening and on weekends."

"Afternoon daycare's only until four. Mothers who use it still have at least three or four hours of quality time every day," Shira explained. "And, you know what? It's enough for a child to have even one hour of real quality time with his mother rather than seven hours where the mother's only watching from the sidelines."

"I disagree with you." My mother rarely disputed what Shira said. "I may be primitive, but, in my opinion, a mother should be with her child as much as possible. A woman who can't raise her child shouldn't have children at all."

Suddenly everyone was looking at me.

"I don't not want children because I don't have time," I replied to all of the curious glances. "I love my job very much, but I'm not exactly a career woman… I don't have any aspirations to conquer the world. I have to say that, personally, I don't really understand parents who let other people raise their children." I looked at my mother and added, "And when I say 'parents,' I mean the father as well." Now it was my turn to mark the word "parents" with imaginary speech marks. "But if there are people who really want children, even though they don't really raise them, I won't judge them for it. I don't want children because I don't want children. I can find the time, but I don't want to. I'm sure that even the busiest parent in the world has endless worries about their child. And that's exactly what I want to avoid.

"Though raising the child doesn't sound like the most attractive thing in the world to me, it's also not something that would be very difficult for me to do. The difficulty is on an emotional level—being responsible for another human being, being their whole world. It's a very heavy responsibility, and I'm not sure it's right for me."

Shira looked at me with gleaming eyes. "Wow, Hadasi, you just said it perfectly. That's the exact difference between a good parent and a not so good parent: we sometimes mistake the external elements with what's really important, what we have in our heart. A good parent can see his child for half an hour each day, but makes the child his whole world."

After I'd relaxed after the meal—especially after the conversation we had—I returned to my humble apartment in southern Tel-Aviv. I was an urban type, and had been so ever since I could remember, I knew I wanted to live in Tel-Aviv. I was not exactly the *Kibbutznik* that moved to the big city. I only moved from Ramat-Gan to Tel-Aviv. Ramat-Gan is a great city, but it doesn't have Tel-Aviv's pulse. Shortly before I graduated from university, I moved in with Yinon, much to my parents' disdain, in an old, quiet two-bedroom apartment not far from Gan Meir in Tel-Aviv. Almost two years later, the homeowner died and his heirs were in a rush to sell it.

Yinon and I were married by then and decided to buy the apartment ourselves. It was sheer luck. Now, the apartment was worth at least seventy percent more. After we separated, I stayed in the apartment and Yinon got his share from me. My mother didn't understand what I saw in an old, two-bedroom apartment on the second floor with no elevator, with a faulty air conditioner and no parking, but I was in love with my old, rundown apartment. The truth was that I didn't mind living in an apartment like that. There was something soothing about living like a slob.

When your apartment looked like a goodwill truck had exploded in it, spewing random furniture and accessories, it didn't hurt too much if there was a permanent ring-shaped watermark on the dining room table, or that the sofa upholstery was almost completely crumbling away. These were two defects I managed to hide from my mother because I made sure to cover the table with a tablecloth and the sofa with a cover on the few occasions when she honored me with a visit. There are things that hurt less if you're simply unaware of them.

I was lucky to find parking right at the end of the street. I slowly climbed up the stairs to the apartment. I was feeling good. The visit to Shira's, the hearty meal and now the excellent parking spot—I was unbeatable!

When I placed the key in the keyhole I was half asleep, but the fact that the door wasn't locked awoke me in a second. Since I'd been involved in the investigation of the infamous Vaserano family money laundering case, a small fear came into my heart that someone would try to get revenge on me, even though the people of the underworld were usually careful about not getting back at police officers. Maybe it was just a thief.

And maybe it was just Yinon, lying asleep on (formerly) our couch in front of the TV screen, flashing the opening credits of *Ferris Bueller's Day Off.*

I felt like waking him up with a kick, but I knew he was going through a difficult couple of weeks. He was preparing for a huge exhibition in Germany and had been working around the clock for a month. So I just took his shoes off and switched off the TV.

I sat on the balcony and read the weekend papers. Tsumi, the stray dog we'd found wandering around near our house three years earlier, was lying on the couch with Yinon, completely ignoring my existence. He hadn't seen Yinon in two months.

An hour later, Yinon awoke.

"Good morning!" I said to him in a partially angry voice. I couldn't really be mad at him, even though he'd come into my apartment, which, until five months ago was also his apartment, without permission.

"To you, too!" He smiled at me and tried to soften my reaction.

"Like to tell me what you're doing here?"

"I'm really sorry, but I lost an important work disc and I couldn't find it anywhere, so I thought it might be here."

"Then why didn't you call and ask me?"

"I called, and I also sent you, like, five texts, but you didn't answer and I was stressing out."

I remembered I had turned my phone off. I always shut it off when I met my family on Shabbat.

"My phone was off."

"Were you at your parents' house?"

"At Shira's."

"What did you lose there?"

"Are you joking?" I gave him an angry glare. "She's my sister!"

"Come on! Since when do you go to Shira's on Saturday?"

"My parents were also there."

Yinon looked at me as if he couldn't understand my simple sentence. "Aren't you all going to Jerusalem together next week?"

"We are, but my parents just had their house sprayed for bugs and Shira spontaneously decided to invite all of us over."

"How's everyone?"

"Great. How are you?"

"Exhausted."

"Did you find what you were looking for?"

"No… I didn't want to go through your stuff too much, but I don't think it's here. I was also searching through the CDs that have movies on them and I found *Ferris Bueller's Day Off*… I haven't watched that movie in at least a year so I decided I have to watch it."

"Do you want something to drink?"

"I'll make us something hot." He slowly got up from the couch and stretched. Tsumi immediately stood up and looked at Yinon with sad eyes. The dog missed his dad.

Unlike me, graced with an excellent metabolism and a skinny figure (although I could eat like a starved truck driver), Yinon was very aware physically and nutritionally. He also had good genes, but he took care of himself. Although I assumed he might, maybe, letting himself go at this busy time in his life, he was still in great shape. He was wearing shorts and an army tank top, and when he stretched, his chest muscles stood out and I suddenly realized that I had not been sexually active in over six months.

You couldn't say Yinon was a particularly beautiful guy. He started losing his hair pretty young, he had a slightly hawkish nose and his eyes were too small. He always dressed like a nerd, button down shirts, at least one size too big, tucked into beige or blue trousers. I was relatively safe from female competition. But I saw what others simply didn't see. In my opinion, his nose and eyes gave him a dark, sexy look. Since I persuaded him that it'd be better to go completely bald than struggle over each hair (less is more), he looked a bit younger and more contemporary. And very few people got to see Yinon's upgraded physique. On the rare occasions that he agreed to take his shirt off on the beach, I could see the sudden, interested looks from other women. Yinon was sort of a caveman. His sex appeal was magnified when he was naked. Every piece of fabric was too much.

But what attracted me most of all, was the fact that Yinon was as beautiful on the inside as he was, at least in my eyes, on the outside. Pleasant, comfortable and not trying too hard.

"What do you want to drink?" he shouted from the kitchen.

"Coffee," I called back and returned to my lounging on the balcony.

When we were married, Saturday afternoon was the best time of the week for me. We almost always spent it in bed, usually after good sex, with coffee and the weekend papers.

I imagined Yinon was thinking what I was thinking when he handed me my coffee over the weekend paper. I wondered to myself if he was already with someone else. I imagined not. A girl would pretty much need to force herself on Yinon for him to get the idea.

"Spoonful, spoonful, half and half," he announced and placed my mug next to me. Yinon was the only person in the world who knew how I liked my coffee without needing me to remind him, and was the only one who could make my coffee better than I could make it for myself. I thought he changed something in his magic dosage.

"So how are you, these crazy days?" He sat down on the floor, stroking Tsumi's head with one hand and reaching for the front page of the paper with the other. The Danilowitz family's story covered a large portion of the opening page, including references to the addendum.

"Difficult story." He gestured towards the headline.

"Yeah."

"Did you see the bodies?"

"Of course."

"Just unbelievable." Yinon shook his head and leafed through the article on the main page. "Everything that's written here… is it true?"

"Some of it. Some less so," I answered concisely. When we were married, I was much more comfortable with sharing confidential issues with Yinon; now I felt I was walking a thin line.

Yinon got up from his perch and sat next to me on the bean bag couch. Tsumi moaned in disappointment. I sat with my back partially turned toward him and he moved closer behind me and warmly embraced me. I lay back in his arms for a moment and then pulled back. "What are you doing?"

He clung to me again, carefully stroking my hair. "I miss you," he whispered. I swallowed, trying to digest his words. "Don't you miss me?" he asked in a cooing voice.

I missed him a lot. The sight of Meir, Hanni and the children's bodies, especially that of little Noa, haunted me. I was in desperate need of human warmth. I turned to him and returned his warm hug. We sat, embracing, seeking solace in the heat of our bodies and in a few seconds Yinon began kissing my neck and his big, skilled hands caressed my back up and down and side to side.

If at any point I had any doubt about Yinon's intentions, it completely disappeared when his hand suddenly cupped my left breast. I let out a little moan. I'd missed this so much in the past months, not only the sexual touching. I missed this intimacy with Yinon. The sex was always good. We weren't world champion acrobatics and we didn't really concern ourselves with how many times a week other people do it. In this area, we only cared about what was good for us, and for us it was really good.

Everything was good except for one giant thing: he wanted kids and I didn't. I remembered our trip to New Zealand, almost a year-and-a-half earlier. Yinon had been sure that we were on our last trip before giving up the comforts of life without children.

During our last week in New Zealand, I lost my packet of

birth control pills and asked Yinon to stop off to get condoms.

"I think it's a sign." Yinon parked in front of a drugstore and refused to get out of the car.

"A sign of what?"

"That we should go for it."

"For what?"

"Finally having a baby." He blurted it out and my heart cringed. We'd taken care not to talk about the subject during the whole trip and I'd hoped Yinon wasn't thinking about it.

I was wrong.

"God, Yinon," I sighed. "We're in paradise; why do you deliberately want to turn this trip into hell?"

"What did I say? That we shouldn't buy condoms?"

"You know very well what you said."

"I thought you changed your mind."

"The fact that I'm thinking about it doesn't mean I changed my mind."

"I can hope." He tried to smile.

"You should know," I looked down, "that I thought about it a lot and I still don't want to and I don't know if I ever will."

Yinon got out of the car and angrily slammed the car door. He returned a few minutes later with two cans of coke and a pack of condoms that was never opened.

About three months after we returned from New Zealand, I joined the police and felt a job satisfaction that I hadn't felt in years. I enjoyed going to work, but coming home every day was horrible. We barely spoke, since every conversation finally circled around to expanding the nest. We hardly ever had sex. The communication between us, which had been so good in the past, just vaporized. We almost didn't see each other. We each made efforts to stay as long as we could at work.

On the weekends, we'd fake being a couple around family and friends, but when we were alone, each of us was on his own. When he watched TV, I read a book. When he was reading a newspaper, I was on the internet. Yinon honestly wanted a family, not only a partner, and I wanted only a partner.

There was no room to compromise here - you can't have half a child. From the minute I met Yinon, I'd prayed this moment wouldn't come, but I knew that if it did, I would have to let go, painful as it was.

A year after we returned from New Zealand, we got divorced. So many kind souls made sure to let me know that a divorce with no children involved is no big deal. It's like breaking up with a boyfriend who you also happened to marry. I didn't doubt for a minute that a divorce where children are involved is more complex than for a couple with no children, but, unlike most divorcing couples, Yinon and I divorced while we were still in love. We divorced despite being a great couple.

Such a great couple that we couldn't stop ourselves on the decrepit bean bag sofa on our—*my*—small balcony.

An hour later, breathless and sweaty on the bed in the bedroom, I knew we had made a mistake. All the love in the world couldn't change the fact that I was not willing to give Yinon what he wanted and was entitled to.

"This was excellent and unnecessary," I said to him when I could breathe again.

"Why are you ruining it?"

"Ruining what?"

"The moment."

"Oh, come on." I got out of bed and went to rinse myself off in the shower.

A few minutes later, when we were washed and dressed, Yinon insisted on bringing it up again.

"So you think it was a mistake?"

"What?"

"What do you mean, 'what'? What we just did!"

"I didn't know if you meant that or that we got married."

"You're not serious?" Yinon opened his eyes in shock. "You know I love you. How could you think any of what we did was ever a mistake?"

"I love you too," I smiled. "A lot, even." Yinon got closer to me and began stroking my hair. "And I don't regret anything we ever did together." Yinon smiled. "But it would be a mistake to stay together."

Yinon's smile disappeared and he stopped caressing me.

"It's hard for me without you."

"It's hard for me too, but there's no choice."

"How many couples do you know who are as good together as we are?"

"It's hard for me to accept that, to stay together, you expect us to become parents."

"I told you more than once that I'm willing to wait as long as necessary."

"And I also told you more than once that it's likely it'll never happen, and I'm not willing to let you wait for a moment that might never happen. It's not fair to me, and it's even less fair on you."

"Then let's adopt. You'll only be in the background. I'll raise the child."

"You really think it would be fair towards the child for his 'mother' not to care about him? That he only has a 'mother' for his ID card? What life would this child have, with a mother who doesn't want him at all? What do you think would be left of us as a couple? Besides, with your work hours, when exactly will you have time to raise this child? I don't intend to switch to the job of being a mother."

"I'll work less." I rolled my eyes. "I'll hire a nanny," he insisted.

"That kills me, not only with you, but with a lot of people. Why bring a child into this world if you're not going to 'enjoy' them. At least I admit, loud and clear, that I get no joy from kids—but those who want kids, and not for religious reasons, but because they claim that children bring them joy or satisfaction—I don't get why they don't bother spending any time with those enjoyable children, but pay other people to do it for them."

"You're taking it a bit far. We don't live in a utopia, and I also need to make a living."

"Then go work a mom job."

"Maybe I'll do that." I rolled my eyes again. No chance of that happening.

"I don’t know about you, but I'd go insane at the thought of someone else touching you." Yinon always was a hopeless romantic. Maybe that's why he was so hung up on this fantasy of a couple with two kids and a dog.

"It'll be hard for me, but I'll learn to live with it," I lied. The thought killed me.

"Would you accept me with a child from another woman?" Yinon had raised the idea numerous times that he might have a child with a different woman and go on living with me, but the idea always had to do with the fact that the child would be outside of the marriage, meaning we'd stay together and he'd raise a child with another woman.

"You mean you'd start a family and then leave your new wife for me?"

"Something like that."

"I find it hard to believe that you'd do that." Yinon was too good a man.

"But would you take me?"

"I don’t know." Honestly, it wasn't a bad idea. That way, Yinon could have kids without me having to be a mother. "Does it seem reasonable to you to deceive a woman like that?"

Yinon looked down. He wasn't the sort of person to do such an evil thing to anyone.

"I want you back."

I knew I had to be strong. In the past, I’d been very close to cracking. Yinon almost convinced me to get pregnant for him, but with the last of my will, I managed to stay loyal to my wishes.

I wanted him to stay overnight, he seemed so miserable and broken, but I knew that if he stayed, it would let him believe that there was still a chance.

CHAPTER 7

Sunday, 5.24.2009

On the first morning of the new week, after a Shabbat that was meant to be relaxing, but ended in frustration and heartbreak, I went to the Leumi Bank branch in Petach Tikva. On the way, I called Riki and asked her to check with the Department of Health if Ariel Danilowitz had a prescription for Ritalin.

At nine o'clock, I entered the branch manager's office. This was where Hanni and Meir ran most of their accounts. Arie Shani was a man of about sixty, stout, balding, with a well kempt comb-over. His shirt was neatly ironed and he straightened his tie from time to time. His office was packed with files and piles of papers. I stared at the piles and wondered to myself if he was really taking care of all this paperwork or if it was only serving as some sort of scenery.

"Did you handle Meir and Hanni Danilowitz's account?" I asked after sitting down.

"No, I don't handle cases for specific customers, nor private homeowners, but I'm familiar with the couple."

"Are you familiar with all of the bank's customers?"

"No, not *all* of them, but I try to know as many of them as I can."

"So how did you know the Danilowitz couple?"

"Meir Danilowitz's parents are very old and respected customers of the bank."

"I understand." I looked through the notes I'd jotted down for myself. "I looked through Meir and Hanni's bank account. I understand they had another account with the Discount Bank."

"Right. Meir worked for Discount Bank, so it was better for him to open the account his paycheck went to there. Even so, each month he transferred money from the Discount account to us, since most of the activity took place here."

"I see the couple had quite a few loans and a credit card overdraft."

"True."

"I thought there was a new law preventing overdrafts on credit cards."

"Right. Customers who make any sort of withdrawal that leads to being overdrawn receive a reminder on the phone from the branch that the withdrawal won't be approved unless they immediately transfer money into their account."

"According to my records, they were tens of thousands of shekels over their credit limit. How could that be?"

Arie sifted through his papers for a long while. "According to my records, on May 15th there was a charge on a Visa bill, which led to being overdrawn. May 15th was a Friday, so on May 17th, Sunday, Meir was contacted about the overdraft.

"The Danilowitz family was murdered the next day."

Arie stared at me with a gloomy gaze. "You don't think the bank clerk pushed Meir to such a desperate act?"

The couple had loans of over two million shekels altogether. It was hard to believe that being overdrawn by 10,000 shekels would push a man to kill his entire family and commit suicide, but the fact that such a phone call took place less than a day before the act was curious and intriguing.

"It's hard for me to believe," I calmed Arie down. "You said Meir had an account at Discount Bank and here as well. Why did he need two bank accounts?"

"As I told you, he received benefits as an employee of Discount Bank, so it was worth his while to open his paycheck account at Discount."

"Then why did he have an account at Leumi? To my understanding, this was their main account, from which credit card bills, mortgage payments and loans were taken. Wouldn't it have been more worth his while to transfer everything to the Discount Bank, where he received employee benefits?"

Arie smiled. "First of all, the account at Leumi Bank is older." He stroked his tie again and went on to gently stroke his round belly. "Secondly, this is the branch that handles the accounts of Meir's parents, Sarah and Natan Danilowitz."

"And what does that have to do with it?" I had no inkling where my parents kept their accounts.

"Natan and Sarah Danilowitz are very wealthy people." I stared at him and he emphasized again, "Very, very wealthy."

I began to understand the connection, as well as the loans which were not proportionate to the couple's ability to repay them.

"I understand the couple had a mortgage loan of 1,400,000 shekels overall and other short term loans of almost 600,000 shekels, in addition to a completely exhausted credit limit."

"True."

"As far as I know, Hanni didn't work and Meir's salary came down to about 10,000 shekels a month."

"Right."

"What collateral did you have to grant the couple so many loans?"

"Against the mortgage, we have the property itself."

"That's clear, but what about the other credit limits?"

Arie cleared his throat. "That's exactly where the family connection comes in."

"Meaning, if I understand you correctly, an average family with Hanni and Meir's earning ability would not have been able to receive loans of such scale."

"Probably not. In Meir and Hanni's case, we knew Meir had

solid backing, so we took the risk."

"Were his parents guarantors on the loans?"

"On one loan, yes. On the others, no."

"So what's going to happen about the Danilowitz family's debt now?"

"We get the money received from the sale of the apartment and turn to the guarantors about the additional loan."

"So the bank doesn't get hurt."

"You say that like it's a bad thing. First of all, there's a likely chance that we won't be able to recover all of the debt. The guarantee was only given on one loan from three years ago, and most of the loan was paid off. Secondly, the more lost debts the bank has, the less stable the banking system will become. As a result of this, there would be an increase in interest rates and commissions, so this conservatism of the banks in Israel is good for the country. The proof of that is all over the world. Banks are closing down every day, but in Israel, the banks are stronger than ever."

I was no financial genius and I didn't want to argue with him, and some of what he was saying did make sense to me, but to my understanding, the rates were already very high.

"So, despite all of this conservatism, you gave Meir and Hanni loans without any guarantee from Meir's parents. How exactly did that happen?"

Arie cleared his throat again. "Meir and Hanni never managed to make ends meet each month, even when his salary was twice as high. In the past, I would call Meir's mother a lot and she would just transfer money to the account. At some point, I guess Meir asked her to stop and they decided to cover their overdraft with the big loan from three years ago, that also paid for renovation of some of their home furniture.

"Then, we also received the guarantee from Meir's parents. After this, Meir asked for more loans to cover their overdraft, and also renewed the mortgage loan to receive further financing, and asked us again not to turn to his parents. I've known that family for twenty years and I didn't panic. I knew that if there was real hardship, they'd help their son, who I sensed was embarrassed by his situation."

"So Meir's parents didn't know the extent of his debt?"

"Apart from the debt they signed off, they had no idea, at least not from the bank, but I have a feeling they knew there were serious money problems."

"Why do you think so?"

"In the last nine months, Meir occasionally deposited money in the account—money that, I believe, wasn't related to his salary."

"Why do you think that?"

"Because the money that was deposited into the Discount account, he transferred through the bank to Leumi, and in recent months he also began depositing cash in round sums."

"Isn't that something that arouses suspicion?"

"It depends on the sums."

"And what sums are we talking about?"

"A few thousand every few weeks."

"So you assumed it was money from his parents?"

"That's what usually happened."

"Then why wouldn't the parents transfer money or write a check?"

"I don't involve myself in the family's business, but it's not a rarity. The reason for it's pretty common. In many cases, one of the parents wants to hide the fact that they're continuing to support adult children from the other parent. A check, or a bank transfer, is something that could be traced. Cash isn't."

When I got to the station, Riki filled me in on the fact that, according to the Ministry of Health's records, Ariel Danilowitz was not taking Ritalin. I guessed Batya's eye wasn't quite as good as she thought.

"Amos said you need to go see him. He has something for you," she added.

I hurried to Amos's lab, hoping he'd discovered something interesting on the Danilowitz family's computer.

Amos Bar-Nir's area was the most spacious and messy room in the station. Computers and cables were strewn in piles all over the room, but I guessed Amos had his own method of organizing inventory since he always knew how to find what he was looking for in the mess he took great care to maintain.

Amos was sort of a domesticated flower child. He was forty years old, married and a father of five. He wasn't a police officer, but a civilian who worked for the police, so the dress and appearance codes that the unit's officers were obligated to maintain didn't apply to him. He had long, curly hair and glasses on a string. He always dressed sloppily and in the summer he always wore Jesus sandals, an item of clothing that does not exist in the police lexicon. I'm far from being a fashion icon, but even I was shocked and appalled by his outfits.

That day, he'd opted for a relatively restrained look, though I discovered that the sandals were out of storage and Amos had returned to airing his toes.

Amos was a doctor in computer sciences and legend had it that he received his doctorate before he was twenty-five. Another legend: when the commander of the unit called him in to explain to him that there was no way he could leave his office every day at four-thirty, Amos forwarded him three concrete job offers he'd received that month, offering him salaries three or four times higher than the salary he got from Israel Police. From that day on, no one said anything to Amos about his working hours.

I first ran into him in the summer, a short time after I joined the police force, on a fun day that was organized for police officers and their families. Yinon and I brought along Ohad and Elad, my younger sister, Ayala's, two boys. We met Amos, his wife and three of their five kids. It was evident that his family was his life. That meaning was etched in my memory, since I rarely met a couple whose relationship with their children was so harmonious and natural. Harmony of the kind that is very hard to fake.

It was obvious to me that when people take to the street,

especially with their kids, there's a considerable element of phoniness there. The Danilowitz family showed, at least to the outside world, a facade of happy family life. But in the Bar-Nir's case, it wasn't fake. They were too easygoing and not trying too hard for it to look like something artificial. All of them, from the baby to Amos and his wife were dressed like a blind stylist threw random clothes that he found in a recycling bin on them.

Their baby son was cradled in a carrier that Amos wrapped around his wide body. Amos's wife was a thin, beautiful woman. She had kind, blue eyes, the kind you'd pour out your heart to. Two additional children, a boy of about three, completely dipped in chocolate ice cream and a girl of about five, who inherited her mother's kind eyes, held their mother's hands. The eldest daughter and the second son, thirteen and eleven, had opted to enjoy the day with kids their age rather than walk around with their parents.

This scene of a humble and happy couple was etched in my memory, and Amos's habit of leaving work early was clear to me; the priorities in his life were clear. He had an interesting and challenging work place, but he didn't allow his work to engulf him.

Because of this, I was not surprised that almost a week had passed since the day the Danilowitz family's computer was given to him.

Amos apologized for the delay. It turned out that, in addition to all of this, he had been away last Thursday because of his younger brother's wedding. He stood by one of the lab tables in his room, leaning one hand on the Danilowitz family computer.

"There weren't too many interesting things here," he said while gently stroking the computer's disk drive. "The computer was used mainly for web surfing. A lot of children's and adult's web games, recipe searches, quite a bit of online shopping sites and also a bit of porn." Amos smiled.

"Anything unusual?" I tried to make my question sound serious, but I struggled against Amos's mischievous smile.

"Not at all, the usual stuff—young models and quite a few

lesbian movies. If I had to guess, and assuming the late Mrs. Danilowitz was not otherwise inclined, most, if not all, of the porn searches were by Mr. Danilowitz."

"But nothing out of the ordinary."

"No."

"Then what do you have?"

"First of all, there was one interesting search the week prior to the murder. I assume Meir ran this search. He was looking for improvised methods to create silencers for a gun."

"You don't say?" I opened my eyes. This fact definitely reinforced the assumption that Meir was the killer, not someone outside the family. It also reinforced the assumption that this was a premeditated murder.

"I also searched their files."

"Did you find anything?"

"Yes, it wasn't particularly difficult seeing as there weren't too many. Most of the files were family pictures and movies. I didn't go through all of them, but I made several CDs for you and for the families. I assume they'll want these mementos." Amos's heart was always in the right place. "There was also one family slide show on PowerPoint and a few Word documents." Amos turned to his desk, poked among the piles of papers for a few seconds and pulled out one page. "Among the Word files, I also found this one." He put on his glasses, perused the page and passed it on to me.

Across the page, one sentence was printed in a giant font: I'm tired of waiting so long, if you don't give me what I asked for, I'm going to the police.

"Wow," I spat out. "Can you tell if it's a file that he received or created?"

"Not for sure, because he could have received this by email and saved it on the computer. I have a log of file creation times, but I don't know if they were actually written on the computer, or only received."

"And what do you think?"

"I'm almost certain that this file was created on the computer and not received. First, I went through all the emails received with attached files over the three-month period surrounding the date this file was created, and there's no such email. Secondly, the file wasn't actively saved on the computer, but written and then erased, meaning the writer, and I presume we're talking about Meir, wrote the sentence, probably printed it and then erased it, or more precisely, didn't save the file."

"If he didn't save the file, how does it exist?"

"Nothing's ever really erased from a computer." Amos smiled knowingly.

"And this is all you found?" I asked as if Amos hadn't just handed me the main puzzle piece in this story.

"As I told you, there wasn't too much in the computer. Whoever erased the files and the history didn't do a very professional job. There's a chance that there were more files that I wasn't able to restore, but I get the feeling that this computer was used by the entire family, so Meir was careful not to use it for secret, personal reasons."

"You mean, he used the computer at work?"

"Maybe. Although, in work places, there's usually more monitoring goes on. Where did he work?"

"At Discount Bank."

"Then I doubt there's anything on his computer. In large companies like banks, for instance, there's very careful monitoring of the workers' computers, for safety reasons like viruses, fear of industrial espionage, that kind of stuff. I assume Meir was aware of the risk of suspicious emails or files being tracked down and avoided using his work computer."

"So where else can we look?"

"I'd look for a flash drive. It's the best and easiest way to save information outside of a computer."

"This changes the whole picture." Alon waved the letter that Amos had found on the Danilowitz family computer. Our assumption was that Meir was blackmailing someone.

"Right," I said, "but I don't think whoever Meir was

blackmailing is the killer."

"Why not?"

"First of all, the gun was Meir's registered gun. All the evidence at the scene, the placement of the gun, the gunpowder marks, all strengthen the assumption that Meir killed himself."

"That doesn't mean anything. We both know that a professional killer knows how to fake a scene and use the victim's own gun."

"Right, but Amos discovered a search made on the family's computer a number of days prior to the murder for improvised silencers for guns."

"What do you mean?" Alon realized the murder was premeditated and not an act of temporary insanity.

He sat behind his overflowing desk and stared at the page printed with the threatening sentence. Alon was the complete opposite of Amos. He was an esteemed, veteran police officer. Since he hadn't been part of on-site investigations in years, he made sure to wear a uniform that fit his broad, muscular physique immaculately. To my surprise, I discovered that he was forty-eight years old this last Chanukah, because he looked much younger. Short, full hair, light brown eyes that charmed quite a few women, and a constant tan, a reminder of the times when he spent full days in the blistering sun.

I looked at Alon bent over Meir's letter. His table was covered with paperwork related to the Georgian Mafia case. In recent weeks, there had been a serious breakthrough in the investigation, following the consent of the Mafia leader's right-hand man, Igor Michaelshvilli, to cross the lines and turn state's evidence against his boss and his uncle on his mother's side, Yitzchak Mirialshvilli.

From that aspect, Meir Danilowitz found the least convenient time, as far as Alon was concerned, to kill his entire family and himself. Alon thought this case was difficult in terms of the scene but simple to decipher. All the evidence found at the scene was unequivocal about Meir's guilt, and the objective of the investigation was mainly to confirm this assumption and find a reasonable explanation of Meir's motives. The letter complicated everything.

"Do you need help?" he asked desperately, but we both knew there was no available manpower.

"Not right now. I still believe Meir's the killer, so I'm not pressed for time."

"There's immense media pressure on this story. We'll have to answer all the questions at some point. There's also a matter of the unit's reputation here."

I nodded, remembering that the police force had its politics as well.

I realized I need to return to Meir and Hanni's house to conduct a more thorough search. Meir had something to hide, and I hoped to find it in the house.

I assumed that if Meir wanted to hide something, he'd hide it among his things and not somewhere where Hanni might find it. This ruled out the kitchen and the two children's rooms. The living room was pretty clean of objects and I moved on to the bedroom. The bedroom closet was full of Hanni's clothes. Meir's clothes were allotted a quarter of the closet's space, neatly folded, just like all the rest of the clothes in the closets.

I imagined Hanni was the one who took care of the folding and tidying up, so the chances of finding something were minute. I decided not to be lazy, and looked through every shirt and pair of trousers. Every pair of socks was examined, and after about forty-five minutes, I had to admit that my presumption was correct. Meir had not hidden anything in the closet.

I moved on to the study. I looked around, not needing another barren search. Still waiting in my office were a few photo albums and a folder of pay stubs. Maybe I'd find something there, but I doubted it. The binder and albums were too available. The closets were very tidy, meaning Hanni's reach extended everywhere. So where the hell could Meir hide anything in this house, if he really wanted to? I looked at the cupboard in the study and tried to think where I would hide my secrets.

Where no one would look, my inner voice told me. The top two shelves of the study storage unit held, in order of height, holy books, dictionaries, atlases and books of pictures of the views of the Land of Israel. I pulled the chair up to the book shelf and pulled down the holy books. Maybe Meir trusted God with his secret. I was wrong. I climbed up again and pulled down the atlases and dictionaries, and was disappointed again. Among the travel books and Israel's views was an album *Horizon,* of aerial photographs of the country's views. On the cover of the album, a greeting card was attached. Meir received the book when he finished his officer training. I opened the large book and a medium-sized envelope fell out of it.

The envelope was addressed to Post Box 50219, Tel Aviv, with no recipient name, only the post box address. The envelope had already been opened, so I peered into it.

Inside the envelope were ten 200 shekel bills.

Bingo. Meir was blackmailing someone.

CHAPTER 8

Monday, 5.25.2009

The envelope immediately went to forensics. A number of finger prints were found on it, some of them Meir's, but none of them Hanni's. Alon decided that the discovery of the envelope and the letter left no choice but to expand the investigation. He had to pull Shachar off the team investigating a suspected case of bribes and fraudulent crimes in a government office, and sent him to Discount Bank. Shachar was the department's jack of all trades. After years in traffic police, he began law school and finally managed to get into investigations.

Our assumption was that there were only two options for extortion: either Meir found out something un-kosher at his work place and began blackmailing someone, or the blackmail was on personal grounds. Shachar, who had a background in white collar investigations, was sent to interrogate employees of the Discount Bank and I continued with the personal inquiries. I asked Shachar to send Amos any electronic devices he found in Meir's office.

Post Box 50219 was located at the post office near Meir's workplace. I showed the branch manager my police badge and the warrant we'd obtained to open the post box.

Meir had started using the post box about ten months earlier—in July 2008. To open a post box, all a person had to do was identify himself and pay a fee of 180 shekels. The branch manager couldn't say how active Box 50219 was, but thought it was probably not as active as boxes belonging to companies. She didn't recall Meir, either. She got chills from the fact that the infamous Meir Danilowitz had a post box in her post office.

Whom was Meir extorting? Did the person being extorted know him? Did he even know the identity of his blackmailer? Maybe Meir was blackmailing the wrong source? Maybe he was blackmailing a criminal element who was getting back at Meir?

Meir's office was located a few meters from the post office, so I decided to go up and visit Shachar. That afternoon, I was finally due to meet with Meir's parents, who finished the *Shiva* that morning, and the meeting at the post office was shorter than anticipated.

Shachar was waiting for me in Meir's office. We asked to speak again with Danit, Meir's department manager, before we began interrogating workers. Danit was late that day and Shachar had to wait for her to arrive. While he was waiting, he went through Meir's office.

"Did you find anything interesting?"

"No." Shachar wrinkled up his nose. He was obviously bored and disappointed with the fact that he was forced to leave the fascinating case he had been working on the last few weeks. "I turned over all the files here and found nothing, no letters or envelopes."

"Did you go through the computer? Find a flash drive, maybe?"

"He had three in the drawer." He collected the three little sticks he found and handed them to me. "There's nothing on them. The first one has family pictures on it, the second has a few files and financial reports and the third's empty."

"Anything interesting in the business files? Anything suspicious?"

"Not at first glance. They're the financial reports of a

medium-sized commercial company called Mega-byte Services Inc., and a few files that analyzed the company's results."

"Did you check up on this company?"

"I did a quick search online. They sell computers and computer parts and provide computer services in the customer's home. Nothing criminal or suspicious. I think he just saved the data on the disk because he had to take it to a meeting."

"And what about the computer? Did you find anything on the computer?"

"I didn't have too much time to look, but I don't think there's anything here. Of course, we need to get it to Amos to be inspected, but—quick glance— nothing there."

Danit's secretary carefully knocked on the door. Danit had arrived.

We shut the door behind us and sat across from Danit. This time, she was a little less emotional than the last time I talked to her. Then, she had still been in shock from Meir's actions.

"Is there anything new that you need me for?" She cut to the chase.

"Yes, there is." I tried to assume a look of utmost importance. "Before I share what I have to say with you, I hope it's clear to you that everything said in this room stays in this room. This is secret, investigative material, and if it gets out it could cause great damage."

Danit looked at me in shock. She had no idea how she could be connected to what happened in the Danilowitz home a week earlier.

"We have reasonable grounds to suspect that Meir Danilowitz was blackmailing someone." Danit's eyes opened in shock. "Right now, we have no idea who he was extorting, or why, and that's why we're here."

"Do you think he was extorting one of our customers?" she said in a voice higher than usual. She was either totally surprised, or she could nominate herself for an Oscar.

"Maybe one of the other workers?" Shachar chimed in.

"Allow me to introduce Shachar Manor, who's supporting

me in the investigation in light of these new discoveries." I introduced Shachar to Danit. "Can you describe for me the clients who worked with Meir and with your department? Did you have any business with any dubious individuals or bodies?"

Danit raised both her hands. "You can stop your assumptions right now! We do not—and never had—any dubious clients or businesses. We make sure to give credit based on legitimate business only."

"What can you tell us about Mega-byte Services?" Shachar shot out.

"Not too much. A very solid company. The owners are young people, very creative and hardworking."

"Did Meir handle their account?"

"Yes."

"Was there any change in the activity with them recently?"

"I'm not completely familiar with their account yet, but Meir was there two weeks ago, when they asked for a significant expansion of their credit limit." This probably explained the reason why the company's data was on the disc. "It's nothing out of the ordinary, it's pretty much the main aspect of our work here," she added immediately.

"Because of new findings in the case, we'd like to question the rest of the department staff," I explained. "Shachar will be conducting most of the inquiries at the bank, and to avoid summoning all of the workers to the station, we'd appreciate you allocating us a small room where we can conduct the interrogations. I assume the interviews will cause a rumor mill. Very few people are aware that we suspect Meir of extortion, and you're one of them. Leaking this information would constitute a serious obstruction of justice," I warned Danit, and she considered it a threat.

"There's no need to threaten me." She seemed angry. "My team and I will cooperate while maintaining the necessary level of secrecy."

"No threats," Shachar decided to assume the role of good cop, "We're just keeping everything clear."

“Everything’s crystal clear.” She smiled a phony smile.

After we left her room, Danit called her secretary who, a few minutes later, led us to a small, stylish conference room at the end of the hall.

"Danit said you need a room to interview people in," she said, and turned on the light. "Do you want anything to drink? To eat?"

"Cold water, please," Shachar said.

"Black coffee," I smiled, "and a list of all of the department staff and their numbers."

"No problem," she said and closed the door behind her.

She returned in a short while with the drinks and the list of workers.

I had a little more time, so I decided to stay and see some of Meir's co-workers before going to visit Natan and Sarah Danilowitz.

In about two hours, I managed to speak with four of Meir's co-workers. Meir did, indeed, spend many hours at work, a fact that apparently didn't improve his popularity within the department. His co-workers didn’t think he was a brilliant banker, but they admitted that he put far more effort into his work than was required of him. One of those questioned admitted that he had been angry at Meir a few months earlier, when, by way of flattery, he stole a client who yielded a handsome bonus from under his nose. It was obvious that the guy was a little overwhelmed by the interrogation itself, and gave this information with no pressure from Shachar or myself. Shachar and I smiled to one another when he left the room—he hadn’t aroused our suspicions.

Although Meir had returned to work at the bank about two-and-a-half years earlier, none of the staff could tell us any personal information about Meir. He didn't connect with anyone, or share his personal life. The worker whose bonus was taken from him told us that, despite his anger, he felt a little sorry for Meir because he seemed like a miserable, lonely guy.

When they worked together on a case, he remembered that Hanni was at the end of her pregnancy and was always bossing Meir around.

"I didn't know him well enough," he told us, "so I wasn't comfortable saying anything about it or asking him, but I'd really never seen a guy whose wife drove him crazy like that. Pregnant or not—and my wife was pregnant too—she never drove me insane like she did him."

Meir's parents and sisters finished the *Shiva* that morning. At their request, I went to their house in the afternoon. Natan and Sarah Danilowitz had lived for the past four years in a private ground floor apartment in Kfar Ganim C neighborhood in Petach Tikva. I asked Shira about it before I went, and she told me it was the most prestigious neighborhood in Petach Tikva, mainly for the religious public.

Even if the bank manager and Hanni's parents hadn't told me anything, I could have guessed that this was a family with money in its pockets. On the outside, the house looked like the rest of the houses on the street. The neighborhood was new, and the style of construction was more or less uniform, but once you entered the house, the visitor had no doubt that a considerable fortune was invested in each and every corner of it. It was a reserved sort of wealth, not ostentatious.

The obituary notice about the death of their son, daughter-in-law and grandchildren was still on the front door. The house itself was deserted. There was no sign of the masses of people who usually visit grieving homes. Natan Danilowitz opened the door and I entered the massive living room that was floored with giant tiles. (My younger sister Ayala is a design buff, and she once explained to me that the larger the tile, the more expensive it is.) Beige hues adorned the sofas and antique wooden furniture.

On the walls and the display cabinets were many pieces of art and Judaica. I couldn't evaluate it, but I got the sense that each item was meticulously selected and cost a considerable sum.

Next to the living room was a giant dining area, a heavy wooden table and a dozen matching chairs. By the dining area was a spacious, lit, fully-equipped kitchen, the dream of every homemaker. Ayala would sell her soul to the devil to live in a house like this. I could only imagine the amount of energy that would need to be invested in cleaning such a fort, although I guessed the family had a full-time housekeeper.

I waited in the middle of the living room while Natan went to the kitchen to get me a glass of water. Sarah Danilowitz entered the living room from the patio door, which led to a well-kept garden.

"Hello." She approached me and warmly shook my hand.

I introduced myself, but she knew who I was. Natan returned with a cool glass of water, and I downed it quickly.

I looked at Natan and Sarah Danilowitz and my heart sank. They'd had to take most of the fire and criticism. They bore and raised a despicable killer. I didn't know them, but they seemed like good people to me. Meir looked exactly like his father. His mother, a small, frail woman with a warm gaze, invited me to sit in the living room or the garden.

"I have to sit with each of you individually," I explained and they nodded their understanding. "I thought Meir's sisters would be here, too. I'd love to talk to them as well."

"They went back home," Sarah explained. "They've been gone almost a week."

Sarah led me upstairs to the second floor. On the second floor were a number of bedrooms. In the large space connecting the rooms was a lounge with a TV and dozens of toys scattered every which way. This was, apparently, where the couple's grandchildren played. I tried to imagine little Ariel and Galit playing with their cousins and grandparents. Sarah opened one of the doors and we entered a study full of books. Another door from Sarah and Natan's bedroom led to a pleasant sun deck overlooking the garden.

Sarah sat on one of the two chairs by the desk and I sat on the other chair. She crossed her legs and gently placed her hands in her lap. Her gaze was slightly lowered and her eyes were sad.

She stated her details almost in a whisper. I asked her to state them again so there would be no problem with the recording and she repeated them in a quivering voice.

"Tell me a little bit about Meir—what kind of child was he?"

"Meir was our little boy. He was born following two girls, Meirav and Michal, who cared for him like he was their little boy. In fact, he had three mothers—his two sisters and me." She broke down in tears and wiped her nose with a tissue from a pack she prepared beforehand.

"Do you want a moment to calm down? I can start with Natan," I offered.

"It's okay." She wiped her nose again. "I can go on. Meir was always a good boy. He was a beautiful boy, very popular, very well-liked. I'm afraid we spoiled him a little bit. After all, he was an only boy after two sisters who were quite a few years older than him."

"How many?" I stopped her.

"Meirav was born in 1966 and Michal in 1968. They were eight and six years older. Both of them married very young, and from about the age of fifteen he was actually the only child still at home, until he got married eleven years later."

"He lived with you until he got married?" I asked in amazement. Meir was twenty-six years old on his wedding day.

"In our circles, it isn't so rare. And, back then, we were living in a private house and had a separate annex for him. I know it sounds like he was spoiled, and I guess he got much more than other boys, but we had it, so we gave it to him. He never took what we gave him for granted. He was always grateful, and as long as he was living in our house, he helped us and followed the rules of our household. He never talked back rudely, not to us and not to his teachers, never rebelled or even tried to rebel. Really a good kid."

"What kind of student was he?"

"Very studious, though I have to admit it wasn't easy for him.

He had decent grades, but he had to work very hard for them."

"Tell me how he met Hanni."

"He met Hanni when he was a guide in Bnei Akivah. He led a group at the Malabes branch and met her for the first time at a Bnei Akivah summer camp. I remember, he returned from the camp completely enamored."

"He told you about it?" I was astonished.

"Of course not," she smiled, "but a mother knows."

"You knew he'd fallen in love with Hanni?"

"I didn't know with whom, but I saw that he fell in love at camp... I didn't have the details. Years later, they met again at university and started going out, and then he reminded me of that summer. He thought it was fate that reunited them. When they met again in university, Meir was in his first year and Hanni had graduated, although she was three years younger than him—she'd skipped a grade and only did one year of national service. Meir was an officer in the army and served an extra year. After the army, he went abroad for a little while and improved his grades and took the psychometric test."

"What did you think of Hanni when Meir brought her home?"

"We thought she was a good girl. A little bit uptight, but a quality girl with a head on her shoulders. She was... still is... was," Sarah was flustered, "a very beautiful girl."

"What do you mean, uptight?"

"Well, it showed in a lot of things, but what I remember from when they started dating is that, from a very early stage, she pressed him to get married. I didn't understand why she was in a rush, Meir had only just begun his studies and she was barely twenty-two."

"You said your daughters also married young."

"Even younger. Meirav at twenty-two, and Michal at twenty-one. But we never pushed them to get married so young, it just turned out that way."

"Isn't it common in your circles to marry at a young age?"

"Religious Zionists are now much more modern than they

used to be. They do marry younger than secular Jews, but we don't run to get married at twenty."

"So, eventually, Meir gave in?"

"There was nothing to give in to. He knew, and also told her pretty quickly, that he wanted to marry her, but he didn't think they needed to rush, especially in light of the fact that he was still studying and she was so young."

"What broke him in the end?"

"After ten months together, she left him, and our boy was just devastated. He really wanted her, but he also wanted to be financially independent, or at least have a degree, before they got married. He didn't understand the rush. He was broken up for a month, until my husband and I couldn't take it anymore and we promised to support them financially, so that they could marry. You need to understand, we had no problem supporting them financially, it was Meir who didn't want us to, he really wanted to be independent, maybe to prove to all of us that he wasn't everybody's little boy."

"Did you support his sisters?"

"Of course. My husband and I were blessed—thank God—with means. My husband owns a pretty successful company importing raw materials for the food industry, and I inherited quite a bit of money and a number of apartments from my parents. Let's just say, we can fully support our three children, but it was always important to us that they know the value of money, so we didn't buy any of them an apartment. We gave each of them half the money for an apartment.

Meirav, my eldest, was lucky, and the other side of the family gave them a similar amount. Michal and Meir were a little less lucky and they had to take out mortgages. But apart from the help purchasing an apartment, we helped each of our children immediately after the wedding, each of them according to their needs."

"How did you and Hanni get along?"

"We didn't mesh well." She looked down.

"May I ask why?"

"Even before Meir and Hanni got married, Hanni was very angry at us. When Meir begged her to return to him and they decided to get married, it was very important to Hanni to have a big, lavish wedding. I know in your circles, that is, in the secular world," (I didn't correct her mistake) "there are many lavish weddings, but in our sector, the weddings are a bit more modest.

"I didn't think for a second to hold my son's wedding at a soup kitchen, but since we knew we'd have to support the young couple, we didn't think it was appropriate to hold an outlandish wedding. Meirav's wedding was certainly grand, but, like I said, her husband's parents were of similar means to us. Michal had a much more modest wedding and we thought that's what Meir and Hanni's wedding was going to be like as well. We also thought, we didn't have the same means as Hanni's parents, and we didn't want to burden them."

"And what actually happened?"

"Hanni wanted a wedding at the Tel-Aviv Hilton, just like the one we held for Meirav. We didn't have to convince her to forget it—her father did the job. Shimon Levin is a successful engineer in Israel Aerospace Industries, but he doesn't have the means to pay for a wedding at the Hilton. If you ask me, Hanni and her mother had no problem with us paying for the entire wedding ourselves, but Shimon had a little more self-respect, so Hanni and Meir had to settle for the Dan Panorama Hotel, which was also, in my opinion, a little out of Shimon and Aviva's scope.

"To this day, they don't know that we actually paid more than they did, even though they had more cash. We didn't want to embarrass them, and we noticed the costs were too high for them. In short, although it was a very beautiful and detailed wedding, Hanni was bitter toward me from the beginning because she didn't have a big, lavish wedding like the one we organized for Meirav."

"And she bore that grudge against you all those years?"

"I'm sure she didn't let it go, but over the years, she found other reasons to get mad at me and feel deprived. Michal—our second daughter—her husband's an accountant. He worked for a medium-sized accounting firm and after a few years he came to work at my husband's company as an accountant.

"The accountant before him was older and retired, and David took his place. This was about five years before Meir and Hanni got married, six years before Meir even finished his economics degree. David may not be our son, but he's married to our daughter. Hanni thought David should give his spot to Meir. She didn't think it was fair that David got his salary from the family business. She ignored the support we gave them over the years with no return, and meddled quite a bit with David's salary."

"She asked you about her brother-in-law's salary?" I asked in amazement.

"Not outright, but she really involved herself in it. When Meir finished his studies, she asked at one of the family gatherings on Shabbat if he intended to go back to work at the accounting firm where he used to work. We were all a bit stunned by the question, and Hanni explained without thinking twice that she thought David was a sort of stand-in until Meir graduated."

"Was there any basis for her to think that?"

"To be fair, there was some basis to it. Giora, our former accountant, surprised us when he retired early. David wasn't depending on this job, but he's great at it, and after all, he's close family. Of course we wouldn't push Meir into such an important position in the company a minute after he finished school. I was glad when Meir found a nice job at the bank pretty quickly after this, and Hanni calmed down. Her comments to David completely disappeared when Meir got a job as a finance manager for that start-up, Fiber-something."

"Fiberlight." I refreshed her memory.

"Yes, that's it. When Meir worked at Fiberlight, we had some peace about this issue, but two-and-a-half years later, when Fiberlight shut down, Hanni involved herself again. I assume she pestered Meir about it. He didn't tell me everything she said to him, but he asked me once how much David earns. I asked him why he was asking, and he made an excuse about wanting to know how much to ask for when he went to job interviews.

"I didn't tell him because I didn't think it was his business and also because I didn't think he could demand David's salary. After all, David was an accountant with thirteen years' experience. Meir was unemployed for six months, they already had two kids and Hanni hadn't worked for two years. I was very surprised with Hanni at that time. She was a trained lawyer, and Galit was already two years old and going to daycare anyway.

"I thought the most natural thing was that she go work, too, and relieve some of the pressure on Meir. But instead of relieving the pressure, she only added to it. Since Meir and Hanni got married, we haven't stopped supporting them. We paid for the wedding Hanni wanted, we paid for half of the apartment for them in Givaat Shmuel, we helped them buy Hanni's car, we occasionally deposited money into their account when they were short, and we asked for nothing in return.

"The only thing we wanted was to see our grandchildren, a right we were entitled to mainly when Hanni needed a babysitter. I remember the time Meir and Hanni went on a two-week vacation to Italy, when Meir was still working at Fiberlight, and we watched Ariel and Galit for a week. I remember daring to say to Hanni that maybe they could go for just one week, not because it was hard for me to watch the children, but because I thought two weeks was too much for two little ones like them. Hanni more or less threatened me that if I didn't watch the children when she wanted me to, I'd never get to see them."

"She threatened to not let you see the grandchildren?"

"Not only threatened…"

"Meaning?"

"In the last year-and-a-half, I saw my grandchildren exactly three times. Meir came with the kids on Rosh Hashanah, at Passover, and at a party celebrating Noa's birth."

"Did anything trigger this excommunication?"

"We stopped supporting them."

"And because of that, they didn't let you see your grandchildren?"

"Yes," she said sadly and lowered her gaze. "It was very, very hard. I loved those children with all my heart. Arieli was an amazing child, smart and incredibly beautiful. He had some difficulties—unfortunately, he didn't get the right help—but I saw beyond his difficulty. The boy was simply a treasure. Galitush was such a sweet and funny girl, she loved playing with me so much. Beyond my personal pain, I was very worried about what this separation would do to the children. I was afraid the children would think they were being abandoned. Abandonment is a terrible trauma for children."

"And you still decided to cut them off, even at the price of separation?" I asked, careful not to sound too judgmental.

"We felt it was a price worth paying, as long as they became more independent. Like I told you, Hanni didn't work. She stopped working after Galit was born. Hanni thought that, because we have the means, we should help her live at the level she wanted. She never stopped comparing herself to others, comparisons that had nothing to do with reality."

"Why?"

"She was very interested in what Meir's sisters were getting, when actually, I can tell you they got less than she did. Even when Meir was working at Fiberlight, I kept transferring them money. Every couple of weeks, they went overdrawn, and Meir or even the branch manager would call me and I'd make a transfer. Hanni was convinced that Meirav and Michal were also receiving money from us on a regular basis, which never happened.

"Apart from holidays and special occasions, they managed on their own. When they were newlyweds, we did help them out more, but only in the first year or two. After that, they ran their households with no help from us. You need to understand that Meirav and Michal were also some years older than Meir. And they married younger than Meir did. Hanni compared herself to Meirav and Michal, who'd been married for over ten years more than her. They'd already managed to create a comfortable life, and Hanni mistakenly thought that she could afford the same things as a couple that's been married for ten years. Besides, Meirav and Michal both work."

"What do they do?"

"Meirav, the older one, manages a chain of fitness clubs. She studied at Wingate and then did an MA in management. She's married to Oded, who owns a successful law firm. Michal studied interior design and owns a nice little business with another partner. They're doing pretty well. Michal's married to David, who like I told you, is the accountant in my husband's company. They're both well-established in their own right. They did have a good starting point and strong financial backing, but I'm very proud of how far they've come. I wanted the same for Meir, but now everything is ruined." She broke out in tears again and I waited for her to calm down.

"What were we talking about?" she asked after a little while, after drying her nose and eyes.

"Meirav and Michal."

"Right," she sniffled and went on. "When Meir was working at Fiberlight and they were doing relatively well, Michal moved into this neighborhood. We'd already bought this house, but it was still under construction. Meirav also lives down the street, in a private house, and Michal bought a penthouse a few streets down. We really wanted Meir and Hanni to move here too, so we'd all be close to one another.

"Hanni's parents live in Ramat Gan, so we didn't think they had any special connection to Givaat Shmuel. Hanni thought we'd buy them a penthouse apartment like Michal's, or a private home like Meirav's, but we refused. We were willing to give them some money, but not buy them a house. Meirav and Michal didn't get anything from us but a fairly generous housewarming present. Hanni understood we weren't about to buy her a new house in Petach Tikva, but I guess it was hard for her to accept that Meirav and Michal have upscale houses and she began expressing interest in private homes in Givaat Shmuel.

"When she realized she'd no chance of purchasing a villa, even in Givaat Shmuel, she kindly agreed to make do with remodeling their current apartment. This was before Passover, so there was a good excuse to paint and remodel the entire apartment. They also refurnished Ariel's room, the dining area and the living room. It was a little hard for me to understand why it was so urgent to refurbish a living room that was only five years old, but I was careful not to say anything about it."

"And who paid for the remodeling?"

"The bank." Sarah smiled sadly. "They took a loan to cover their overdraft and the cost of the decorating and we were the guarantors for their loan. I thought—hoped, really—that it would keep Hanni quiet for a little while. As we'd covered their overdraft so many times, Hanni promised Meir, who was very embarrassed every time he had to come ask us for money, that this renovation was the end of it, that she'd feel more comfortable in the house and be calmer."

"And did she calm down?"

"For a very short time. Three months after the remodeling, Fiberlight was closed and Meir lost his job. It took him six months to get back to work, and in that period we, again, supported them—even more intensively. My heart would break every time Meir came to me to ask for money. It was very humiliating for him, a thirty-two year old man with two kids, coming to bum money off his parents."

She started crying again, but calmed down more quickly than expected. "Maybe we were wrong," she said in a quivering voice. "Maybe we shouldn't have waited until he asked, maybe we should have given it to him without him even asking," she said without waiting for a comment. "I know there are kids who receive constant financial support from their parents, even though the kids are already grown people with their own families—even people less well-off than us, and surely those like us, too."

"Do you think that if you'd gone on supporting Meir and Hanni, this whole tragedy would have been avoided?"

"If you ask me, I think so."

"Your wife told me she believes that stopping supporting Hanni and Meir financially was what brought Meir to commit such an extreme act," I told Natan after he recited his personal details for the record. It had become difficult for Sarah to go on with the interview, and I decided to obtain the rest of the information from her husband and, if necessary, pick up with her another time.

Natan pursed his lips and thought for a moment. "I don't know. Maybe."

"So you think it's possible?"

"I really don't know. It sounds too extreme to me."

"Maybe you could tell me a little bit about your relationship with Meir and Hanni. I understand from your wife that there was a rift between you because of you cutting them off."

"Right."

"Can you expand on that?"

"I don't like to speak ill of the dead, but my young daughter-in-law brought out the devil in me. Who knows what she could bring out of Meir? Right from the start of her relationship with Meir, I got the sense that she was walking around feeling like she'd caught a fat fish, that she was marrying a bank account."

"She didn't love Meir?"

"The truth? I've no idea. I'm not sure. He was very attached to her. She was a very pretty girl, very smart, charismatic, but also petty, lazy and exploitative."

"Elaborate, please."

"She was always busy comparing. Especially with Meir's sisters. Had to know how much everyone was getting, and constantly convinced that she was being discriminated against when, in reality, it was the other way around."

"You said she was lazy."

"It's a trait that I simply detest, and I think it was the root of the problem of her behavior. A young, healthy, smart girl who has a degree, but sits at home instead of getting a job—"

"Being a housewife is also a job." I quoted my mother and recalled Hanni's immaculately tidy home.

Natan snorted in disdain. "Hanni knew how to impose jobs upon others. She had a housekeeper, and she sent the kids out to daycare from a young age. The only thing she did was occasionally cook on Fridays, but she bought most of their meals. Forgive me, she may be dead, but for many years she made my blood boil. I admit, I hoped more than once that he'd divorce her."

"Did you share these hopes with your son?"

"Even when they were still engaged and she drove us all crazy about the wedding, I told him it wasn't too late to call the wedding off."

"And how did he react?"

"He was really mad at me."

"Because he was in love with her?"

"Yes." Natan lowered his gaze. "Believe me, I've no idea why. Because despite all of the beauty and charisma, when you live with a person, all of the masks come off. And I've no doubt that life wasn't easy with that girl."

"What do you mean?"

"When they still used to come here, she'd just bully him: 'Get this! Go there! Come here!' If he dared ask anything of her, she'd plant him a hundred meters into the ground. It's not easy for any parent to admit it, but she definitely surpassed my son intellectually and rhetorically, and he was a sucker for her. She talked down to him. That's one of the reasons I suspected she married him for the money. She didn't look like a woman in love, while he was extremely devoted to her."

"But, after all, there wasn't so much money."

"Not as much as she hoped. In my opinion, they got above and beyond what they needed. I know it's a painful issue, especially for my wife, who, with a very heavy heart, joined me in my refusal to support them, but I felt like there was no other option. I started my company alone. My wife came from a very wealthy home, but I didn't have too many luxuries growing up, so my expectations from the kids are different.

“My wife's parents died about fifteen years after we were married, and by then we managed by my own means. Following their death, my wife inherited a great fortune, but we were already financially comfortable. I never asked for money from my in-laws, and I admit that they gave without our asking and it was very convenient, but I actually refused substantial sums from them while they were alive. I felt it was their money and I wasn’t supposed to enjoy it. That's also how we raised our children, Meirav, Michal and Meir. We had a bad example in our background and it was very important to me not to spoil my children too much."

"What example?"

"My wife has a brother, who inherited a sum similar to Sarah's. He relied on his parent's assets all his life and after their death, when he inherited half of their fortune, he was spared the need to ask them for it. He spoiled his children, who grew up to be quite the freeloaders. My wife's parents had a considerable fortune, but not a vast one. For a couple, it was a significant amount, but don't forget that the fortune was split in two.

“After a few years, they used up a substantial part of their share of the inheritance and today they're barely speaking to their kids, who refuse to pay them back even a small portion of what they received. They have to live very humbly. Because of Sarah's brother's story, Sarah agreed to stop supporting Hanni and Meir."

"Why stop? Maybe you could have reduced it?"

"We tried to cut back the support, but what happened was that Meir would go to Sarah behind my back and she'd take pity on him and transfer him money."

I recalled the bank manager who told me that cash deposits often occur when one parent isn't willing to finance the child and the other parent keeps supplying him with cash. "Did she transfer it through the bank or give him cash?"

"Both, and sometimes checks too. When she really wanted to hide it from me, she withdrew cash for him, but I always knew in the end."

"So what caused you to completely cut them off?"

"All these years, there was my wife's brother in the background. We're very wealthy people, but not so wealthy that our kids could live only off the inheritance, and certainly not after dividing it between the three families. We worried what would happen after we die, how they'd manage. We weren't so worried about Meirav and Michal, mostly about Meir."

"Why? He was working most of the time."

"It's important to me to be as honest with you as possible, so I'm not going to sound like a particularly encouraging father: my Meir was a lovely person, but I didn't expect him to be very successful, not as a businessman, and not as a salaried employee. He got lucky with that start-up company who employed him in a position that was ten sizes too big for him, but I estimated that that sort of luck wouldn't hit him twice. He was a good, hardworking young man, and I'm sure he would have worked to retirement, but not in very lucrative jobs."

"What's wrong with that? Not everyone’s a manager."

"Right, but Hanni thought that the fact that her neighbors and Meir's sisters, who are both married to men with very high managerial and earning potential, lead a certain lifestyle, meant that she should live like that, too. She ignored reality and lived a lifestyle that didn't match Meir's earning ability."

"How did this manifest itself?"

"Meir didn't share the little details with us, he just asked for money, but the girl was addicted to shopping. For herself, for the kids, and for Meir here and there. I never saw her wear the same dress twice on Shabbat, and she had dozens, if not hundreds, of pairs of shoes. The kids were always dressed in the nicest, newest clothes."

"Was she a good mother?" I try to get a compliment out of him.

"I don't know. I don't think showering the children with clothes and toys is proof of good parenting. I don't remember even one occasion when she played with the kids when they were here. She was always sitting and talking to Meirav or Michal, and Meir would watch the kids and play with them. I remember, I once dared to say something about it to her and she was so insulted that she threatened she'd never come visit us again.

“After an hour of flattery from Meir and Sarah, she agreed to come back in the house and didn't look at me the rest of the Shabbat. Meir told me that she watched the kids all week long, so he enjoyed being the responsible parent on Saturdays. I, personally, didn't buy it. Meir would often come home early and put the kids to bed, so she wasn't really 'carrying the load' during the week like she tried to make out. Besides, Meir wasn't exactly resting during the week."

"And she was?"

"Yes, definitely yes. Although, the last few months, she was taking care of the baby, before that, for years, she sat at home all day for hours doing nothing until Ariel and Galit came home from school and kindergarten."

"It sounds like you have a lot of resentment towards your late daughter-in-law."

"Certainly. She made my son's life miserable."

"So you think that's the reason that pushed him to kill her and their three children."

"It sounds insane to me, but there's no way of knowing how far she pushed him."

"I want to go back to the matter of the support that was cut off. You said that, in light of Sarah's brother's story and Hanni's squandering, you decided to completely cut off your support."

"Right. That was about a year-and-a-half ago. November 2007, as far as I recall."

"Was there any trigger?"

"Yes. For years, since Hanni and Meir got married, including when he was with that start-up and making a very handsome, fat salary, we paid off Meir and Hanni's overdraft. The busiest time was after Meir was fired from the start-up company and was unemployed for about six months. Hanni didn't get a job and didn't even try to cut back on her spending. Six months later, Meir returned to the bank, but his salary was far from what he was paid at the start-up company. And again, instead of adjusting, Hanni went on spending disproportionally.

"What caused things to reach a boiling point was the new car she bought in October 2007. Meir had a company car and Hanni had a private car in their name. I didn't understand from the beginning why a woman who doesn't work and has both her kids in school near home needs a car just for herself, but I suppose it's a minimal convenience. She had a 2001 Suzuki Euroswift, which, in my opinion, was enough for her needs. It was a great car, barely gave her any trouble, mainly because it was hardly used, but it was very important to Hanni to replace it with a big, fancy car."

"What kind?"

"I don't remember the exact model, but it was a Mitsubishi. She did buy one that was two years old rather than a new one, but that entire purchase was completely unnecessary."

"Maybe the Suzuki was too small for three kids?"

"First of all, a Suzuki Euroswift may not be a large car, but it's relatively spacious, and besides, don't forget that Noa was born only four months ago. In October 2007, Hanni wasn't even pregnant yet. There was no reason to buy a bigger car other than the fact that other people had one and she didn't."

"So after they bought the new car, you decided to cut them off?"

"Yes. Sarah was finally convinced that only drastic action would change anything. We made the decision with a heavy heart. All parents want nothing but good for their children, but we thought Meir and Hanni would only become independent if they realized they had no one to rely on other than themselves."

"So what did you do? Tell them that you weren't going to cover their overdraft?"

"No. First we asked them to return the new car."

"And did they agree?"

"You think? Hanni went crazy! She couldn't shut up about the new car we bought David, Michal's husband, who's my company accountant and has been working there for almost fifteen years. I didn't do anything I wouldn't have done for any other senior employee. David's car was becoming a wreck and I decided to treat him to a good, executive vehicle. All of our attempts to calm her down and explain to her that David got a car because of his position and not because we favored him in any way were in vain, so we explained to them that if they chose to keep the car, they could pay for everything themselves."

"And what was their reaction?"

"There was no reaction. I think they didn't believe we were serious."

"And once they realized you were serious?"

"It happened pretty quickly. After about a month, Meir asked us to help them out because their Visa account was maxed out and they were into overdraft."

"And you said no?"

"Right."

"And then what happened?"

"I've no idea. I assume Meir closed it with a loan or something of the sort."

"I mean what happened between you? I understand Hanni cut you both off."

"Of course. That threat became a reality. Meir felt really bad for us, but we decided not to cause any more tension. After all, his life was with Hanni, not with us. He explained to us that Hanni thought grandparents had not only rights, but also duties, and if we weren't willing to help out, she saw no reason to allow us to see our grandchildren."

"Didn't you try to coerce Meir?"

"I told you, we didn't want to cause any tension."

"You didn't even talk to Meir? You've no idea how he felt about it?"

"My wife was very scared to talk to him about it. I was a little less timid."

"Well… what did he say? How did he feel?"

"Horrible. He was very uncomfortable. We're a very caring, tight knit family and this disengagement was hard for all of us. On more than one occasion, he tried to sneak the kids over to our house and we stopped him. Children are too innocent, they would have told Hanni and all hell would have broken loose. He was pained for the children—they missed us and didn't understand why they didn't visit us anymore."

"So, you hadn't helped Meir and Hanni financially for a year-and-a-half."

"Right."

"Are you one hundred percent sure that Sarah also stuck to this and didn't sneak them money?"

"One hundred percent. We have joint bank accounts, and I know about every shekel that's withdrawn."

"So how did they manage in the last year and a half? Did they start being more frugal?"

"I doubt it."

"Why do you think so? You haven't been as close to them as you were."

"We weren't completely disconnected. Although Hanni went on without a job and Meir was still working at the bank, they didn't exactly live modestly. Last August for example, they flew to Holland with Ariel and Galit. When Noa was born, they threw her a lavish *brita* [naming celebration]. Simply raising a baby entails a lot of expenses."

"So maybe Hanni's parents helped them?"

"I imagine they did, though Hanni's parents didn't have the same means as us. They're both pensioners."

"So do you believe their money worries could lead Meir to get up one morning, kill them all and commit suicide?"

"I really have no idea. Maybe he really was badly in debt… that sounds like madness to me. I raised and educated that boy. I didn't educate him to be a murderer. I didn't educate him to any sort of violence. I understand all the evidence is against my son, and I'm trying to cope with reality, but it's difficult for me. I'll admit, I can't stop thinking the killer could have been someone from outside the family. Maybe he got in trouble with the gray market, and someone took his revenge?"

Since we'd been through the financial information we had, we had no doubt that there was no criminal factor involved. I planned to recheck the financial details, so I decided there was no harm in letting this miserable man go on dreaming.

"If you'd known he was in such an extreme state, would you have given him money?"

"Is there any doubt in your mind? I'd give everything I own for all of them to be back."

"And do you think he knew that?"

"I really don't know. I hope he knew that. After all, we're his parents and if there were very serious problems—a matter of life and death—we were still here for him, despite all of the past problems."

I wondered. Maybe this wasn't financial hardship. True, the parents cut off their support, but children of wealthy parents know that bottom line: when you reach the point of no return, mom and dad are there.

"Are we done?"

"One more question: did you know Meir had a postbox?"

"The kind they have at the post office?"

"Right."

"No, I didn't know."

"Can you think what would cause him to open one of those post boxes?"

"Maybe he'd started working independently?"

"You don't know if he became self-employed?"

"As I told you, our contact wasn't very steady."

"According to the information I have, he wasn't self-employed. Do you see any reason for him to open a post box?"

Natan shook his head. "No, I really don't," he said.

When I got in the car, I called Riki. "Riki?"

"Hadas?" she asked in her friendly voice.

"Yes, do me a favor; I don't have a phone number on me and I'm already on my way home."

"What do you need?"

"Can you call Mrs. Aviva Levin?"

"Hanni Levin's mother?"

"That's right, to schedule another interview with me at the station."

"When?"

"As soon as possible."

It was time for Mrs. Levin to stop hiding things. It was so important to her to be interviewed a few days ago, yet she hadn't said one word to me about the estrangement between her daughter and her in-laws.

CHAPTER 9

Tuesday, 5.26.2009

"I'm really sorry, there's nothing here." Amos passed me a bag of evidence holding the three memory sticks and the cell phone that Shachar found in Meir's desk.
"Are you certain?"
Amos seemed a bit insulted by my question. "There's no such thing as certain. If you format a digital appliance, there's always a chance that we'll never manage to restore the data that was erased, but with a pretty high level of certainty, I can tell you that there was nothing here but family pictures and work data."
"And what about the cell phone?"
"There was almost nothing there, but bear in mind it's a new phone."
"You mean it's very advanced?"
Amos laughed. "I mean, it was taken out of the box about three months ago. Meir's old phone was lost. There's almost nothing on the new one."
I smiled awkwardly and returned to my office. A short conversation with Shachar revealed that his investigation had failed to turn up anything new. Meir was a devoted worker and a pretty discreet guy. His co-workers hardly knew anything about his private life, as he didn't talk a lot about personal matters. All the accounts Meir was involved with were

completely Kosher, without any financial problems or suspicion of criminal activity.
Shachar hadn't finished interviewing everyone he wanted to, or looking through all the necessary material, but he estimated that his investigation wouldn't reap many further rewards.
The conversation with Meir's parents still echoed in my mind. There was a deep and serious rift in the family. Meir and Hanni were used to enjoying the support of Meir's parents and when it stopped, it lit the fuse of the bomb that exploded last week.
Meir and Hanni fanatically guarded their private life. No one knew that their financial situation was so bad, including Hanni's parents; no one knew their son needed therapy. There was something very rotten in Meir and Hanni's home, but instead of dealing with the problem, they kept sweeping everything under the rug. The most important thing was that no one should know.

The radio in my room was on. The sequence of songs was replaced by a short commercial break. A credit card company was offering a loan to anyone who wanted it, with no security, for any purpose. Practically America. How easily the banks gave credit... no wonder so many households were in debt. If someone was giving it away, we'd take it. An overdraft had become a status symbol. No one wanted to be left behind.
We all treated our financial issues as if they were the country's nuclear secrets. On one hand, everybody was curious to know how much money their friends were making and on the other hand, they fanatically safeguarded the secrecy of their own private financial information. People could tell their friends their deepest secrets, but not reveal their salary.
It reminded me of Tali, the wife of Yinon's friend. She was an accountant in a medium sized high-tech company. She enjoyed a right that few get to enjoy. She knew how much other people were paid because she took care of the payroll. She claimed she'd rather not know. Everybody was dying to know how much their friends were making, but really there was no joy in

such knowledge, which can only cause bitterness.
She claimed it took years for those preparing the paychecks, especially if they were also doing their own, to stop comparing themselves to others. A salary is a very, very simplistic but efficient tool with which to rate people. If you're in demand you'll get x and if you're less in demand you'll get less than x. The problem is that, in reality, it often occurs that quality people get paid less than those who are less qualified. She claims that, just as everyone thinks, those who know to demand more also get more, and sometimes there's no relation between how high the salary is and how efficient the worker is.
I knew that it was a very sensitive issue for the Danilowitz family. I decided to thoroughly check Hanni and Meir's bank accounts. The bank manager and Meir's parents told me that, in the past, there'd been constant support coming from Natan and Sarah, but the bank manager said round sums were still being deposited in the account. It was clear to me that Meir was blackmailing someone. But who? Over what? And, no less importantly, for how much?
I spread out the bank statements and started rummaging through the numbers.
Throughout the entire period I checked, the Danilowitz family lived on their overdraft and a cycle of loans. In October 2007, there was the loan taken out to pay for Hanni's car, the loan that put an end to the support from Meir's parents and began Hanni's lock out. Up to that month, there were quite a few cash deposits from Meir's parents' account.
From the month the car was purchased, the cash deposits from Natan and Sarah's account stopped. On August 12th, 2008, a deposit was made of 15,000 shekels in cash to the account. It was the first deposit of a round sum since September 2007. Meir received this sum from someone other than his parents.
Who?
The cash deposits continued, and, besides the first deposit, a few more deposits were made to the account of an overall sum of 145,000 thousand shekels, all of them deposited in round

sums.

These were clearly not gray market amounts. From the gray market, you take one big sum, not numerous, relatively small ones. Despite its stigma, money from the gray market isn't exchanged in cash envelopes, but in a regular bank transfer.

I stared at the negative balance of the account which almost never reached zero. How does a bank allow people to live like this? I think every adult person, of sound mind and body is responsible for his own actions, but still, it was hard to ignore the fact that the bank gave Meir and Hanni credit that they couldn't pay back. A bank is a store for money. Just like I couldn't walk into a supermarket, load a cart full of goods and leave, so a bank could not allow people to take credit if there was no way of paying it back.

On the day of their death, Meir and Hanni had loans and overdrafts totaling almost 2,150,000 shekels.

How could a family of five get into this kind of debt? The bank statements showed me general earning and spending. I knew a great deal of the spending was actually paying off loans, but the family's monthly consumption was very high, disproportionate to the couple's earning ability. The credit card company prepared a report for me dividing the expenses by category of business.

The fact that the couple was up to their neck in loans didn't stop them (apparently Hanni) from buying clothes for thousands of shekels each month. I thought to myself that that was my *annual* clothes budget. There were many expenses on restaurants and cafés. Twice a year, there were vacation expenses in Israel or abroad (including the family trip to Holland in August 2008), substantial payments to toy and gift stores and, of course, electricity bills, tax payments, and grocery shopping.

After hours of surveying and analyzing the bank accounts, I felt like my brain was about to explode. I tried to understand how I'd managed to sit in an office for all those years and go through exhausting purchasing agreements, and could not believe I'd

been able to do it.
I went out to get something to eat and when I returned, Riki told me that Meirav, Meir's sister, called the station and asked when she needed to come in. Her parents probably told her that I wanted to speak to her as well. I called her and, to my surprise, she agreed to come to the station immediately.
Less than an hour later, she was sitting across from me in the interrogation room.
From the first second I saw her, I knew I liked her. She reminded me of my sister, Shira. Not in appearance—Shira was a short, chubby girl, dressed in "comfortable" clothes, as she liked to describe them. Meirav was tall, good-looking and immaculately dressed. They both had an inner charm that worked just great on me. Just like my sister, Meirav also seemed like an easygoing, direct person. They both had kind eyes, a calming smile and dimples that graced their cheeks whenever they smiled. I wanted her to invite me to her kitchen for schnitzels and mashed potatoes.
Meirav told me that she always loved physical activity, so when she finished her year of service she decided to study an unusual profession for girls from religious households—physical education and personal training at Wingate College. After she got married and had two boys, she decided to change courses, enrolled for a Master's in Business Management and was now the manager and part-owner of a chain of fitness centers.
"Meir was almost like a son to me," she smiled longingly, a tear sparkling in the corner of her eye. "I was eight when he was born, and from that moment I was crazy about him. He was an amazingly beautiful boy. It was torture not to hug and kiss him."
"Was he a spoiled child?"
"He was coddled, but he wasn't spoiled. He was always considerate toward my parents, never thought he deserved any special treatment. He served in a combat unit and was an officer—it's not exactly what a spoiled person does."
"Was he a violent child?"

"The complete opposite; he was very kind and gentle. The only thing that comes to mind is that sometimes he'd store anger and tensions inside and show nothing, and then suddenly explode, with no warning and with no proportion to the specific event."

"Do you remember one of these occasions?"

She thought about it for a few seconds. "I can't think of something from recent years. I remember one occasion when he was in tenth or eleventh grade. He was a guide in Bnei Akivah. There was an organizational Shabbat—it's a Shabbat when an age group is raised a level and there are shows and torch processions," she explained to me without knowing that I had taken part in countless organizational Shabbats.

"In short, most of the other guides blew it off and all of the load fell on him. He took everything on himself. In the end, it was a great event for the kids, all of the guides were happy and only Meir was exhausted. He had a big math test at the time and he failed it. A month later he had to redo the test.

"It happened to fall on Chanuka and the other guide went on a vacation abroad with his parents. He didn't say anything to Meir and again, all the load fell on him. When the branch coordinator told him that he had to be in charge of the activity on Shabbat because there were no other guides, he almost broke a chair in his rage. At that moment, there were young kids in the branch who witnessed Meir's outburst of rage and I understood some parents demanded Meir be expelled from the branch."

"Did that happen?"

"No, everything calmed down."

"Did your parents tell you there was a rift between them and Meir?"

"Of course. It was the main topic of our conversations in the last year."

"Tell me a little bit about this rift."

"Since Meir and Hanni got married, our parents helped them out. Financially, I mean. Don't get me wrong, it's really not something that unusual or special. In our circles it's very common, especially because we marry very young and there's still no real income. They helped my sister and me out too, but as they say: there's no such thing as a free lunch, and at some point everybody gets on their feet and gets by without help from their parents. They occasionally give something, but it's not really support, but more of a gift.

"With Meir and Hanni, it wasn't like that. The support never stopped. This also wasn't a rarity; I hear about quite a few adult children being supported by their parents, but it's certainly not accepted in every household. My parents are very wealthy people and, maybe in wealthy families it's more acceptable, but my parents, in principle, thought it unhealthy and educationally wrong to support adult, educated people."

"And yet, they did."

"They really had no choice. I don't know all the details. I don't think they gave them a permanent, monthly stipend, like other parents do, but transferred them money when they needed it."

"Right," I observed.

"Don't get me wrong, I'm all for parents supporting their children. Any kind of support. There's something very Israeli or Jewish about it. I don't think there's this amount of family involvement in their adult children's lives in other western countries. In the United States the relationship between family members—even immediate family—can come down to as little as a greeting card on holidays, but I think Hanni thought she was marrying an open bank account. She saw and heard around her, or thought she saw and heard, that wealthy people financially support their adult offspring and thought that's what they should do for her."

"How do you know that's what she thought?"

"Out of everyone in our family, I think I had the least bad relationship with her. Honestly, it didn't come from me—she sought me out. I don't know if she was really interested in me, or just felt the need to compare herself to me."

"Go on."

"It started with their wedding. When they got married, she really involved me with the preparations, like my opinion mattered to

her. She said I was like the sister she never had."
"But Meir has another sister. She didn't connect with her?"
"There was no great love there. My sister, Michal, is a very quiet and humble woman; I'm more bubbly and extroverted, like Hanni. Hanni also didn't like the fact that David, Michal's husband, works for my father's company in a job she thought Meir should have. Soon after the wedding, she was already pregnant and Ariel was born less than a year after they were married. In this matter, she also really valued my opinion.
"She asked me to come shopping with her for baby equipment, and once Ariel was born, she asked me for advice a lot. I wasn't sure why this honor was bestowed upon me. I'm not the most maternal type. Michal's much more maternal than me, but I became Hanni's shoulder to lean on. I remember that it bothered me a little that she esteemed my opinion so highly and disregarded the advice of my mother, for instance.
"We could have said the exact same thing, but when it came from me, she listened. When she was expecting Galit, she gained a lot of weight. Of course, after Galit was born, she turned to me to help her get back in shape. At that time, I was already managing Fitroom, so I set her up with discounted membership and even came to work out with her a couple of times. In short, we were close compared to her relationship with the rest of our family."
"Can you, maybe, shed some light on the split in the family?"
"Like I told you, Meir and Hanni received financial support. My parents were torn on this arrangement. It wasn't financially difficult for them, but emotionally difficult—they wanted Meir to be independent. They really deliberated whether to give them a set allowance, or just transfer them money when they asked for it."
"But that didn't happen."
"I'm not totally up to date on this, but I think, as time passed, they had to give them more and more support. Eventually it all exploded."
"With the purchase of the car?"

"Right. As long as it was small purchases, you could maybe think it was lack of attention, but when she bought the car, it was clear to all of us that she expected my parents to pay for it. It was a leap too far and when my parents asked her to return it. It was an extravagant purchase, after all. She managed to cross all the red lines and spit in the well she'd drunk from for years."
"What did she say?"
"I wasn't there, but from what I understand, she told my parents that she was through with the fact that they favored us—me, and particularly Michal—over her. That in every normal family, especially ones with the financial ability to, they support their children and that all they ever did was insult her and make her feel like she didn't belong. She claimed she didn't ask them to pay for her car and that's why my parents' demand upset her so much."
"And what do you think? Was there any truth to what she was saying?"
"There was some. My parents had definitely had enough of her, but they tried their hardest not to show it. And, to say it lightly, she completely brought it upon herself. She was just ungrateful. How could she claim that she was mistreated or wasn't getting enough? Besides the financial support, she'd boss my mother around endlessly to watch the children."
"So they kept the car, your parents cut them off and there was a cutting off of relations."
"Something like that."
"Did you believe it would really happen?"
"At first, not at all. First of all, I thought Meir also had a say in their household. Secondly, she used my mother so much as a sitter that I didn't think she'd withstand the punishment she basically inflicted on herself."
"But she withstood it?"
"Yes, unfortunately, she did."
"I want to understand something. Didn't she know her financial situation?"
"She knew, but she wasn't informed in all of the little details.

Meir was an accountant, and he was the one that dealt with the bank."
"But she was a lawyer. She wasn't uneducated or unable to understand."
"True! That really drove us all crazy."
"Did you try talking to her?"
"Of course, but there was no one listening."
"Was the connection to you and Michal also severed?"
"With Michal, there was no real connection in the first place. The relationship with me dwindled, mainly because it was difficult for me to pretend everything was okay."
"Then why did you talk to her?"
"My mother was glad that I stayed in contact with Hanni because she wanted to at least be updated, and she hoped that, someday, everything would sort itself out," she said in a quivering voice and then broke into tears.
She calmed down after a couple of minutes. "Where was I?"
"You said your mother hoped everything would sort itself out."
"Right, since I was still in contact with her, my mother could find out from me what was going on with them, especially with the grandchildren. My mother was very worried about Arieli."
"Why?"
"He had a lot of problems, mostly discipline, but it stemmed from something deeper. I think he had some untreated emotional problem."
"Are you sure he wasn't getting help?"
"No, I've no idea what they were doing with him. I can only say that I got the feeling his unruly behavior toned down a bit in recent months. Maybe it's just a feeling, seeing as I barely saw him."
"Was he given Ritalin?" Maybe he had an illegal prescription.
"I don't know."
"So you stayed in touch with her for your mother's sake?"
"Yes."

When we were done with the interview, I did what I had never dared to do before, and asked Meirav if she wanted to go out for a cup of coffee.

I guess she liked me, too, and about half an hour later we were sitting in a small coffee shop in Tel-Aviv.

She was very interested by the fact that I chose to work in the police, leaving behind a law firm and fat paycheck. I reminded her that she also made a professional transformation from a fitness trainer to a businesswoman, and she laughed. She thought that while she'd settled down, I'd done the reverse, from a respectable job as a lawyer to a tough cop. I laughed.

She asked about my family situation and I told her I was recently divorced.

"Oh," she made a sad face. "Why?"

"Because my husband wanted children and I didn't," I answered simply. I usually just said that it didn't work out between us, when that was far from being the real and even true answer. I felt like Meirav would understand me.

"Really?" She seemed impressed, not surprised, and I liked that.

"Yes," I smiled.

"I really admire you." I knew it was not for nothing that I liked her. "A lot of people don't really want to be parents, including myself." She shocked me. She smiled at the sight of my stunned face. I'm not used to being stunned in these conversations. "I surprised you, huh?"

"Completely."

"I have two boys and I'm crazy about them, but I really don't love being a mother." I nodded in understanding. "I married young and got pregnant right away. That's how it's done in our circles."

"I know," I added. "I'm also originally from a religious home."

"Really? I wouldn't have guessed it."

"What do you mean? You can guess who used to be religious?"

"Usually I can," she laughed, "There's something about people who used to be religious that's very obvious. I think it may be their need to flaunt their secularity. You don't try too hard."

I smiled, trying to understand if that was a compliment.

"Anyway, a year and three months after I got married, when I was twenty-two, I had my first son and discovered I'm not as maternal as I was expected. My sister, Michal, knew how to take care of her young nephew better than I did, and she wasn't even pregnant yet. I didn't enjoy anything, not even things that supposedly were meant to cause me great joy, like his first step or first word."

"Maybe you had post-partum depression?"

"I suspected that, too, at first, but I soon realized it wasn't depression, I was just not enjoying parenthood."

"Then why did you have another child?"

"Excellent question," she smiled in embarrassment. "As time went on, it was easier for me to connect with my son. He grew and was very communicative and that's much more fun than looking after a tiny creature that just eats, poops and sleeps. I still didn't find much interest in kindergarten parties and was bored to death every time I had to play with him.

"I didn't have anything in common with other mothers who were busy with development issues, sicknesses and educational activities. As soon as Ophir turned two, my entire environment seemed to tell me I should have another baby. At first I wouldn't even hear about it, I was still in shock, but as time went on, the shock subsided a bit and I felt like I was doing my son wrong by keeping him alone."

"You think it's doing a child wrong to raise him without siblings?"

"I don't know… there's a six-year gap between my eldest son and my youngest. They're not really the best of friends. They don't fight or anything, but they don't have too much in common, either. I think the main reason I had another child was to not be unusual, though only two kids in a religious family is fairly unusual, since the minimum is three and these days, four kids are the new three. Two is still considered 'a family,' though." She marked up air quotes when she said "family."

"And one isn't?"

"If you ask me today, with the mind I have today, I'd say

anyone can define their family as they wish. If two men who live together adopt a dog and they see themselves as a family unit, they're a family. I can't tell anybody what family is to them."
"You're very liberal."
"For a religious person." She completed the sentence for me. "Yes, I know," she smiled.
"But - do you love your children?"
"Very much, and now it's also much easier because they're grown up and completely independent and I can talk to them like I do to any other adult, but when they were little, I didn't enjoy myself."
"So maybe it's worth suffering in the beginning to enjoy them when they're older, to have a family, to not be alone?" I raised arguments I didn't believe in.
"Maybe. I'm not sure about that. Nobody promises your kids will become your best friends. Maybe they'll move to another country… maybe they'll be leeches?"
"Like Hanni, for instance?"
"For instance!" She laughed a bitter laugh. "Here, look at my parents, they brought three children into the world and they got so much grief from my brother, God rest his soul." Her eyes filled with tears again.
This wasn't an interrogation and we weren't in the station. I got up off the chair and went over to her. I bent over and gave her a long, warm hug.
"You're changing everything I think about cops," she said after she finished blowing her nose.

The next morning I went to Tsumi's veterinary clinic. The dog had a nasty skin problem that demanded monthly cosmetic treatment, which included getting his fur washed with a medical shampoo.
The treatment was scheduled ahead of time and was like a thorn in my side, but I knew I had no choice because Emily, the dog groomer who treated him, was about to fly to South America for two months and I knew it wouldn't be wise to postpone.

My furry ball of energy was happy as could be when he discovered I was taking him out of the house. He walked with his head held high and tail wagging, as if saying, "Today, I'm specially loved." His sheer joy was replaced by horror once he realized the purpose of our trip was the vet's clinic. He did not stop crying from the moment we walked in to the blessed moment we walked out.

I sat in the waiting room and ignored his non-stop crying while he was being washed. I leisurely read a newspaper, completely ignoring his ceaseless pleas for my attention. I couldn't do anything, not even pet him, because he was completely covered in the medical shampoo.

To my great surprise, despite the relatively early time of day, there was another young woman in the waiting room. She was waiting for her beloved dog, which had undergone emergency surgery to remove a malignant tumor. She was constantly calling her partner and her mother and informing them of every single detail.

I sensed she was looking at me with an accusatory gaze. How could I sit so leisurely while my dog was undergoing such torture? That feeling was replaced with knowing a few minutes later. Emily had now gone outside with Tsumi to comb and dry him off.

"Is that your dog barking out there?" She roused me from a titillating article about twenty-one ways to improve your sex life (but not one tip about how to *get* a sex life).

"Yes," I answered without lifting my eyes from the paper.

"Why's he barking?"

"Because he doesn't like being combed."

"But he's not being combed," she said, shaking her head in repulsion.

I went outside. Emily had tied Tsumi to a pole and gone back inside the clinic. I hadn't noticed, since I was so absorbed in the paper. I released Tsumi and brought him into the waiting room with me.

Tsumi rubbed up against me and licked me hysterically. He was

finally rescued from the hands of the terrible Emily and back with Mommy.
"You see?" she said. "He wanted you! Why weren't you sitting with him?" she added, rolling her eyes.
I didn't answer. What could I say? She was right, but I'm not as evil as I appeared to her. During the treatment, Tsumi needed to see me as little as possible, because I couldn't touch him. When he was crying outside, I hadn't noticed he was alone.
I thought about Hanni—how much criticism I'd heard from those close to her in the last few days. It seemed that everyone approached parenting in his own way.

CHAPTER 10

Wednesday 5.27.09

I was ten minutes late to the meeting with Aviva, Hanni's mother, at the station. She was fifteen minutes early, so she ended up waiting for me for almost half an hour.

She sat at the entrance of the station, with an angry glare and her crossed leg jiggling in irritation. I asked her into the interrogation room.

"You know I waited for you for forty-five minutes?" She rounded up her waiting time.

"I apologize," I lied. "I'm currently working on solving your daughter's murder. I don't have so much control over my schedule, and besides, we made our appointment for twelve, so I was ten minutes late."

She noticed no hint of apology in my voice. "You could be a bit more respectful toward me. After all, my taxes pay your paycheck."

"I want a raise then!" I smiled.

Aviva didn't think I was funny and she demanded to see my superior.

Fifteen minutes later, Alon came out of the interrogation room with a look that said, "Why must I deal with this kindergarten?"

"Apologize to the lady and we'll be done with this."

"No problem." I looked down; I had not an inkling of regret about what I'd said.

"She wanted me to replace you, you know that?"

"Really? Why?" I was surprised.

"She thinks you're not impartial."

"What?" I didn't believe it.

"You knew her daughter."

"So? That means there's a chance I'm a suspect? I haven't spoken to her daughter in fifteen years, and even when we were in high school together, we weren't exactly best friends."

"You don't have to convince me; I told her there was no reason why you shouldn't run the case and that, anyway, there's no other available manpower and it would be a shame after all of the hard work you've done."

"And was she convinced?"

"I don't think so, but she understands she doesn't really have a choice."

I sat down across from Aviva, whose face bore such a sour expression that I knew nothing I could say would calm her down.

"I apologize," I said in a weak voice. She rolled her eyes. "We have the same objective. I want to understand who killed your daughter and grandchildren and why."

"I thought the 'who' had already been determined."

"It's true; the chances are your late son-in-law killed your daughter and grandchildren and committed suicide, but we want to be certain there isn't a killer walking among us, and also to try and understand the motive that led to this horrible act."

"This won't bring them back," she said sadly.

"True, but in my experience, it's easier to deal with these kinds of situations when the picture's clear."

"Okay." She brought her hands together on the table. "What did you want to ask me that you haven't yet?"

I sifted through some of the papers I had brought. "Did you know there was a deep rift between Hanni and Meir and Meir's parents?" She heavily nodded her head. "I need you to say it for the recording."

"Yes." She answered almost in a whisper.

"What did you know?"

"I knew she didn't get along with Meir's parents, especially with his mother."

"Why?"

"Sarah Danilowitz is a good woman, but she kept involving herself with Meir and Hanni's life. I have three sons, besides Hanni. All of them are married and I really try to stay out of any business of my daughters-in-law." I had a sense that reality was far from what she was describing. "I understand you're divorced," she added.

Turns out Mrs. Danilowitz had done some research about me, a pretty simple thing to do in religious circles, where everyone knows everything about everyone.

"So you used to have a mother-in-law." She went on analyzing my personality. "You surely know how irritating it is to have your mother-in-law meddling with everything, even if she's right."

To be honest, Hava, Yinon's mother, didn't involve herself in any aspect of our life. She was one of the few people who didn't drive me crazy with the pregnancy issue, for instance.

"How was this meddling manifested?" I got back on track.

"Comments about how to clean and do the laundry, how to raise the children, where to shop, questions about their financial situation."

"But don't you think that if they were supporting Meir and Hanni financially, it was her right?"

"To tell her how to raise the children?"

"What did she have to say about how the children were raised?"

"Mostly comment about how much shopping she did and all sorts of recommendations about Ariel."

"What recommendations?"

"Sarah thought Ariel needed therapy."

"What kind of therapy?"

"She didn't know, but she kept pressuring Hanni to send him to be evaluated."

"And did they evaluate him?"

"Not because Sarah told them to. The boy was having trouble in class, so we went to a children's psychologist."

"And what did the psychologist say?"

"He sent them to a psychiatrist."

"And what did the psychiatrist say?"

"He recommended the boy be given Ritalin."

"Ariel was given Ritalin?" I was surprised. According to the Department of Health's listings, there was no prescription for Ritalin on his name.

"No, of course not. Hanni didn't want to drug her child. She went to another institute and they told her she could forgo Ritalin and administer alternative treatment."

"What kind?"

"May I know what this has to do with the investigation?" she asked angrily. She was right, and I decided not to start another front with her.

"You're right. My question is, don't you think it was Sarah's right to make comments to Hanni since they were still supporting them?"

"I think if you give, you should give wholeheartedly and unconditionally. From what I understood from Hanni, they didn't even give them that much, surely far less than they were able to."

I decide to confront her with the numbers.

"Between 2005 and 2007," I looked through the pages again to be sure, "Natan and Sarah transferred about 300,000 shekels to your daughter and son-in-law." It was evident by Aviva's face that she was surprised. She didn't know we were talking about such a large sum.

"Very nice," she said.

"You didn't know how much money they'd given them?"

"No."

"Hanni didn't share these things with you?"

"No."

"You never asked her about it? After all, there was a period when Meir was unemployed."

"I can't remember… maybe I asked her about something, but she never willingly shared that subject and I never asked her about it."

"Are you telling me you had no idea they were deep in debt?"

"Deep in debt?" she asked in wonder. "They were deep in debt? From what exactly?"

I sift through my pages again. "They owed banks over two million shekels."

"What?" She almost yelled in her shock. It was clear she didn't have any idea how bad Meir and Hanni's situation was.

I looked at her as she processed the information. "How did they get into such a state?" she finally asked. "They didn't live a very luxurious life."

"They went on a family trip abroad, bought a fancy new car, remodeled their house, bought a lot of clothes and toys." I tried to explain the balance.

"Which is what everyone does," Aviva shrugged, "so does that mean everyone's in that kind of debt?"

"I don't know; I haven't conducted a survey. You have to understand that, in addition to all their expenses, they kept recycling loans and were actually paying more and more interest and returns for previous loans. This was from the end of 2007, when Meir's parents stopped assisting them financially and their situation got even worse."

"Wow, I didn't know."

"You didn't know Sarah and Natan stopped supporting them?"

"That, I knew." She grimaced in disgust. "That was the last straw for Hanni, after all of Sarah's intrusions. Hanni stood up for herself, so they decided to stop helping them."

"And Hanni reacted by freezing out Meir's parents?"

"I must say I didn't like that. Parents are parents, but she was so hurt that I didn't butt heads with her over it. I hoped that, in time, the anger would subside and both sides would calm down. In fact, she recently invited them to the party she organized for Noa's birth."

"Why was she so hurt?"

"She always felt rejected at their house, that she was always disrespected, discriminated against."

"How was her relationship with Meir's sisters?"

"She really liked his elder sister, Meirav. She had less of a connection with Michal, but the unpleasantness she sensed wasn't from her sisters-in-law, but from her father-in-law."

"And how did Meir feel about all of this?"

"About how his parents treated Hanni?"

"No, about the fact that Hanni cut his parents out?"

"I've no idea. I'm sure he didn't like it, but I think that he, like myself, thought she'd get over it."

"To what extent was Hanni involved in managing the family's finances?"

"Not too involved, I think. I think she would have told me they were so deep in debt if she knew. We hardly kept any secrets from one another."

"You mean Meir kept this situation from her?"

"I think he did."

"Why?"

"I really have no idea. Meir was a very quiet, introverted guy, maybe he was embarrassed that he couldn't manage the bills."

"And maybe she was embarrassed and chose to hide it?"

"I don't think so. Hanni wasn't afraid to ask," she smiled. "I know some grandmothers love to complain, but I love being a grandmother and my daughter, bless her, knew to ask for my help, and since she stopped asking Sarah for help, all the load was suddenly on me." She sighed. "Not that I'm complaining, of course."

"You mean you helped with raising the children?"

"Of course. What did you think I was talking about?"

"She never asked for financial help?"

"Here and there, nothing out of the ordinary. I can tell you one thing for sure, if my husband and I had known what a mess they were in, we'd have given them everything we could, which might not be as much as Sarah and Natan could give, but it's substantial," Aviva clarified.

"In the last year, did you give Meir or Hanni cash?"

"No."

"Are you sure your husband didn't either?"

"A million percent. In our house, I'm the one who handles the money. I worked as a bookkeeper for a few years."

"According to the data we have, about 145,000 shekels in cash was deposited into your daughter and son-in-law's account in the last few months. Do you have any idea where that came from? Maybe something Hanni and Meir were doing on the side?"

She shook her head. "Hardly, they didn't have a minute."

I decided to reveal some more cards. "We have reason to believe that Meir was extorting someone."

"What?" she gasped, putting her hands on her chest, as if trying to keep her heart from leaping out from the scare.

"So Meir could be a victim, just like my daughter and grandchildren?"

"I wouldn't jump to conclusions. All the signs still point to Meir killing them all and committing suicide."

"But it's possible to fake a suicide."

"It is possible, but we doubt that's what happened."

"But you're telling me you think Meir was extorting someone and the fact is, Meir deposited a lot of money into their account."

"Right."

"So there's a chance that whoever killed my daughter, grandchildren and son-in-law is walking among us?" I wasn't sure if she was happy that the tarnish of a murderer for a son-in-law had been removed, or angry that the killer was still free.

"There's such a chance, but the forensics team are skilled professionals, and if they determine this is a suicide, then the likelihood is that they're right."

"But these things have happened."

"They have." I sighed. I somewhat regretted revealing this information to her. My objective was to discover whom Meir was blackmailing, not stir her hopes about Meir being innocent. "So, do you have any idea who Meir could have been blackmailing?"

"Not at all." She shook her head. "Maybe someone from work?"

"We're looking into that. I'm asking you in the context of friends and family."

"Not that I know of."

"Did Meir and Hanni have close friends we haven't spoken to?"

"I've no idea who you've spoken to."

I went over the list of those interviewed with her and she immediately interjected. "You didn't talk to Iris Green?"

"Who's that?"

"She was like a sister to Hanni. They met in the Civil Service and became a pair of kindred spirits. If there's anybody who could tell you what Hanni was going through, it's her."

"Where does she live?"

"She lives in Raanana. There are a lot of Anglo-Saxon Jews there. Iris's husband came here from England with his parents twenty years ago." She dictated Iris's cell and home phone numbers to me. The name and number looked familiar.

"Is it possible that Iris is out of the country right now?" I remembered Iris's number from the phone records, and that when I tried to call, I was asked to type in a secret code.

Aviva thought for a moment. "Yes, of course, how could I forget? She called me during the *Shiva*. They went to visit her husband's family in England. Some cousin got married. They should be back right after the holiday."

Aviva left the interrogation room thinking Meir was innocent. I felt this line of thought made it a bit easier for her. Meir had been her son-in-law for years, and it's hard for people to see their relatives as vicious killers. It's easier to get caught up in a fantasy about an anonymous murderer. I would also be happy to discover that it was a different killer. The thought of a father shooting his children like that is beyond understanding, but I knew the chances of any alternative were slim. The evidence was unequivocal, and the chances of faking them tiny.

CHAPTER 11

Thursday, 5.28.2009.
Shavuot Eve

Yinon called in the morning and said he was stuck at work and would come pick Tsumi up the next day. I explained to him that I had to leave early because I was going to the Inbal Hotel in Jerusalem with my family, a fact that I thought was well known to him, since it was the reason I'd asked him to take Tsumi over the weekend. I had the feeling he was doing everything he could to not see me again, after what had happened the week before. He may have thought there was a chance of us getting back together, and been very hurt when I made it clear that it was a mistake I wouldn't repeat.

He promised to pick Tsumi up in the afternoon and return him at noon on Saturday, before I got back. On the one hand, I didn't like the fact that my ex-husband still had the key to my apartment, but on the other hand, it was very convenient. I didn't feel like seeing him either. I'm not made of steel.

When Yinon and I were married and my parents invited us over for a holiday or Shabbat at a hotel, we would always leave a minute before the holiday began and leave the hotel before it had ended. My parents didn't like this, but they would rather we come, and desecrate Shabbat, than not come at all. Now, divorced and alone, I left for my parents' house at one o'clock, a solid five hours before the holiday began.

I never liked going out of town, and, of all the places in the country, the one I least liked going to was Jerusalem. That city confused me. In the absence of a husband or driver, I had to go with my parents, who refused to come into Tel-Aviv in order to pick me up.

There's something a little sad about sleeping in a hotel room alone. I'd been living alone for several months, but it felt far less lonely surrounded by all my personal objects. The neat, cold, hotel room made me feel lonelier than ever, and I decided to go down for a dip in the pool.

I passed through the lobby, which was filled with guests who had come to celebrate Shavuot in Jerusalem. All the guests, without exception, were religious, most of the of the knit skullcap variety. The Haredi Jews, who stay in hotels on the three high holidays (Sukkot, Passover and Shavuot), aren't the average Haredim. Most Haredim live, more or less, around the poverty line and can't afford a long weekend in a five-star hotel in Jerusalem.

The few that came to these hotels were usually wealthy pilgrims from the United States. For the knit skullcaps, it's a social event, which is meant to categorize you socioeconomically. Those staying at the King David Hotel were the elite, the cream of the crop. All the rest stayed in the other hotels around the walls of the old city in the direction of the Armenian quarter.

My parents had booked rooms at the Inbal Hotel, which was an excellent hotel near Gan Hapaamon. It was also horrendously expensive (but not as expensive as the King David Hotel), a price many pay in order to be part of the social elite of the Religious Zionist community. In short, if you weren't there, you didn't really exist.

In the past, my parents had been more insistent that we

attend these social events in Jerusalem on Shavuot. That was when we were still very young and it was important to my parents that we were well known in society. Just like in Jane Austen novels, in the Religious Zionist public, there was a need to present the girls who have come of age to "society." A substantial portion of the hotel guests were families whose kids were over eighteen, and this was an effective and elegant way of fixing up young people.

Even if you didn't leave with a date or a phone number, it was always possible that someone had spotted you and could tell someone else who was looking for a match. When you explain this whole operation to a secular person (say, Yinon), they're pretty shocked.

The Religious Zionist public was perceived by the secular public as open and liberal, and the fact that most couplings came to be made by way of matchmaking astounds them. The word *Shidduch* (matchmaking) was associated with the Haredi world, where a guy is matched with a girl and after three dates in a coffee shop, a wedding hall is booked. For the knit skullcaps, *Shidduch* is the most effective way to meet a partner. No one has any expectation that the couple will get engaged after three meetings.

Just like in the secular world, the knit skullcaps also go on dates and get to know the partner before they make fatal decisions. If the Haredim need two or three dates to decide, among the knit skullcaps there's a whole range of customs surrounding this, from those who observe *Negiyah* [abstaining from touching the opposite sex until marriage] and will meet only in public places (so as to avoid being alone together—*Yichud*) to "Religious lite" who, in some cases, may marry not as virgins.

The need for *Shidduch* stems from the simple fact that those wearing knit skullcaps are completely integrated in the secular social life. They don't work and study only within the community, hence the difficulty of meeting a religious partner in everyday life.

In short, a long weekend in Jerusalem was a great way to see and be seen. The modest and humble daughters of Israel arrive wearing their finest attire and tear up the lobbies of all the hotels in the area. When I walked through the lobby on my way to the swimming pool, I was glad I wasn't there anymore, inside that boiling pot. Not that I ever really belonged.

The hotel pool was relatively empty for such a weekend, which usually involves many knit skullcaps. The knit skullcaps could be divided into several movements of pool goers: those who won’t go to a mixed gender pool on Shabbat or holiday; those who won't go only on Shabbat; those who would go on Shabbat, but not in a hotel where so many religious people are staying; and, of course, the "Religious lite" gang, who are only slightly different than completely secular people. My parents belong to the third group: whenever we went to Eilat for a family vacation, they had no problem with us going to the pool even on Shabbat, but when we went to Jerusalem for Shabbat, when it was clear that everyone around us would be religious, my mother didn't even pack my swimsuit.

Once, on Shavuot, when I was sixteen, I really wanted to sunbathe and I was annoyed with my mother because she took away the bathing suit I had stowed deep in my bag. While my parents were sitting, chatting with their friends and Shira was doing what was expected of her, I decided that, in the absence of a bathing suit, a bra and panties were the solution. I thought (and still think) that there's no real difference between a bikini and a matching bra and panties set, and I proceeded to tan on the balcony adjoining our room. Ayala and Evyatar, who were then ten and twelve years old, were horrified to find me lying on the balcony, reading, in my underwear.

"Aren’t you ashamed?" Ayala cried out.

"Of what?"

"Lying like that!" she said, pointing at me.

"What's the problem?"

"You're outside! Dressed in a bra and panties!"

"Who's looking?"

"They are!" Evyatar whispered and pointed to a group of boys who were enjoying their view of my balcony.

Ayala ran inside and returned with a heavy wool blanket that she threw over me. I flung the blanket off in anger.

"Are you insane?"

"No," she said. "You are!"

"Aren't you embarrassed the boys saw you in your underwear?" Evyatar asked.

"They didn't see anything they haven't seen on the beach or at the swimming pool right below us."

I made my two little siblings swear they wouldn't say anything to my parents. It cost me quite a bit, but it was worth saving the lecture I would have suffered. Of course, I told Shira and she relished the story.

"You crazy bitch!" she laughed. "All the girls walk around the lobby dressed up and made-up to the nines, and you take your clothes off and get all the boys!"

When I returned to my lonely room, I saw that my mother had tried to reach me on my cell phone approximately ten times.

"Did something happen?" I asked her in an impatient tone when she picked up the phone, half asleep.

"Where've you been?" My mother is the world champion, or at least the Polish champion of answering a question with a question.

"In the pool."

"Are you insane? You could catch cold. This is Jerusalem, not Tel- Aviv! It isn't summer yet."

"The pool's heated... "I tried to calm her down, knowing that the chances of that were slim, especially when it had to do with me.

"Are you in your room right now?"

"Yes," I answered.

"I'm coming." She hung up and was in my room a few seconds later.

"Show me what you brought," she commanded.

"What?"

"Come on…" she also had an impatient tone. "Show me what clothes you brought."

"Mom, I'm not looking for a husband," I calmed her.

"Very funny." She didn't laugh. "First of all, you never know," *(she's got that right)* "but I want to know that you came with normal clothes and not something we'd be ashamed to sit next to in the dining room."

I put my trolley case on the bed, and began taking out the clothes I'd shoved into it in disarray.

"If you can't pack properly, you could ask me to pack for you," she said, picking out a shirt. "Look, everything's all wrinkled! Why didn't you put it on a hanger as soon as you got in the room?"

"It's a pajama top." I tugged the shirt from my mother's hands, "besides, nothing's wrinkled." I scattered the clothes I had brought with me on the bed and my mother examined them carefully.

"You're not leaving the room wearing that—" she pointed at a shirt with cutoff sleeves, "and those—" she pointed at flared trousers that I had bought with her two years ago, "—just don't fit you well. Where's the other suitcase?" she asked and I looked at her in wonder.

"Don't tell me that's all you brought?" she said, panicked, "There are clothes here for two-three meals, tops. You remember this is full board and there are six meals between tonight until Saturday noon?"

"There are clothes here for two days, maybe even three," I pointed out. "I never change outfits three times a day, and I don't intend to begin to this weekend."

"Hadas'ile…" My mother started speaking slowly and quietly. "If it's hard for you to spend money on yourself because…" she began stuttering, "uh… well… you know, because you're a cop, then tell me and I'll take you clothes shopping."

"Thank you, Mother." I strained all my facial muscles to produce a smile. "Even when I was working as a lawyer, I didn't buy clothes as a hobby. You know very well that shopping's torture for me and that even if you bought me half the mall, I'd still only wear maybe two items."

She shook her head in disagreement, knowing I was a lost cause. "It's such a shame, with a figure like yours, to walk around like something from *Les Miserables.*"

"I'm hardly a *miserable*," I said, and held up one of the shirts I had brought, a shirt I had purchased only three years ago, a purchase that had earned my mother's praise. That hardly ever happened. "Look what a nice shirt this is." I tried to pry a compliment out of her.

My mother was on the verge of tears. "Ayala wouldn't wash the floor with that shirt."

"And what about this one?" I pulled out a shirt I really love.

"I wouldn't even use it as a rag."

Eventually, I was led, head down, to my parents' room; my father was sitting on the couch, perusing the holiday and weekend papers.

"What have you done now?" he asked me with a smile when he saw my mother's grouchy face.

"It's just like I told you!" my mother answered for me. "She brought all her rags just to spite me."

"Why do you love getting your mother upset?" he looked at me over the rim of his glasses. "You know she just wants you to look good."

"Really?" I answered angrily. "I thought she was just ashamed to be seen in public with me."

"Oh, come on," she said and pulled a bag from her favorite boutique out of the closet. "Since you've been avoiding my calls all week—"

"I'm in the middle of an investigation," I tried to explain and she shushed me.

"I didn't take the risk," she explained, "and I bought some shirts and a skirt for you at Zehava's."

I looked over the clothes, nothing I would choose for myself, but I really didn't have the energy to spend the holiday and

Shabbat arguing. I decided this weekend would be the short and inexhaustible substitute for the vacation abroad I had planned on taking.

CHAPTER 12

Friday, 5.29.2009.
Shavuot Day

My dream of a vacation completely dissolved when Shira and my dad dragged me to the Birkat Kohanim at the Western Wall at four in the morning. I maintained a grumpy expression the whole way, though privately, I had to admit it was a special experience.

"It's just horrible; how could a person do such a thing, kill his own children like that, and that tiny, sweet little baby girl?" I was surprised to hear a female voice that wasn't Shira's, who'd fallen asleep next to me, talking about my case in the quiet little corner we stood in at the edge of the wall's floor.

"What does Iris say about all of this?" a nasal voice asked.

"What can she say?" the first voice sighed. "She's just in shock."

"Poor thing."

"She is. Hanni was her best friend. She's just devastated."

"She couldn't come back from England?"

"She really wanted to, but still, it's a family wedding."

Of all the places in the world, the mother of Iris, Hanni's

best friend, was sitting next to me on the morning of Shavuot near the Western Wall. In a world where everyone somehow knows everyone, I was not very surprised.

"But what does she say about that Meir?" the nasal voice returned, "Was he the violent type?"

"I don't know; she never talked about him. I met him maybe two or three times and he seemed like a completely normal guy."

"All serial killers seemed normal once," the nasal voice commented.

"I really don't know what happened there. Iris is so shocked that she's barely functioning. Luckily, they're coming back on Sunday. I could help her a bit."

"Poor thing."

"Such a horror. Hanni was such a beautiful and vibrant girl. Iris loved her so much. They'd been friends since they did their Civil Service."

"I know."

"Iris tells me they had a bit of financial trouble."

"Well… who doesn't these days?" the nasal voice was commentating again. "My youngest still gets a monthly allowance from us. Young people today can't make ends meet."

"Yes, but you know, Meir's parents are one of the richest families in Petach Tikva."

"*You don't say*?" The nasal voice accentuated each syllable.

"Yes, it's well-known."

"I didn't know. So, what drove him to it?"

"I've no idea. I'm dying to hear what Iris has to say. She must know something."

I was also dying to speak with Iris, and to my joy I now knew that she was returning from overseas this Sunday. I deliberated whether to reveal myself to the two ladies sitting near me, not noticing I exist. My police badge was deep in my sweater pocket. Should I jump up in front of them, waving my badge? What did I need to ask them? I had Iris's details, and her mother and her nasal friend didn't really interest me. Who would I impress?

While I pondered this, Iris's mother and her friend were joined by two men who urged them to move quicker. A few minutes later, my father and Yehuda, Ayelet's husband, also emerged from the crowd and we went back to the hotel.

If Iris's mother knew Hanni and Meir had financial difficulties, Iris was probably an essential witness. Hanni kept up the perfect act for the outside world. None of her neighbors really knew what happened inside Hanni and Meir's house, but all of us put on an act when we're out in society. Shavuot in Jerusalem is basically one big masquerade ball. Everyone comes with one objective, to present themselves and their families as successful, happy, and beautiful. The failures, disappointments, shouting and ugliness are left behind locked doors.

I wondered if this was only a trait of religious society, or if secular people also kept up this kind of façade. It was a bit difficult for me to answer, since I didn't have kids and I had no idea how secular families with children behave. I assumed everyone was pretending, but that the pretense in religious society was greater. In secular society, there was less pressure on marriage and children, so the need to sweep flaws and problems under the rug was less necessary.

But to what extent can you leave everything under wraps and closed off? Every person needs to have an escape, a wall where they can unload all of their secrets and unease, and Iris was, apparently, Hanni's wall.

CHAPTER 13

Saturday, 5.30.2009

To my surprise, during that day and the Shabbat following it, I didn't meet any more direct or indirect acquaintances. This may have stemmed from the fact that I dedicated a considerable amount of my time to sleeping and watching TV in my room. Shira kept me updated on mealtimes, and I mostly kept annoying my mother.

"You're allowed to brush your hair before you go down to the lobby," she said sadly, aware of the fact that the battle has already been lost.

"I did," I replied in despair. "That's my hair. You can only blame God."

"Ayala has more difficult hair than yours and she always looks neat."

"I don't intend to cover my hair!" I almost yelled.

I sat down next to Ayala and hugged her, lest she think for one moment that I was belittling her or her hair.

"Who are we waiting for?" I asked impatiently.

"Not you, for a change!" My dad took a dig at me.

"We're waiting for Moshe. He took the kids for a short walk

in Gan Hapaamon," Shira answered calmly.

I made myself comfortable on the couch and looked around. I was looking for people I might know. I was hoping to see Iris's mother again. Maybe I could get some more details from her.

I didn't know if I was even interested in running into someone I knew. In the last two weeks, I'd seen so many acquaintances from my past, I felt I was overdosing on nostalgia. Unmarried, childless, not religious or even traditional, I had nothing in common with these childhood friends. When I was still in school with them, and attended Bnei Akivah with them, I didn't feel like I belonged, so now, when my life was so different from theirs, I had even less in common with them. In the movies, reunions offer the chance to show everyone how successful you've been and how you've conquered the world in the years that have passed.

In the ideal movie, the geek has become a multimillionaire, and the evil captain of the football team has turned into a fat bum. I was definitely the geek, the honor student, the slightly ugly loner. Years later, I wasn't a millionaire, nor had I undergone comprehensive plastic surgery to transform me into a stretched-out Barbie doll. At a class reunion, I'd be considered a failure in religious society terms: divorced, no children, hardly getting by on a police officer's salary.

However, that was exactly the point. In my mind, I was an incredible success story, because I was spending my life doing only what was good for me and not what was expected of me by others. How many of my classmates and acquaintances worked in a job that gave them such great satisfaction? How many of them had three or four kids because they really, really wanted them, and not because that's what everyone did?

I had no intention of saying what I thought to my childhood friends. People don't like hearing the truth, but I also didn't have the energy to deal with the looks of pity I received when people heard I was a single, childless old maid.

I didn't see anyone I knew around me, or maybe I just didn't recognize them under all of the fancy clothes, dolled up hats, makeup and falsity. Still, it had been fifteen years since we parted ways. I wore the clothes my mother bought for me and still managed to look like a waif. It turned out I managed to pick the shirt that least matched the skirt, which was two sizes too big. It was meant to be a tight skirt, but on me it looked like a shapeless sack. My hair was more disheveled than usual, and I was wearing a pair of sandals that had seen better days.

"You couldn't look in the mirror before you left your room?" My mother still hadn't given up.

"I think I look great."

"I didn't buy you those sandals, and you could have worn something else with that top. You can't see that skirt's huge on you? Since when did you get to be such a small size? Why aren't you eating? Since you joined the police, you've just neglected yourself. Believe me, state security won't be harmed if you go out to eat a normal lunch once a day." My mother was firing off rounds.

"The last time I checked my ID, I was already over eighteen, so you can stop worrying about how much I'm eating and how I dress. Just say the truth, Mom - you're embarrassed I don't fit in with this whole performance." I waved my hands around me.

"All of this," Ayala tried to imitate my gestures, "is a performance for you?"

"More or less."

"What exactly are we performing?" I had a feeling Ayala was insulted.

"You know that case I'm dealing with now, a family that was outwardly dressed up to the nines and completely functional, but inside, apparently, everything must have gone rotten if, one day, the father can get up and slay them all."

"Wow, that's just too much." Ayala was practically stewing when she talked. I'd really managed to upset her. "If we dress nicely it means we're covering up something rotten?"

"No, that's not what I said." Ayala managed to confuse me.

"But that's what it sounds like." Shira surprised me by joining

Ayala and my mother's team. Shira, herself, is not exactly a role model when it comes to color matching and ironed clothes, but she was a little better than me and when it came to events or weekends, she made an effort to fall in line with my mother and Ayala.

"I'm just saying that pretty clothes don't mean anything. If I'm a slob, then that's how I want to look," I lied. I didn't want to look like this, but I didn't know how to dress differently.

"You're talking nonsense." My mother pulled back an empty chair and sat down next to me, careful not to talk loudly, so the other people in the lobby, some of whom were already intently listening to our conversation, wouldn't hear what she had to say. "A person who's dressed well conveys something about himself. It's true that sometimes it's a lie, but a lie is destined to come out, just like what happened in the shocking case of the Danilowitz family."

"But maybe if people didn't work so hard covering up their lie so perfectly, things wouldn't explode in such a horrible way? If Hanni and Meir were busier sorting out their issues rather than covering them up, maybe this whole story would have ended differently."

"Are we still talking about clothes?" Ayala wondered.

"Yes, among other things, but not only that, I've a feeling that a lot of people, not only Hanni and Meir Danilowitz, are too busy with how those around them perceive them, rather than being true to themselves."

"Not everyone can afford to leave everything and start working for the police." My mother explained the facts of life to me.

"Why not?" I played dumb.

"Because most people have a mortgage and children and they can't do whatever they feel like all of a sudden."

"But the mortgage and the kids are part of it. Where does it say that you have to have three kids and a mortgage?"

"So we're talking about the having kids again?" My mother rolled her eyes. "I thought you didn't want to talk about that with us anymore."

"In my opinion," Ayala interjected before I could answer my mother, "you've turned being a slob into a way of life. You perceive anyone who goes through the trouble of matching their shirt to their pants as someone who wastes their time in vanity. But the truth is, you're no better than those trying to cover up emptiness with beautiful clothes.

"You dress the way you do because you're trying to show that you're better than everyone. That you, unlike all of us, have a life and an important job, so you can't waste your time on insignificant things like shopping or manicures." Ayala, my younger sister, was the exact opposite of me, especially when it came to grooming.

"I assure you my sloppiness isn't deliberate," I said, almost in a whisper.

"I also don't dress nicely to cover up something dark, I just like to be aesthetic. I think personal grooming's important. If you look good on the outside, you usually also feel good on the inside."

"No doubt." I smiled at her. I didn't feel like fighting, and I also didn't think she was wrong. Still, I felt that when someone is excessively busy with appearance, it's often to make up for internal, substantial problems. I decided not to continue with the argument, and fortunately, my cell phone rang just then.

It was Yinon.

My father gave me an angry look, and before he could launch into a tirade, I got up and found a secluded corner of the lobby.

"What's up?" I asked.

"Everything's great." He was breathing hard.

"What's that? Where are you, huffing and puffing like that?"

"I went out for a jog with Tsumi. The poor dog's really out of shape. Do you ever walk him?"

"Yes," I said, almost in a whisper. I wasn't lying, I did walk him. A walk around our back yard is also a walk.

"Listen, that dog's so cute you could eat him."

I smiled. I loved that dog, although I hadn't cared for him

properly in a long while.

Yinon went on, "This week I had lunch at a restaurant and one of those deaf people came by, selling little dolls. I usually ignore them, but because I remembered I'd be taking Tsumi for the weekend, I bought a little teddy bear so he'd have a new toy from Daddy. Anyway, he's completely in love with this little bear, doesn't leave it for a second. I even had to take the bear on our run."

"What a cutie," I laughed.

"Yeah… I wish I could keep him longer. The day I bought the teddy bear, I went to the gym and left it in my locker, so I only really gave it to him this morning."

Yinon went on talking and describing the dream weekend he had with Tsumi, but I found it hard to listen. I remembered Meirav, Meir's sister, owned a chain of gyms. How did I not think of this earlier? Maybe Meir was hiding something in his locker.

I anxiously waited for Shabbat to end so I could call Meirav.

"*Shavua Tov* [good week]," she answered.

"*Shavua Tov.* Meirav?"

"Yes. Who is this?"

"It's Hadas Levinger, from the police. We met this week."

"Yes, of course." I could hear her smile. I knew she liked me, too. "How can I help you?"

"Do you remember you told me that you gave Hanni a membership to your gym?"

"Yes."

"Was Meir also a member?"

"Yes."

"Did they have lockers?"

"I don't know. I'd need to check."

"When could you do that for me?"

"Tomorrow morning, but in any case, I can't let you open a locker without a warrant."

"We already have a warrant to search the house and car, and

it also applies to lockers."

"No problem, darling. I'll get back to you in the morning."

CHAPTER 14

Sunday, 5.31.2009

Meir had a locker.

Meirav called me at eight-thirty and said she checked with the gym in Kiryat Ono where Meir and Hanni had memberships, and it turned out they each had a locker.

"When do you want to go there?" Meirav inquired.

"Straight away."

"Do you need me there?"

"No, not at all. As long as someone can identify the locker for me and open it, if that's possible."

"What do you mean, if that's possible?"

I smiled. "I'll get it open anyway, but I think it's better to keep the lock whole."

Meirav laughed. "No problem, honey. If there's any trouble let me know."

I usually didn't like to be called "honey" or "darling" by women or men. Even my mother and Shira were careful not to call me by nicknames, but coming from Meirav, it gave me a nice feeling that she liked me.

On my way to Kiryat Ono, I got a call from Iris, Hanni's good friend, who had finally returned from England.

"Is this Hadas Levinger?" she asked in a hesitant voice.

"Speaking," I said in a singsong voice. I was in a good mood.

"You left me a message."

"Who is this?"

"Iris Green."

"You're the friend of the late Hanni Danilowitz?" I asked as if I had not been looking for her for days.

"Yes, I was Hanni's friend," she said sadly.

"I understand you just got back from England."

"Sure, we were at a family event."

"I need to ask you a couple of questions. Can you come to the station?"

"Of course."

"I just left, so could you come by in about four hours?"

"No problem."

The last time I visited a gym was during the compulsory sports lessons at university. I chose gym because it just worked out in my curriculum. Luckily for me, the grade was pass or fail and you had to really make an effort to fail this course. What I remembered from those lessons was a dark gym in the university's bomb shelter, and a fitness instructor who had very little to do with health. He used the breaks between the lessons to smoke cigarettes and maintain his potbelly.

Twenty years earlier, he'd been a renowned coach in Belarus, but in Israel he had to choose between cleaning stairwells and training in the university's broken-down gym. His gym was equipped with apparatus that was considered old even in his heyday in Belarus.

The Fitroom Health and Fitness Center was completely different from the distant memory I had of the university gym. The gym, located in the new shopping mall, was well lit and ventilated. The equipment was state of the art and spotless. Bulky fitness instructors walked around among the different apparatus, their main clients at this time of day—late morning—being mostly pensioners and bored housewives.

A tall and muscular guy in a tight T-shirt embossed with the word trainer in large font, leaned against the reception desk. He had a fashionably disheveled forelock, a chiseled chin and blue eyes. I made a mental note that I could stand to work out every once in a while.

I approached the desk. He turned to me and smiled. I was blinded—I really have to start working out.

"I'm looking for Mirit." I tried to sound as nonchalant as possible.

"She went down to the grocery store for a minute. We ran out of milk." He managed to talk without losing his smile for a second. I smiled. Without showing my teeth. I was reminded that I hadn't seen the dentist or dental hygienist in over a year.

"She'll be right back," he leaned over the counter to grab something. You could put a picture of him in the dictionary next to 'firm buttocks.' "You can fill out your details in the meantime." He handed me a clipboard with a personal details form.

For a minute, I considered becoming a member. I ignored the fact that this gym was in Kiryat Ono and that I have at least five gyms within walking distance from my house and workplace, and the sad fact that I can barely walk 200 meters at a slow pace without beginning to have suicidal thoughts.

"Thank you," I returned the form to him and held my toothless smile. "I'm not joining the gym."

"Really?" he rounded his eyebrows. He seemed really surprised.

"I'll wait here for Mirit." I sat down on a couch at the corner. I had a hard time remembering when I'd last sat on a couch this uncomfortable. I guess they do anything here to keep the customers from sitting down for even a moment.

A few minutes later, a young, smiley woman skipped joyfully to the reception desk and handed the trainer a plastic bag filled with cartons of 1% milk, which, to my knowledge, is more or less white, colored water. From the other bag, she pulled out a pack of rice cakes. I tried to understand why a size-36 girl has to torture herself with something that tastes and smells like Styrofoam. The charming instructor collected the plastic bag and pointed in my direction.

"Hello." Mirit revealed perfect, white teeth. She really seemed happy; I guess she was also on in a constant endorphin high.

I pulled out my badge and placed it on the counter. "I'm Hadas Levinger from Israel Police." A couple of pensioners who were standing a few meters from me, enthralled with the June activity schedule, immediately went into listening mode. "Meirav Avni referred me to you."

"Oh, the Danilowitz lockers." The smile was erased from her face.

"Correct."

She led me toward the dressing rooms. The lockers were just inside. She gave me the key to Hanni's locker.

"It'll be a problem for you to go in to open Meir's locker. I'll get Niv to open it for you, if you'd just tell him exactly what you're looking for."

"I have to open Meir's locker myself," I said decisively.

"But women aren't allowed to enter the men's dressing room."

"You don't have cleaning ladies here?"

"They clean after activity hours."

"Listen, I'm going in, whether you clear out the locker rooms or not. You can be sure I've seen it all before." Actually, I hadn't seen that many, but I didn't want her to think that I was some rookie who could be disregarded.

Eventually, I began in the women's dressing room with Hanni's locker. In the meantime, Niv asked the men showering to hurry up, while Mirit asked other gym members to wait outside the locker room for a few minutes.

Hanni's locker was nearly empty. In it were a towel and a change of clothes.

A few minutes later I moved on to the men's locker room. In it was a pensioner, drying his hair, completely disregarding my dramatic entrance.

I was disappointed to find that Meir's locker was almost empty, too. Here, I also found a towel, a change of clothes and an old health magazine. I put it all in the bags I'd brought, although I didn't know what the forensics department would be able to find. Deep inside the locker was a pair of rolled up socks. I reached out my hand to get to them.

Once I touched the socks, my heart started beating wildly. Hidden inside the rolled up socks was a flash drive.

Without knowing what was on the disk, it was clear to me that it was something important, otherwise what reason would Meir have to hide it in a ball of rolled-up socks in the corner of his locker, far from everyone's eyes?

I raced to the office. I was impatient. I wanted to know what Meir had to hide in those socks. The whole way, I prayed that the disc was readable and that there was something on it that would finally give us a lead.

I stormed into the station, carrying the bags of Hanni and Meir's clothes and towels. The flash drive was sitting on top of the pile. I'd pushed it back into the socks; I didn't want something to happen to it on the way.

Riki was blocking my way. Her face looked like she had hot gossip to tell.

"Riki, I'm really into something. Is it brief?" I said tensely.

"Just one second… I just want to warn you."

I stopped. This sounded interesting. "What?" I was curious.

"Alon's mad."

"Tell me something new." I kept walking and Riki trailed after me.

"I know, but today a little more than usual. He even yelled at Amos earlier."

That was unusual. Alon was careful not to start any unnecessary wars with Amos. I stopped again.

"What happened?"

"That's it," she rolled her eyes and rubbed her hands together, "I don't know for sure, but I heard that, over the holiday, Alon's ex-wife introduced him to her new boyfriend."

"So?" I didn't see what the problem was. The fact that Alon and his ex-wife have a relationship that's far from over, even after eight years of divorce, is not enough of a reason, in my opinion, to get Alon screaming at everyone, especially Amos.

"Her new boyfriend's a firefighter," she said with a meaningful gaze, "and he's also at least five years younger than her."

Now, that definitely sounded problematic. Dorit had a younger boyfriend, and even worse, he was a firefighter. Alon had a thing about firefighters a strange little battle of ego.

I made extreme efforts to make myself invisible, especially when I passed by Alon's door. It didn't do me any good.

"Levinger!" I heard him shout and knew there was nowhere to run.

I entered his room and lingered in the doorway.

"Come in, come in," he said angrily and gestured. "You have nothing to be scared of."

Oh, but I do… no reason other than the fact that Alon was furious and was looking for someone to pour his rage out on, and I, unfortunately, was the latest victim.

I took two more steps and placed the bags of evidence on his desk.

Alon stretched out in his chair, as if loading his gun before firing it. "Could you explain, please," he fired the first shot, "how it's possible that nearly two weeks have passed since the event and a whole week since we found Meir's extorting letter, and we still have nothing? Just nothing? All I hear is that you're wandering around endlessly—going to the bank, to the school, the public library—and conducting interviews at witnesses' houses.

"How many times do I have to tell you: ask the people to come here. We don't have time for unnecessary trips. If you have nothing, it's no shame. Just say the word and we'll transfer you to a different case or give you another one… I don't exactly have too many people to spare here."

"But you also told me numerous times that the best way to

understand a case is to search as closely as possible to the scene. You, yourself, also told me you gave me the case because I have a religious background, and it would be easy for me to understand this family. This is no ordinary homicide. We're not looking for a murderer, we're looking for a motive, and since Meir's letter was found it's become clear to all of us that the story here's a bit more complicated than a family feud.

"How do you want me to get into Meir's head in my office? In order to understand Meir, in order to get to know his family, I have to meet the family, the friends, the teachers, the neighbors and, in my opinion, nothing beats getting to know them and understand them in their natural environment."

"I didn't say you shouldn't." Alon was probably surprised by the fact I answered him back, and his voice softened a bit. "But still, two weeks with almost nothing, just more and more questions… can you please explain to me where you disappeared to this morning? What's that bag, for instance?"

"I went to the gym Hanni and Meir used."

"May I ask what for?" He resumed his angry tone.

"Because I found out they had lockers there." Alon's look changed again; I could see my latest discovery intrigued him.

"And did you find anything there?" he asked in an appeasing tone.

"I found this." I picked up the rolled-up socks.

"You found a pair of socks. Good job, Levinger, I'll update the chief commissioner." In spite of his anger, he managed to smile at his own joke.

"What's interesting about this pair of socks," I went into a dramatic tone, "is what I found rolled up inside them."

I pulled out the disc and waved it in Alon's stunned face.

"Then why didn't you tell me you'd found a very suspicious piece of evidence?" he scolded me, but I knew he was happy.

"Because you haven't stopped yelling at me from the minute I came in."

"Okay, okay, okay," he gestured for me to come closer. "So what's on this?"

"I've no idea, I just got it here."

"Give it." He reached out his hand and I gently placed it in in his palm. He grabbed it and plugged it into the USB slot of his computer.

Within seconds the computer identified the device and the file library was opened. There was one file on it.

A video.

Alon double clicked on the file and the video opened. I breathed a sigh of relief. I was afraid that it would be another dead end. Within a few seconds, I stopped breathing. The sense of relief was replaced by a sense of unease and discomfort.

The video was taken by Meir, a year earlier, on Independence Day. Meir's voice was heard, urging Galit, his four-year-old daughter, to tell him what holiday it was today and then he asked her to sing *My Flag is Blue and White.* The video was shot outside and I recognized the location as a playground not far from Shira's house in Givaat Shmuel.

Galit giggled at the camera and ran toward the slides. There were not many children there. When Galit ran, Meir lowered the camera. There was a shot of the ground for a few seconds. Although Galit ran toward the slides, Meir was walking in the opposite direction. At first it was unclear why, and after a few seconds you could hear what Meir probably heard himself: the sounds of a man breathing heavily in excitement.

The camera lens was raised in the direction of some tall bushes. It was possible to dimly hear the man's voice and the thin voice of a little boy or girl. In a short while, there was some stirring from within the bushes. The camera shot the ground again. Meir apparently ran in a different direction. The camera's lens was again raised in the direction the voices were coming from. A young boy of about eight came out from the bushes, wiping his hands on his shirt. He seemed embarrassed and flustered, but not as upset as I'd expect of a boy who had just undergone what he had, just moments earlier, apparently.

I thought to myself, what's he supposed to feel like? I'd never talked with a child who'd been sexually abused, much less seen one seconds after he had undergone this difficult experience.

It was hard to identify the boy. The camera hadn't captured such good quality footage, and it was far away. The boy turned in the opposite direction and ran. A few seconds later, a man emerged from the bushes. He was about forty years old. His face was also hard to clearly identify, but I assumed anyone who knew him would be able to recognize him easily. The man was wearing a knit skullcap, and was zipping his pants and adjusting his shirt. He began walking toward the playground and Meir immediately turned the camera away and stopped the recording.

Alon and I exchanged glances in silence. I assumed Alon had already encountered sexual assault investigations, but it was a first for me.

"Play it again," I said.

We watched again. This time, I talked us through the video and identified the location of the playground for Alon.

When the man emerged from the bushes, Alon froze the image.

"Do you know him?"

I looked intently at the blurry image. It was a man of medium height, a bit chubby, slightly balding, wearing eyeglasses. He was dressed in jeans and a green polo shirt. There was no detail differentiating him from dozens of other men who look, more or less, exactly like him. Despite the standard, clichéd appearance, I had the feeling I knew him, or had seen him somewhere before, a perfectly reasonable feeling in light of the fact that he was probably a resident of Givaat Shmuel, a city that I visit pretty often.

"No, I don't know him, but I've a feeling I've seen him before."

"Maybe in Givaat Shmuel?"

"Probably."

We were silent again. I was distraught and confused from the difficult footage.

Alon huffed. "It's not easy to watch."

"Not at all."

"Were there any complaints filed to the police by Meir or Hanni?

"Neither of them ever filed a police complaint."

"You mean, Meir walked around for at least a year with this video shoved in a pair of socks and didn't tell anyone a thing?"

"Not as far as I know. None of the relatives even mentioned anything that comes close to what we saw."

Alon shook his head in disbelief. It was hard to believe that Meir had captured such footage and didn't run to the police with it

"Okay," Alon huffed again. "Find this pervert. I think we can guess now who Meir was blackmailing." I nodded. "Once we know who this is, maybe we'll be able to understand what brought Meir to do what he did."

I gathered up the socks, Alon placed the disc in a new evidence bag, and asked me to make at least three copies of the video and send one to him.

I was about to leave the room when he called my name.

"Levinger." I turned around.

"Good job."

I smiled shyly and ran to my room.

I had a hot potato in my hand and knew that I couldn't talk to anyone—not even at the station. Stories of this kind had a tendency to get to the press at the speed of light.

I watched the video a few more times. I tried to understand where I knew this man from and tried to produce a clearer photo of the boy. A chill went down my spine each time I watched it. I thought of Elad, my sister Ayala's eldest son. This wasn't Elad, but he reminded me of him: a skinny, curly-haired boy. Elad's skullcap, just like this boy's, was also always hanging and not lying on the top of his head. In Elad's case, it was because he was hyperactive. In the case of the boy from the bushes, I didn't know whether he was mischievous or not, but I assumed the skullcap was hanging for other reasons.

I thought of Elad again. I loved that boy. It may be because he was Ayala's complete opposite, and gave her hell. In character, he took more after me than my sister, a fact that was no doubt costing Ayala her health. Elad was a beautiful boy. When he was a toddler, he was even in a commercial for a dairy product for toddlers. The thought of someone hurting him and destroying his innocence drove me mad.

Elad was not my son. I tried to imagine what had gone through Alon's mind, as a father of two boys, when he watched the video. How could you have a job like ours and not get emotionally involved? How could you be cold and objective?

I made copies of the video and printed out some copies of the pictures of the man and child. It took a while, because I tried to capture a frame where they didn't look as if they had just committed a sexual act. The boy turned around too fast, so I cut the picture in a way that only showed his face. As for the man, I had a full body shot and a face shot. None of the pictures were clear enough, but I assumed that someone who knew them would be able to recognize them.

I wasted too much time on fiddling with the pictures and I regretted not involving someone else. Amos surely would not have told anyone, and I could have used his professional services. I thought I'd manage to run over to Shira to show her the pictures. I imagined that if it was someone from Givaat Shmuel, she could identify him for me, and be as discreet as possible.

By the time I was done, it was already three-thirty. I told Iris we'd meet at four, so I couldn't manage to get back to Givaat Shmuel.

I went out to have a falafel and when I got back, Iris was already waiting for me. We entered the interview room. Iris sat down and immediately broke into tears.

I ran to my room and brought her a packet of tissues.

"I'm sorry," she said and blew her nose. "This whole situation, me sitting in an interrogation room and having to talk about Hanni's death—it's horrible."

I tried to muster my most sympathetic look. "I understand," I said in a whisper, and sat across from her. I allowed her to calm down. Even though she was crying, it was hard to ignore the fact that she was a beautiful girl. Long, smooth, black hair, gigantic blue eyes, a tiny nose and a perfectly drawn mouth. The girl could have been used as inspiration by whoever drew Snow White.

"Tell me how you met Hanni." I decided not to start from the end.

"We both did our civil service at Sieff Hospital."

"In Zefat?" I was a bit stunned. Hanni didn't seem to me like the kind of girl who would go to the other end of the country to do her year of service.

"Yes," she replied. She noticed the slight surprise in my voice. "We both did one year, and we decided to do it somewhere far away, so we'd feel like we were serving. My parents are from Tel-Aviv; Hanni's are from Ramat Gan, so we'd always travel there and back together. I know that for many people, doing only one year of service doesn't really count, but I believe what we did there in one year was equal to, or even more than, what an office worker does in the Tel-Aviv headquarters in two years."

I had no intention of getting into an argument with her. I also thought she had a point.

"We shared a room in a civil service apartment in Zefat and became best friends," she went on. "I don't know how to explain it, but right from the beginning we felt a real closeness to one another. Both of us only had brothers and we were like sisters to one another." She burst into tears again.

After she calmed down, I asked, "What can you tell me about Hanni and Meir's relationship?"

She thought for a moment. "If you ask me, she didn't love Meir."

"Ever? Or did the love fade?" I tried not to use the word “died,” so as to avoid another flood of tears.

"I don’t think she ever did." She surprised me. "See, Hanni

was a very practical girl, Meir was a guy from a wealthy family and she wanted to live in comfort." I looked at her, astounded. "I know it sounds bad, but we both know why I'm sitting here, and I want to help as much as I can." Frankly, she amazed me; the weeping girl from moments earlier just disappeared.

"So she married him for the money?"

"You didn't know her when she was younger." I decided not to correct her. "Hanni was very beautiful, I mean, she's beautiful now, too…" She paused for a second and corrected herself, "I mean, she was beautiful." I prayed she wouldn't start crying again, and she went on. "But, what I'm saying is that, when we were in civil service, she was very, very beautiful and very, very sought after.

"She met Meir back in Bnei Akivah, but they didn't connect until she was in university. Up until she met Meir, there were a lot of guys interested in her, some had more money, some less. What I'm trying to say is, Meir wasn't the only admirer she had from a wealthy family and that she liked, and the fact that she finally chose him says something."

"What?"

"That it wasn't just for his money."

"But you said that you don't think she married out of love."

"Right."

"Why?"

"I think she never got over the love she had when we were in Zefat."

"Can you tell me more about that?"

"When we were in Zefat, we occasionally stayed for Shabbat in the civil service apartment. Mainly families live in Zefat and the only young people you can see there over the weekends are civil service girls and guys from the Hesder Yeshiva. On our first Shabbat there, we met Avinadav. You could say it was really love at first sight."

"Between Hanni and Avinadav?"

"Of course, I was already engaged to Jeremy. I met my husband at a Bnei Akivah camp when we were seventeen and we decided to get married once Jeremy finished the army. I wasn't single, but Hanni was a hit in Zefat. A lot of guys were interested in her. Why wouldn't they be?" she said longingly.

"She was so beautiful, and also smart and opinionated, everyone wanted to be around her, but only Avinadav managed to really get close to her. He was an amazingly good-looking guy, very tall, broad shoulders, dark curls and almond colored eyes that melted everyone. He was also a smart student. Everyone in the Yeshiva was impressed by his knowledge and debating ability."

"So… what happened?"

"After a couple of months of lots of nightly conversations and a lot of butterflies, he proposed to her, but Hanni said no."

"She didn't want him?"

Iris snickered. "She was in love with him with every fiber of her being."

"Then why did she refuse?"

"I already told you, Hanni was a practical girl and she didn't believe love could pay the bills. Although Avinadav was the epitome of her romantic dreams, a world-class hunk, very intelligent, and very romantic… you should have seen the letters he wrote her, even I skipped a beat when she read them to me."

"But..?" I tried to move her along.

"But he had no money, and was also too religious for her. For instance, they never touched one another, because he was *Shomer Negiaa*." I was astonished. I knew the phrase, but was amazed at the thought that there could be a couple that longed for one another so completely, but never even kissed.

"Did she also observe *Negiaa*?"

"No, don't get me wrong, she was married a virgin—of that I'm certain, because we told each other everything, but she fooled around with Meir, for instance, before they were married, and I think there were at least three other guys that she kissed before she started seeing Meir, so the thought that she didn't get to touch Avinadav specifically was pretty disappointing for her."

"So they didn't get married because he was too religious?"

"I told you, he also had nothing. Hanni deliberated a lot about this point, she was very practical. She saw quite a few people around her who married out of great love and the love eventually died. She didn't want to find herself raising six or seven kids, with a husband studying in Yeshiva."

"I thought he was a Hesder student."

"Right, but all kinds come to Yeshivat Hesder, and Avinadav wanted to go on with his studies in the Yeshiva. He also planned to go to university, but not to study something practical. Hanni didn't want to clip his wings. She loved him very much. She thought that if she demanded that he become, say, an engineer, he'd hold it against her their entire life."

"Where is he now? Any idea?" I wanted to talk to him.

"He was killed." She surprised me. "The year after Hanni's year of service, when Hanni was already in law school at Bar-Ilan, he was very closed off and refused to meet any girls. A year later, he apparently softened, was introduced to a few girls and ended up marrying someone, I've no idea who. When we heard he got married, Hanni was depressed. She probably hoped in her heart they'd eventually get married. After that, we didn't hear about him for years. We only knew he moved to some godforsaken Moshav in Galilee, and that he led a very spiritual life style.

"In the Second Lebanon War, he was recruited to the reserve forces and was killed. Then we saw his picture in the paper and there was an article about him and his family. He had six kids, two boys and four girls, very close in age. He had a small Galilee vineyard and he continued studying and teaching in a Yeshiva. There was a picture of him; he'd aged a bit, but was still handsome. Hanni didn't stop talking about him for days after that article was published following his death."

"What did she say?"

"She mainly tried to convince herself how right she was not marrying him, that she didn't see herself raising six kids in some hole in the north, and how happy she was with the life she had."

"And was she really happy?"

"Depends when you're thinking of… like all of us, really, who's happy all the time?" she asked. I didn't answer and she went on. "Avinadav was killed a few weeks after Meir was fired from the start-up company. It wasn't such a pleasant time for them. Meir had a dream job and, suddenly, all of their dreams were shattered."

"So she was lying to herself when she said she was happy with her life?"

"I don't think so. Hanni was a very optimistic girl. At least, at that time, she still believed Meir would find another job as good as the start-up, if not better."

"And it didn't work out in the end." I filled in what I already knew.

"Right, it didn't work out and Meir went back to work at the bank."

"How did Hanni take it?"

"Hanni didn't like that too much. She thought Meir would get a job that was a bit more respectable and rewarding."

"Working in a bank isn't respectable?" I asked in wonder.

"It's very respectable, but there's an environmental element. A lot of very successful people live in Givaat Shmuel, Meir had gotten there, and now had to regress to his student job."

I already knew all that. I wanted to try and get an insider's view of Hanni and Meir. "How was Hanni and Meir's relationship? Did they fight a lot? Was there verbal or physical violence?"

"Not that I saw. That's why I'm so shocked. Hanni and Meir seemed to me like a completely normal couple. They fought quite a bit, mostly about money, but I know a lot of other couples who fight about money." Interesting. I didn't know even one couple like that. Iris noticed my difficulty in understanding and she explained. "In a lot of relationships, there's one side that squanders a bit more and a side that's a bit more frugal—opposites attract, as they say."

"Were Hanni and Meir complementary opposites?"

"In that field, of course. Hanni was a bit frivolous with money, but Meir was very tight fisted."

"And they fought about it?"

"Wow." She rolled her eyes. "Endlessly!"

"And who do you think was overreacting?"

"I think Meir, but, of course, I'm not objective. Hanni was like a sister to me and I only heard her side."

"And what did she tell you?"

"That he wouldn't stop telling her off about everything she bought."

"Can you give me an example?"

Iris thought for a moment and then began. "This is the latest example I have, from just a few weeks ago. On the Tuesday before this horrible murder, we celebrated Galitush's birthday. Believe me, it wasn't anything too extravagant, just a party in the community room in their building: some snacks and a local clown who does magic tricks and Meir just gave her hell about it. I've been to so many birthday parties that cost the parents a fortune, and Meir was raging when she also booked a clown.

"He wanted to just have games like in old times, without an outside host, because it cost 450 shekels. It's not like she booked an expensive activity, they have someone in the neighborhood who's great with kids and does birthday parties as a sideline. I thought it was great, worth every shekel. You get what I'm talking about - he came down on her about sums like those."

"Maybe she did too much shopping? Maybe 450 shekels here and 500 shekels there, and together it adds up to a lot of money?"

"I already told you she was quite a spender, but I don't think they led a lifestyle that was too extravagant or showy, no more than I did, anyway." I realized that Iris was actually a sort of gauge of standard for Hanni.

"May I ask what you do for a living?"

"I have a degree in education and bible studies."

"You mean you're a bible teacher?"

"No," she smiled. "I'm a full-time mom."

"What does your husband do, if I may ask?" It interested me to know how a family in Israel could manage with one salary.

"My husband studied law and business management, but he works in his father's investment firm." Now everything was clear.

"Hanni shared their financial issues with you. Did you know, for instance, what their financial situation was after Meir was fired from Fiberlight?"

"From where?"

"The start-up."

"Huh," she nodded, "you think I saw their bank balances? Of course not…" she smiled "that's highly unacceptable. We were like sisters, but even my brothers don't know how much money I have in the bank. Besides, I don't think Hanni herself knew how much money she had in the bank."

"How do you explain that? Hanni was a lawyer, not exactly someone who couldn't handle a bank account."

"I don't know. Hanni never liked bills, she left that to Meir. Don't forget, Meir was an accountant. He was good at it. Too good. He drove her crazy about it."

"Maybe he had good reason to? Maybe she really was spending too much?"

Iris stretched out in her chair, a gesture I noticed she repeated every time she was about to say something she wasn't very comfortable with. "I told you—Hanni married Meir also because of the money. Meir could have sat at home and not worked, and it wouldn't have changed anything. His parents are sitting pretty, as they say. He had no reason to be so stingy."

"Maybe he was uncomfortable asking his parents for money?"

"I know there was some issue there," she stretched again. "Hanni didn't like talking about it too much because it was a sensitive subject. I think she was barely speaking to her in-laws, but she and I both had no doubt that, if the situation was very bad, they'd have their back."

It was already five-thirty. Talking to Iris was interesting. I discovered some interesting things, mainly the story of Avinadav, but most of the things I'd already heard in earlier interrogations of family members. I wanted to have time to go to Shira's and show her the picture.

Iris was already at the door when I decided to see if she knew the man in the picture. I have no idea why I did it, I didn't think that Iris would know the man at first, but I suddenly got the idea that maybe he was a mutual acquaintance.

"Do you recognize the man in this picture?"

Iris got closer to the table and looked at the picture thoroughly. It was evident in her eyes that she recognized him immediately. "Of course I know him," she smiled. "It's Chubby Yigal, that clown I told you about. He's excellent."

She was curious to know why I'd be interested in a children's entertainer, but I rushed her out, curious to find out more about the clown.

I was surprised. The information Iris gave me about Hanni, though interesting, did not add a lot to work with. The quick identification of the rapist in the bushes moved our investigation along significantly. I shuddered at the thought that (Chubby) Yigal was a children's entertainer, but it didn't especially surprise me. Many pedophiles choose to work or volunteer with children. Yigal, apparently, had the right approach was familiar to a large number of children, who, presumably, trusted him fully. I thought about Shira and my precious nephews. Did they also know this clown from hell?

I stopped myself from calling her. I'd get the answer to that soon. I was sure of it.

I went to the computer, and after a quick web search, I reached Chubby Yigal's fairly impressive website, which included pictures of Yigal, photos from birthday parties and recommendations from parents. Chubby Yigal, or, by his full name, Yigal Einav, explained to those interested in an activity for a birthday party, that he did "Simple activities like the old days, without any effects or bouncy castles—just laughs and magic that children love."

In most of the pictures, Yigal wore especially colorful clothes, but without any makeup, which was why Iris was able to identify him so easily. On the site was a link to a page where Yigal talked about himself. On the side of the page was a clear image of Yigal in "regular" clothes. I had no doubt that this was the man in Meir's video. It turned out that Yigal was also, (well, mainly) an electronics engineer. From a young age he'd been an amateur magician and his love of children (I cringed when reading this) led him to perform and host activities for children. It began with volunteering in children's wards in hospitals, and, due to great demand, he began performing for a low fee. Yigal had been married to Dina for sixteen years and they had three daughters.

At the bottom of the page was his contact information: phone number, email address and home address.

Yigal was from Givaat Shmuel. Just as I thought, and probably why he looked familiar to me.

CHAPTER 15

Monday, 6.1.2009

I knew the video alone would not be enough to keep Yigal under arrest, and was certainly not enough to indict him. I knew I could manage to get a warrant for his arrest, but any rookie lawyer would be able to get him out on bail in less than twenty-four hours. Actually, the video didn't show anything. If I hadn't found it rolled up in Meir's socks, I may have not jumped to conclusions. On the other hand, an arrest warrant and a warrant to search an apartment are the kind of warrants that can bring an investigation down, because this is when the suspect knows he's under investigation and is able to tamper with evidence.

Alon and I decided to keep everything very secret. The fewer people knew about the story, the easier it would be to get quick results without anything leaking to the press.

Shachar had finished his investigation at the bank empty-handed. It was now clear to us that investigations at the bank were pointless, and Alon sent him to tail Yigal. Shachar didn't ask too many questions, and, in fact, wasn't aware of why he was following Yigal, except that he knew it had to do with the Danilowitz family investigation, of course.

I rushed to court in the morning and requested a warrant to

inspect Yigal Einav's bank accounts without his knowledge. I knew that if we could link the cash deposits in Meir's account to cash withdrawals in Yigal's account, we'd have a good base.

Yigal had two bank accounts. I requested printouts of the last two years, and was promised they'd be on my desk by noon, so I decided to go visit Shachar, and maybe get a close look at Yigal.

Shachar was happy to see me. Following Yigal was turning out to be especially boring. Yigal got up in the morning, drove his two younger girls to school and went to Ramat Hachayal, where he worked as an electronics engineer for one of the global media giants. The judge had also given us a warrant to bug him, which allowed Shachar to monitor all Yigal's cell phone calls. There was nothing to report. Another day of a typical high-tech slave.

"Can you tell me why I'm being subjected to this tedium?"

"I promise you that today, tomorrow tops, you'll know everything. We decided it'd be best if as few people as possible know what this is about."

The call-monitoring device beeped. Yigal was receiving a call.

Shachar tuned into it immediately:

"Are you here?"

"Yes, I'm sitting in the coffee shop where we sat last time, right across from your building."

"I'll be right down."

The caller hung up.

Across from the building were a number of coffee shops. Shachar got out of the car and waited for Yigal.

A few minutes later, Yigal came out of the building. He was, indeed, chubby. The picture on the site was taken when he was at least twenty kilos lighter than his current weight. Even compared to the person in the video, it was evident that Yigal had gained weight in the last year. Compulsive eating is often a sign of emotional distress. If Yigal was being extorted in the past year, he was certainly under distress.

According to our records, Yigal was forty-two years old. If I hadn't known this, I would have guessed he was at least fifty. A fat, balding man, Yigal refrained from shaving his head completely bald, unlike the current fashion, which made him look even older. He wore a tailored shirt and a tie that matched his pants. Yigal was a senior engineer.

Shachar waited across from the coffee shop and went in after Yigal, who joined another man sitting at a side table. On his way to the restroom, Shachar managed to stick a tiny bugging device to Yigal's table. When he came out, he collected the two cups of coffee he'd ordered for us.

"I hope you like yours with a lot of foam," he said as he climbed back in the car.

"Did you bring sugar?" I asked.

"Yes," he passed me three packets of sugar and was astounded to see me pour all of them into my coffee.

"It's a big cup!" I reasoned.

Shachar flipped to another channel in the receiver of his car and we could now hear Yigal's conversation with the other man.

".... I hope this is clear to you," Yigal whispered.

"Don't worry, we understand it's sensitive."

"And how can I be sure you'll wait for me?"

"As far as we're concerned, you can start tomorrow. We're willing to pay you that bonus as soon as today, if you want."

Yigal huffed. "I wish I could, but I'm completely tied up in my contract. I can't work for the competition for at least six months after I leave. I'd have to sit at home for six months without a salary."

"I heard you're a pretty good clown."

Yigal snickered. "Your kids got a birthday soon? I'll give you a good price."

The other man laughed. "Don't worry, you'll get severance and unemployment, and in six months, when you start working for us, you'll get a welcome bonus that'll make up for your six months of unemployment."

Yigal finished his cup of coffee and collected a chocolate

croissant on his way back to the office.

Yigal was planning on transferring to a rival firm for a very high salary. Was he doing this because of the extortion?

My cell phone rang. Riki informed me that the material I'd requested from Bank Hapoalim and Bank Mizrahi arrived.

I'd noted down the sums of the unexplained deposits to Meir and Hanni's account in the recent year in advance, so now I searched Yigal's bank account for withdrawals of similar amounts in the days leading up to the date of the deposits.

The Mizrahi Bank account was relatively dormant and there wasn't anything to see in it, but after short consideration of the Hapoalim Bank statements, I had no doubt. Yigal was giving Meir the money that was being deposited into his account.

Not all the sums were identical. It's possible that Meir didn't deposit all the money he was given, or that Yigal didn't give Meir all of the money he withdrew, but against every deposit there was a withdrawal from Yigal's account of a similar or identical sum, about a week before the deposit in Meir and Hanni's account.

It was still circumstantial, but I knew I had to move forward, and the only way to do that was to take out a search and arrest warrant for Yigal.

Since Shachar was already in Yigal's vicinity, I decided that he could conduct the arrest and take his personal computer for investigation. I took two patrol officers with me to help me, in case of resistance, and drove to Yigal's house. I wanted the search and the arrest to happen simultaneously. If Yigal had something to hide, he wouldn't have the time to hide it.

The other implication of a search and arrest was the fact that it was only a matter of time before our dear friends from the media found out what was going on. It had already been two weeks since the murder/suicide, and, all of a sudden, we were holding a search and arrest warrant of a Danilowitz family neighbor, an outstanding family man and an executive in the high-tech industry.

On the way to Yigal's house, Shachar updated me that the

suspect was in custody. We didn't say any more because the suspect was in the police car with Shachar. I was curious to know how he reacted to the arrest.

When we arrived at his house, it was one-thirty in the afternoon. I had no idea if anyone was at home, but I hoped someone was.

Yigal lived in one of the private homes at the edge of the neighborhood. I imagined it was a pretty expensive piece of real estate. I didn't look too deeply into the numbers I had received earlier from the bank, but I remembered his paycheck was especially big and he had quite a bit in savings and investment accounts. Yigal was a wealthy man. Meir knew who to extort.

I rang the doorbell.

"Who's there?" I heard a woman's voice.

"Police," I replied.

A few seconds later, the door opened. Dina Einav stood in front of me, a look of awe on her face.

"How may I help you?" she asked. She had no idea what was going on.

"Mrs. Einav?" I asked and she nodded. "Dina Einav?" she nodded again, she was getting nervous. I assumed the first thought that was running through her head was that something had happened to one of her relatives, so I immediately continued. "I'm Inspector Hadas Levinger from Israel Police. I have a search warrant for the home of Yigal Einav, your husband. Please open the door and let us in." I handed her the search warrant that I had received a short while earlier from the judge on call.

I placed the warrant in her hand and she didn't look at it. Her stunned gaze was fixed on me. She stared at me with her eyes agape. She had no idea how she was supposed to act. This wasn't exactly a drug baron's wife, used to having her house searched.

After a long while, she snapped back to life and said, "Wait here for a moment. I'll just call my husband."

"Your husband was taken into custody just a few minutes

ago."

Her face turned white and I realized she was about to lose her balance. I caught her before she fell and asked one of the officers who had come with me to help me take her inside.

She sat on a chair in the spacious dining room. I went into the adjoining kitchen to get her a glass of water. While she sipped from the glass, I took the chance to get a look at my surroundings. The house was carefully furnished, very clean and tidy. Next to the dining room was a heavy wooden cupboard with a glass vitrine. Through the glass shone heavy and expensive silverware, candlesticks for Shabbat candles, a giant Menorah, Kiddush goblets and a decorated plate. A few baby toys were scattered about the living room. That seemed a bit strange to me. Dina and Yigal had grown-up daughters, but not old enough for the couple to have grandchildren.

Dina was thirty-eight years old, fairly pretty and well groomed. Although she'd spent her morning at home, she was dressed and put together. When I spent my morning at home, I looked as if I'd just been yanked out of bed, disheveled and dazed. The only items of clothing that gave away the fact that she was in her house were the slippers on her feet.

She wore jeggings and a wide, slightly kitschy sweatshirt. Her hair was carefully pulled back, her nails were painted red. She wore little jewelry, but it was obvious that each ring or bracelet was pretty expensive. She seemed like a real *balabusta*: one of those women who manage to keep both themselves and their house in tip-top shape. I was certain that if I opened the fridge, I'd find it full of homemade food.

Dina emptied her glass and placed it next to the search warrant, which she'd put on the table earlier. She placed her hand on the search warrant and asked in a low voice, "Could I call a lawyer first? Is it possible you come back later?"

"No," I replied in a calm but assertive voice. "You can call a lawyer if you want, but we're not leaving this apartment before we finish the search."

"I have two little babies here; I don't want you to wake

them."

I looked at her in shock. According to the information we had, the couple had three daughters aged seventeen, twelve and nine. "There are babies here?" I asked, surprised.

"I run a sort of nursery."

"If you don't get in our way, I promise you we'll be quiet."

Just as I finished the sentence, the door swung open, and Hagit and Noga appeared, home from school. Tears came to Dina's eyes. How could she explain the awkward situation that she was in to her young daughters? She looked at me desperately.

"Do you have any neighbors they could maybe go to for an hour or two?" I whispered.

She thought for a second. "My mother lives not far from here, I can call her."

"Go ahead," I replied.

She went to her daughters who stood frozen over their school bags, whispered something and hugged them and then went into the kitchen and spoke briefly on the phone to her mother.

A few minutes later Hagit and Noga were already on their way to their grandmother's house.

"You have another daughter, an older one?" I asked Dina.

"Yes, Avigail. She'll be here in about two hours."

"Where does she go to school?"

"I don't believe you'd know it. It's a small high school in Ramat-Gan."

"Haro'eh High School?"

"You know it?" She was surprised.

"I went there," I smiled and immediately regretted it. This small talk was redundant.

I didn't know if she was impressed for the better or worse. She went to the warrant that was waiting on the table; she perused it and thought for a few seconds.

"Okay," she sighed. "Look for whatever you need, but try not to wake the babies, and, please, finish as soon as possible."

"Do you have a study here or a room where you keep a computer?" I asked immediately.

Dina led me to a room in the basement. In the room was a large library, a treadmill, which, based on the amount of objects that were hanging and placed on it, had clearly not been used in a long time, and a large desk. Everything was neat and tidy.

"Yaniv," I called one of the officers who accompanied me. "Please disconnect the computer and take it to the car."

Dina jumped immediately. "You're taking the computer?"

"We'll return it after it's inspected."

"But it's our home computer. The kids use it to play."

"I promise we'll return it as quickly as possible." I tried to calm her down.

One of the babies started crying and Dina rushed to him.

I gestured for the other officer to come to me. "Omer," I whispered. "Don't let her out of your sight. I don't want her to try and throw our search. I don't think she has any intention to, but just to make sure we avoid any glitches." Omer nodded and stood in the doorway, watching Dina soothe one of the babies.

I went to the bookshelf and searched among the books and drawers. Maybe there was a letter from Meir, maybe an envelope identical to the one we found at Meir's house.

Yaniv was done disconnecting the computer and placed it in the doorway. I asked him to go upstairs to the bedroom and search through the closets.

"What am I supposed to look for?"

"Anything that doesn't belong in a bedroom."

"Like what?" he asked. He had no idea what the search was about.

"Letters, money, pictures."

"No problem, boss," he said.

The search in the study was barren. I went up to the girls' rooms and took a look inside them. Each of the girls had her own room. I did a superficial search because I didn't think I'd find anything there. I went down to the kitchen again. Dina's kitchen was spacious, neat, fully equipped and clean. I opened the refrigerator not to search it, just out of curiosity. As I expected, Dina's fridge was full of bounty. The cupboards, the refrigerator and the pantry were incredibly tidy. I didn't imagine I'd find anything there. The kitchen looked like Dina's personal kingdom. If Yigal were hiding something, it wouldn't be there.

"Hadas." Yaniv surprised me from behind, just as I took another (longing) glance at the cream cake in the fridge.

"Yes?" I turned around and smiled an embarrassed smile. I was caught red-handed.

"I found this in the upper closet." Yaniv handed me a laptop computer, a pretty old one.

"Oh, wow," I said to myself and took the computer to the living room. Dina was sitting on the carpet, playing with the baby who had woken up.

"Mrs. Einav," I said in an authoritative voice and she raised her eyes to me. "Can you explain this is to me?" I waved the computer. "Just to remind you - I specifically asked where the computer is."

She looked at me, surprised, "Uh… umm…" she faltered. "I really wasn't trying to hide anything." She sounded sincere. "I totally forgot about that computer. It's my husband's old computer. I don't even know if it works." It was clear that she really hadn't thought about the computer. For her, it was just an old computer that could be discarded, not a computer a demon could come out of.

Immediately, I knew that what we were looking for was there and not on the home computer. If Yigal had something to hide, he wouldn't hide it where his wife and three daughters played and use the Internet. He'd do it on a hidden computer no one used or remembered.

I looked at Yaniv and Omer. "Load 'em up!" I commanded and they took both computers to the police car.

"Can you please explain to me what this is about?" Dina stopped me from leaving.

"Do it without me," I said to Omer and Yaniv. "I'll be right there."

"I'm really sorry," I told Dina, "I've no doubt that it wasn't pleasant for you to have three cops come into your house and go through your personal belongings, but I assure you that we did this because we have cause to believe that your husband has committed a serious crime."

"Crime?" she echoed. "Serious?"

"Yes." I looked down.

"What crime are you talking about? My husband's a law abiding citizen."

"I'd appreciate it if you could come to the station tomorrow morning for an interview. If it's difficult for you to get there, we can come to pick you up."

"I can get there," she said immediately. "But what for?"

"I need to ask you a couple of questions, and maybe I can give you a couple of answers regarding the suspicions we have about your husband."

She looked at me, her eyes gleaming with tears. I really felt bad for her. She was headed toward even more difficult times.

She simply married the wrong man.

When we arrived at the station, Yaniv helped me take the computers to Amos's office.

"Put them there," he pointed to a random spot in the room without lifting his gaze from the computer. Yaniv placed the computer on the floor, and I took the laptop to Amos.

"It's urgent." I stood in front of him.

"Everything's urgent." He still didn't look up.

"Do you want Alon to tell you it's urgent?"

He sighed and finally lifted his gaze from the computer. "What I'm doing right now was also urgently requested by Alon."

He managed to confuse me. We called Alon, who asked Amos to give first priority to the computer I'd just brought in. On the one hand, I didn't like bossing Amos around like that, but on the other hand it felt pretty good to be top priority.

Amos tapped something on the computer he was working on

and then put it aside.

"What do we have here?" he took Yigal's laptop from me. “Hmm… a real archive specimen?"

"A laptop’s an archive specimen?" I marveled.

"Everything in life is relative; this laptop’s at least ten years old, which is certainly some type of dinosaur."

He looked the computer over from every angle. "So, what exactly do you want me to do?"

"As a first step, I'd like to open it."

"What's the problem? Here, you press here." He pointed to the "on" button.

"Very funny," I smiled. "I'm not that stupid. I turned the computer on already. I just can't open it because there's a passcode."

Amos gave me the look of a genius asked to do novice mental exercises. "That's the only problem?"

"I don't know what’s on the computer. I assume, or actually, hope, that we'll find something useful on it."

"What?"

It was useless to withhold information from Amos, and he wouldn't run off to tell anyone. I told him briefly the direction the investigation was going in. "In short, I want to find something that can tie Yigal to Meir's extortion. A letter, maybe."

"No problem. Do you also want me to look through the other two computers?"

"What two computers?"

"The one you just brought in and the one Shachar brought in earlier." I realized Shachar had confiscated Yigal's work computer.

"Yeah, sure, but this one first. If Yigal had something suspicious on a computer at all, I’d bet it’d be on his home computer rather than his work one."

"Okay." He stretched and settled to his work.

I found Shachar in the smoking area.

"May I join you?" I sat down next to him and he handed me the pack of cigarettes.

"No, thank you."

"Do you even smoke?"

"Only second hand."

He smiled and blew a bubble of smoke in my direction.

"Tell me how the arrest went."

Shachar took a final drag from the cigarette and stomped it out with his heavy shoes. "I can't say it was particularly pleasant."

"Is there a pleasant arrest you can tell me about?"

"Look, it's not every day I go into a fancy high-tech company and arrest one of the executives. Let's just say: when we arrest a member of one of the organized crime families, they're a little less surprised."

"So… tell me how it went down."

"The building he works in has two receptionists. My cat probably has a higher IQ than both of them put together."

I smiled. Shachar didn't seem like a cat person.

"It took about twenty minutes for them to tell me what floor Yigal works on and let me in."

"You didn't show them your badge and warrant?"

"Of course I showed them, but they had to call the security officer, who was at lunch. Eventually I went up. The offices there are amazing, like the kind you see in movies. I didn't believe there were places like that in Israel. At the entrance to Yigal's floor, there's another receptionist, a bit more intelligent than the two sitting downstairs, and also, if I may, much better looking."

"And I assume you already have her phone number," I added.

Shachar flashed a telling smile. "We have a date tomorrow night." I laughed and he went on. "She escorted me to Yigal's office. Listen, that guy's seriously big there. He has a corner office with a huge window. He was with two other people. I went in and asked him if he's Yigal Einav. He said yes and asked for me to wait outside because he was in the middle of an important meeting. I told him it couldn't wait and he got angry."

"What did he say?"

"I don't remember exactly, just got annoyed and said anything could wait until the meeting was over. I flashed my badge and he immediately got rid of the two guys who were sitting with him. They were shocked."

"So, once you showed your badge, he stopped the important meeting?" Yigal wasn't completely surprised to see an officer before him. He'd known this day could come.

"Yes. The two left, and Yigal closed the door behind them. I showed him the warrant and told him I was taking him in for questioning. He asked if it could be postponed to another day, and I told him the warrant was immediate. I pulled out the handcuffs and he started to cry."

"He cried?"

"Full on tears, like a little kid."

"Wow."

"Wow indeed. It was very awkward. I explained to him that there was no choice, and that he had to come with me, cuffed."

"I'm sure it's uncomfortable to leave your office handcuffed and accompanied by a police officer."

"Very."

"Where is he now?"

"In Holding Room 2."

"Take him to the interrogation room near my office. I'll be there to interrogate him in a minute."

"Will you just tell me what this dork did?"

"I'll tell you later, I promise."

I went to my office to get ready. Amos called me.

“Come in here, now!” he said excitedly.

“I have to go into an interrogation right now.”

“Whose? This Yigal guy?”

“Yes.”

“Then come here first. Believe me, it's urgent.

I rushed to Amos's lab. He sat looking at Yigal's laptop, shaking his head.

"Just horrendous." He looked at me when I came in.

"I see you've cracked the code."

Amos smiled as if I'd told an old, bad joke. "It is a pretty old computer, but it's been upgraded pretty well. The hard-disk and screen card have been replaced. Of course, the password wasn't really a problem."

"So—what did you find?"

"I didn't have to look too hard," he said and gestured for me to sit next to him.

"I checked what took up the most memory and got to the video file."

Amos clicked on the "My Videos" file. Dozens of videos popped up. Amos clicked on one of them. A young boy of about eight or nine was sitting on a red couch. The voice from behind the camera instructed him in a foreign language, German or Dutch, and the boy undressed in front of the camera.

"Wow," I exclaimed in horror.

"This is a soft one."

I didn't want to know what a "hard" one was, but Amos left nothing for me to imagine. He looked through the video library and found a video of a handsome boy, no older than ten, performing oral sex on a man and later being sodomized by another man.

Amos fast forwarded the video just so I could get a sense of what we were watching, but just a few seconds in fast forward was too much for me. It was just horrible.

I closed the laptop and shut my eyes. I tried to erase what I'd seen from my memory, but I knew the pictures would stay etched in it forever.

We sat in silence for a few moments. I could only imagine what these sights were doing to Amos, who was such a devoted father.

"The owner of this computer is sitting right down the hall." I finally broke the silence. “I don’t need to tell you about the hotheads here in the station who’d beat him to death if they saw these videos.”

“I could kill him,” Amos whispered.

“I’m asking you to keep these videos between us. Please make a copy of the file for me. I’ll have Shachar try to find Israeli videos. In the meantime, try to find out where Yigal gathered this disgusting collection. Besides, I’m reminding you that we’re also investigating the Danilowitz family murder here, so try to find any letters he may have written to Meir.”

I left Amos's office enraged. The pictures kept running through my head. I consider myself to be a pretty calm person, but I felt like going into the interrogation room and shooting Yigal.

Shachar was waiting outside the interrogation room. "The suspect's inside," he said when he saw me.

"Is the door locked?"

"No."

"Then lock it. I want to talk to you first, but first I'm going to speak with Alon."

Alon was sitting in his room, looking through follow up reports on the Mirashvilli case. He seemed defeated. The media kept talking about how poorly the police were handling the case. Despite the amount of evidence they had, the police still hadn't managed to formulate an indictment.

"Yes, Levinger?" he looked at me with an almost sleepy gaze.

I updated him about what we found on Yigal's computer. This woke him up immediately.

"I'm updating Shachar about everything. I want him to go through all the videos. It's enough that he just sees a second or two of each of them. I want to see if there are any homemade or Israeli videos in there. Amos is working on the computer as we speak and looking into the sources of this disgusting collection."

"No problem."

"I just want to know how I go forward from here. We started on the Danilowitz case and now we have a different case altogether."

"Look," Alon began tapping on his computer, "these are not exactly separate cases. I think it's clear to all of us that Meir was blackmailing Yigal because he caught on to his sick hobby. I think we have no doubt that Meir himself killed his wife and kids and then took his own life, so Yigal's not a murder suspect, but who knows what kind of trigger he was for this act?"

I nodded, and Alon continued.

"Start with the pedophilia and we'll get to the extortion from there. Maybe it'll come from him eventually. I'm connected to the camera in the interrogation room. I'll be watching, so if there are any problems, I'll come in."

"No problem," I said and left the room. I felt my heart beating all through my body. I'd never interrogated a pedophile, let alone in such a complex case.

Shachar waited for me by the interrogation room. I pulled him to Amos's office and updated him about all the details of the investigation. I saw the blood go to his head when I told him about the videos.

"I'd like to beat this disgusting pervert to a pulp," he said and I just held him still. "Here I was, feeling sorry for him, arresting him at work like that. If I'd known about this, he'd have seen what humiliation is…"

I was glad Shachar hadn't known anything until now. That was the last thing I needed right now, a hotheaded cop putting on a show at the heart of the high-tech industry.

"Anyway, stay here with Amos. He'll transfer Yigal's library to you. I want to know if there are any videos in there that were shot by Yigal, or videos of Israeli origin. Maybe we can reach other pedophiles ."

"Do me a favor," Amos added. "Watch that abomination with headphones on, I don't even want to hear it."

I entered the interrogation room and looked up at the

camera straight away. The red light was on. Alon was watching us.

It was the first time I'd met Yigal. He seemed stunned and humiliated, but not surprised. I've interrogated quite a few people and, apart from a small number of good actors, the difference between innocent and guilty ones was that the innocent ones looked confused. They didn't understand what they were doing in an interrogation room, because they really weren't supposed to be there.

Yigal knew very well why he was sitting in an interrogation room; he seemed defeated and ashamed, but not confused. He looked a bit tired, probably because he had cried quite a bit. He was wearing the same clothes he'd had on in the morning, except for the confiscated tie. Shachar would have now happily handed him a noose.

I introduced myself and then asked him his name.

Silence.

"Yigal, I need your personal details. You have no reason to worry about giving your personal information."

Silence.

It wasn't the first time I was confronted with silence. Any time that someone refused to talk, without exception, they had something to hide. Five minutes later, which felt like an eternity, Yigal said, "I want a glass of water and an attorney."

I left the room. Alon came out of his room and caught up to me at the water fountain. "The little shit came prepared."

"What do I do?"

"Give me that." He yanked the cup of water from my hand and went to the interrogation room. I thought I saw him spit into the cup before he entered. I ran to his office to watch him.

"Here's your water, Mister Yigal Einav." Alon slammed the cup onto the table. Half of it splashed on Yigal. "You have to understand that not all the cops here at the station are as sensitive and respectful of human rights as Inspector Hadas Levinger. I have a few investigators here at the station who'd hang you out to dry for a long while if I let them watch the perverse collection of videos we found on your laptop."

Yigal looked up in shock. He didn't know we had searched his house.

"Yes, yes, dear Mr. Einav. We've searched your home and your secret computer is in our possession."

"I want a lawyer," Yigal said, almost whimpering.

"First, answer a few questions for us."

"I want a lawyer!" Yigal started to cry.

"You'll get a lawyer after you answer a few questions for us."

Yigal was silent, probably in an attempt to stop his crying, and then said again, "I know my rights. I want a lawyer."

We switched back and forth like that a number of times. I was the good cop; Alon was the bad cop. It didn't work. Yigal was completely mute except for his pleas to get a lawyer.

After about an hour of this, we gave up. Yigal wouldn't even confirm his personal details for protocol. Of course, he didn't want public defense, and he called a criminal attorney who had handled cases of incest and pedophilia in the past.

Yigal had his phone number ready in advance. He knew this day could come.

CHAPTER 16

Tuesday, 6.2.2009

Yigal spent the night in Abu-Cabir. We could have left him at the station, but he was giving us a hard time, so we decided not to take it easy on him.

I felt sorry for his wife, who had no idea what this was about, why her husband was arrested and why her house had been searched. Just before he was taken to Abu-Cabir, I allowed Yigal to call her in my presence.

"Hello?"

"Dina?" Yigal said gently.

"Yigal?" Dina broke into tears "Where are you? What's going on? Do you have any idea how many reporters are standing outside our house? My phone's ringing non-stop."

It had not taken the leeches long to make the connection between the arrest of a high-tech executive and the fact that he lived in the Danilowitz neighborhood.

"I'm sorry," he joined her in crying, "I'm really sorry." It was hard for him to calm down. I took the receiver from him.

"Mrs. Einav?"

"Who is this?" she asked in a voice choked up with tears.

"This is Inspector Hadas Levinger. I was at your house

today." I heard her blow her nose. "We've issued a warrant for your husband's arrest for forty-eight hours. I assume that we'll extend it tomorrow. We'll be arranging to pick you up to be interrogated first thing tomorrow morning."

"Can you tell me what this is about?"

"Tomorrow," I replied and hung up.

The gag order on the investigation didn't deter the press photographers from accompanying Dina on her way to the police station. No newscast could afford to miss this giant story the second the order was revoked. On some websites, the fact that the Danilowitz family's neighbor had been arrested was already out in the open. I knew it was only matter of time before the whole story blew up.

Dina entered the station accompanied by two police officers. My heart went out to her. It was evident that she hadn't slept all night. Her eyes were red with tears and surrounded by dark circles. In spite of the difficult situation, she was dressed nicely in a short denim skirt and a trendy wrap blouse. Her hair was down and tied with a ribbon that matched her top. She was a pretty woman, and very well kept.

I tried to think how I would look if I was summoned for an interrogation after my husband and the father of my daughters was mysteriously arrested. I escorted Dina to the interrogation room. I was curious to know if she was going to answer my questions. Yigal had already contacted a lawyer, who had, apparently, advised him to remain silent. I assumed the lawyer had briefed her as well.

She sat down where Yigal had sat the day before, crossed her arms and legs, and waited for me to speak.

"Would you like anything to drink before we start?"

"Water, please."

I looked toward the camera; I knew Alon was watching us.

"It'll be here in a minute," I assured her.

"Are we being recorded?" she asked in astonishment.

"Of course. This is a police investigation. Neither of us wants any dispute over what we said or didn't say."

"No problem."

"Have you already spoken to your husband's lawyer?"

"Yes."

"So you're aware of the fact that you may reserve your right to silence if you're afraid of incriminating Yigal? This is your right by law."

"I'm aware of that, but I still have no idea what this is about."

"Would you like to proceed with the investigation?"

"No problem; I can't incriminate my husband since I have no idea why he's even under arrest."

Riki came in with a cup of water. Dina thanked her and took a drink.

"Okay," I said, and opened a blank pad of paper. "Let's get started."

"Can you start by explaining to me what I'm doing here?"

"In a minute. I'd like to get to know you first." Dina shrugged and I went on, "Please state your name, age and address for the record."

"Dina Einav, thirty-eight years old, from Shivaat Haminim Street 7, Givaat Shmuel."

"Please tell me what you do for a living."

"I have an in-home nursery for toddlers aged six months to two."

"How did you come to open it?" It didn't exactly interest me, but I wanted to let her loosen up a bit.

"I opened it when we were still living in Givatayim. Before I started the nursery, I worked for an insurance agency. But after I had the girls, I preferred to stay at home, so I took on a few more kids to watch and I found that I loved it."

"I understand you moved from Givatayim?"

"Yes, we moved to Givaat Shmuel five years ago."

"Please tell me how you met Yigal?"

"I did my civil service in the maternity ward in Tel-Hashomer. I met a nice girl from Elkana there. I went to her house for Shabbat one weekend. Yigal's parents are the neighbors of that friend's parents. Yigal's mother saw me and immediately wanted to introduce me to Yigal."

"Your friend didn't think to make this match herself?"

"She didn't even think about it. She said he was a very quiet and introverted guy—a little strange, played with magic. She didn't even think about introducing us. She thought I was looking for someone who was good-looking and dominant, but she was wrong. I didn't want someone who'd play games with me. I was looking for a good husband."

"How old were you?"

"I was nineteen-and-a-half."

"Isn't that a bit young to think of marriage?"

"In our circles, that's the age you start thinking about marriage. Ever since I can remember, I wanted to be a wife and mother."

"What can you tell me about Yigal? What kind of person is he?"

"What do you mean?"

"Is he a good father?"

"He's a great father."

"Does he have a tendency to get irritated? Angry?"

"No, I can't say he never got angry or annoyed, but he's definitely a calm, easygoing person."

"What's your relationship like? How open are you with one another?"

She hesitated before replying. "Yigal's a wonderful husband. We're happy together. I thought we were very open with one another, but apparently not enough, if I'm sitting here without understanding why."

I decided to take it up a notch. "How's your sex life?"

She threw her head back, as if I had slapped her. It was like I'd punched her. "I don't think I want to answer that question. I'm sure it's none of your business."

I thought for a minute and then pulled out a photograph of one of the children found on Yigal's computer. An eight-year-old boy, completely naked, holding an erect penis.

I placed the photo in front of Dina. She leaned in closer to see what it showed and immediately twisted her face in horror and disgust and pushed the photo away.

"We found this picture on your husband's laptop."

"Which one? The computer that was in the bedroom closet?"

"Yes."

She thought for a few seconds. I couldn't decipher her expression. She was undoubtedly shocked by the picture, but it seemed as if she was trying to figure out her place in this story.

"Don't get me wrong," she eventually said, "the picture is absolutely horrid, but if that's what you found on Yigal's computer, I think this whole ordeal is a bit much. There are a lot of people with shocking photos on their computer. Not all of them are even real."

"Dina, I really hope you don't think we arrested your husband and searched your house because of one picture, horrible as it may be."

I turned behind me and switched on the television set that was in the room. The movie we had seen came up on the screen, the boy conducting oral sex and then being sodomized. I fast-forwarded the movie, so Dina would get an idea about the severity of the material we found on Yigal's computer.

She shut her eyes and begged me to turn the TV off.

"This is one video out of over a hundred on Yigal's computer." Dina put her hand to her mouth; her eyes and cheeks were wet with tears. "Our computer specialist located some of the sites Yigal downloaded the videos from. The only good thing I can tell you is that all the videos and all the sites were from abroad. Meanwhile, we've forwarded the information we have to Interpol and police forces in the countries these sites operate from."

She looked at me, stunned.

"Would you like some more water?" I asked and she nodded. It was hard for her to speak.

I went out to fill her cup and get a fresh pack of tissues.

She sipped her water slowly, as if she was drinking scorching hot tea. Then she blew her nose.

"I thought you arrested him because of the whole Danilowitz family story, I really had no idea how he could have anything to do with this whole ordeal, not that what you've shown me now isn't shocking in itself. Believe me, I'd no idea I had this in my home."

"We have reason to believe that Meir Danilowitz, God rest his soul, was extorting your husband."

"What?" she gasped.

"Do you have any idea about this? Maybe Yigal told you he was being blackmailed? Do you know about any sums of money Yigal withdrew from your account without any explanation?"

She opened her eyes wide and shook her head. "Wow, I really have no idea. Yigal didn't share anything like that with me."

"And you didn't notice inexplicable sums of money withdrawn from your account?"

"I'm embarrassed to say I never check our bank account. I always trust Yigal completely. I'm not good with numbers."

"Did Yigal seem agitated this year?"

"He was blackmailing him for a year?" she asked, astonished.

"We're still not a hundred percent sure if he was, indeed, blackmailing him, but if he was, that was more or less the time frame."

"But how did Meir find out about these videos? I lived with Yigal and I had no idea."

I bit my lip. Dina didn't yet understand that the videos were the least of it. "Meir was blackmailing him about something else."

"What?" She couldn't even imagine that there could be something worse.

"We suspect Meir caught Yigal molesting a child."

This time she covered her face with both her hands and began to sob. Within minutes, the man she married at the age of twenty, with whom she raised three girls and built a magnificent house in Givaat Shmuel, had become a dangerous sex offender.

I felt sorry for her. She was also a victim in this horrible story.

I felt the need to get close to her, to let her feel and understand that I saw her as a victim. She was the set-up for a dangerous person. She was Yigal's cover story. I got up from my seat and sat down next to her. I felt a bit strange. I'm not an especially sentimental person; I never had any female friends that I felt comfortable enough to cry with and hug in times of crisis. I gently stroked her hair and gave her some more tissues.

Before I could understand what was happening, she just leaned into me and hugged me tightly. I'm sure she didn't feel close to me. She needed a shoulder to cry on, and I was there. I held her for a few minutes. It quickly became very uncomfortable for me. The position was forced, and she wet my shoulder with her tears, but I had enough compassion to know that I couldn't move until she disengaged from me herself.

She leaned away from me at last, and said, quivering, "I married a deviant and a murderer." I knew it would be said eventually, more or less.

"Murderer?" I asked in amazement.

"You also suspect he killed the Danilowitz family, I suppose?"

I got up and returned to my chair. "Dina, we don't suspect your husband killed the Danilowitz family. We're pretty convinced that Meir killed his family and committed suicide."

"But why?"

"That's what we're investigating. During the investigation, we found your husband."

She thought for a long while and then asked, "Am I a suspect or anything?"

"No."

"I lied to you before." She surprised me.

"When?"

"When I told you we had a good relationship. You asked me before how our sex life was… the truth is, there was no sex life." I was stunned by her frankness. I let her go on. "The last time I had sex with my husband was two years ago, maybe three. This must sound shocking to you, but you have to understand that Yigal hardly ever touched me before that, either, even when we were newlyweds and were supposed to be in love and overcome with lust. It bothered me, but I never talked about it.

"In our circles, you just don't talk about that. Occasionally people even tell dirty jokes, but no one ever *really* talks about it. It's sort of… taboo. I assumed that was what it was like for everyone. I suspected we might be different because of what I saw on television and in the movies. I really love that show *Everybody Loves Raymond*, for instance, as it always seemed to me like a show that talks about subjects that anyone can relate to.

"Like all kinds of problems with kids and family. Yigal's mother can be pretty bossy, like Raymond's mother. The only thing that bothered me was how Raymond was always begging for sex and willing to do anything for his wife so she'd agree to sleep with him. I wasn't familiar with that. Yigal never, ever, begged for sex. The only times it was important to Yigal that we have sex was when we planned to expand the family. The only other very few times, it was something very, very planned and dispassionate. I sometimes felt that he was doing it to please me because it bothered me and I spoke to him about it, so he slept with me to shut me up."

"And that didn't seem strange to you?"

"As I told you, we don't talk about those things in our society. I married very young and was very inexperienced. Every time I brought it up, Yigal told me that's what it's like for everyone and that I should stop believing what I see on TV. Otherwise, he really had to be forced to sleep with me."

She lowered her gaze. She seemed so humiliated. Again, my heart pitied her.

"I sensed it wasn't meant to be like that," she continued. "Now I know I was right all along… he just didn't want me. I was some kind of cover story for him."

I looked at her. Despite her puffy eyes and red nose, she was a very attractive woman. I had the feeling that quite a few men would have been happy to be with her, but instead, she had spent years in an emotional prison.

"So why did you stay?"

"Because I believed him when he said it's like that for everyone. I thought that if we separated, I'd only lose out. Except for the intimacy issue, I was pretty comfortable with him. He's a kind, calm man. We raised our girls in relative harmony. He was a good father." She was suddenly reminded of her daughters, and her expression changed. "*I'll kill that dog if he touched our girls!*"

"I doubt that," I tried to calm her down. "We didn't find one video or picture of a girl—just boys."

She closed her eyes and prayed or thanked God.

About an hour after Dina was released, Yigal returned to the station after his night in Abu-Cabir. I hoped it would break him. After all, it was hardly an easy experience, especially for a senior high-tech engineer used to the good life, but, unfortunately, Yigal went on with his silence. He had already been briefed by his lawyer, whom he met in that morning at Abu-Cabir.

We slowly revealed to him the material we had. I had wanted to avoid this, because a confession made without the suspect's exposure to the evidence is stronger, but there was no choice. I wanted to rattle him, to let him know we were on to him.

But he was silent.

It was evident from his expression that nothing surprised him. Maybe there was even some sense of relief there that criminals sometimes feel when they're caught and the burden of concealment is lifted from them. I had no doubt Yigal had done horrible things and that he had something to hide. Otherwise, he would not refuse to speak.

Keeping silent is no easy feat… sitting for hours across from an investigator who asks you the same questions in different ways… all that you're trying to conceal being slowly revealed to everyone. It's not easy for the investigator either, that I can confirm. It's very frustrating. You try to touch the right spot, press the button that will make the suspect talk.

In the evening, after six hours of silence, we sent Yigal back to Abu-Cabir.

I sat down at my computer, defeated, massaging my temples. My head was about to explode. I'd been in the interrogation room since first thing in the morning, initially with Dina and then for hour after miserable hour with Yigal.

My cell phone danced on the table. I had a message. I'd switched it to vibrate in the morning. My mother had called me just as I'd started interrogating Dina, so I'd switched off the ringer and later forgotten about it on my desk.

I picked up the "museum piece" (that's what Nurit, Shira's daughter, called my cell phone). I had ten missed calls from my mother and another five text messages, four from my mother, and the most recent one from Shira.

"Hello?" My mother answered in a suspicious tone. I was calling from the landline in the office and she probably saw an unidentified call on her screen. She hates it when I call her from an unidentified number; as she claims telemarketing sales representatives constantly bother her.

"Mom, it's Hadas. You were trying to get hold of me?"

Her tone of voice immediately changed. "Where are you?" she cried out. "I've been looking for you all day."

"I've been in the station all day."

"I know," she said angrily. "I called two hours ago and they told me you were in an interrogation."

"Right, I've been in an interrogation all day long, I didn't have my phone with me and I didn't know you were looking for me."

"Then why don't you take your cell phone with you? That's why you have one."

"I don't have it so my mother can interrupt me in the middle of an investigation. I have it so I can be reached when I'm not at home or at work. I was in the station all day, Mom. You could have left a message."

"I did."

"When?"

"Two hours ago."

I looked at my desk. It was so messy that it had to be quite a task to leave me a message that would be seen. I noticed the note that had been taped to the computer screen and fallen off. It said to call my mother, with three exclamation marks.

I could lie and tell her there was no message, but I knew that would give my mother ammo about how the people who go to work for the police are irresponsible and disorganized and how I was wasting my talents there.

"Sorry, I didn't notice. There is a note here," I confessed.

"I don't understand why, on a day like today, I have to worry about you instead of about what's important."

"What's happened?" I panicked.

"Don't worry," she suddenly giggled. "Something good happened. Evyatar is getting married!"

"Congratulations," I said in a tired voice. I was happy for my little brother, but I was simply exhausted.

"You could sound a little happier for your brother," my mother reprimanded me.

"I really am very happy, I'm just incredibly tired. I've had an exhausting day."

"So go get a nice cup of coffee and get yourself together because there's a *Vort* [betrothal] party at the bride's parents' house."

"When?"

"In an hour."

"You're kidding me."

"Not at all."

"Since when do the groom's siblings come to a *Vort* party?" I remembered the *Vort* Shira and Ayala had. Only the couple and the parents participated in the occasion where the couple usually introduce the parents to each other and they discuss the dowry each one will receive. "I thought only you were supposed to meet the bride's parents."

"We met with them yesterday. Lovely people. Real salt of the earth," she said, satisfied. "It's customary for them to have a small party right after the meeting with the parents and invite the close relatives and some good friends."

"And that's how they invited you? At a moment's notice?"

"Yes, you know how it is. You don't talk about it until everything's settled between the parents, to avoid the evil eye."

"Just like the Middle Ages," I blurted out.

"Hadasi!" my mother protested. "Listen to yourself!"

"Come on, Mom… really, what's this 'evil eye' nonsense?"

"I'm sorry we're not all as enlightened as you."

"Okay, okay, this is no time to fight."

"You're right." My mother returned to her pleased voice.

"Do I have to come?" I tried my luck. "My head's exploding."

"Take a pill and come, it won't be for long. We'll have a toast and some nice cake and go home." She tried to lure me with food. "Don't you want to meet your new sister-in-law? Her parents? Her brothers and sisters?"

Actually, I wasn't anxious to, but I knew that was the wrong answer.

"Yes, of course," I lied.

"Good." My mother rejoiced and dictated the address of the bride's parents' house in Tel-Aviv's old north.

Evyatar, my little brother, was born when Shira was seven-and-a-half years old, I was six and Ayala was a year-and-a-half. Allegedly, my parents kept it consistent and had another child a year-and-a-half apart, "because that way the child grows up with a friend," as my mother says. (By the way, her theory only proved successful with Shira and I. Ayala and Evyatar never got along). Actually, I always had the feeling that my parents just wanted a boy, and after Ayala was born they tried their luck again.

Evyatar never got any privileges for being the youngest and

the only boy. He helped clean the house like all of us, washed dishes and cleared the table. The only thing he didn't do was cook, but I almost never helped my mother cook, either. Besides being the only male, Evyatar stood out from all of us because of his looks.

Ever since I can remember, that boy turned heads. He had a light lick of hair and two huge almond eyes that could melt any human with one long gaze. Evyatar never had a single moment in his life when he looked bad. He never had pimples; he was never too skinny or fat. In fact, he even went through adolescence looking amazingly handsome.

Toward the end of high school, he began to grow some muscles. He wanted to be a paratrooper and began working out more seriously. I don't think I've ever seen a paratrooper as hunky as my brother. He was devastating. With the uniform, the beret, the hair, the eyes and the muscles, it was very hard for girls to resist him. When I moved in with Yinon, Evyatar was already in the army. He came from the base that Friday and helped me move my things from my parents' house to our new apartment. He took his shirt off and was in a white tank top and his uniform pants. I had to wipe the drool off all Israel's women as they watched him loading and unloading my stuff from the car.

After he'd finished in the army, he took off to South America and the US for a few months. I doubt he saved himself for marriage, surely not on that trip, when he was far from home and the inquiring glare of the religious community. When he returned from his travels, his *kippa* [skull cap] got smaller, as did the number of his visits to the synagogue. He started studying electronic engineering at Tel-Aviv University and I thought he was on the right path out of religion.

But at Tel-Aviv University, of all places, he met some religious guys. They started a group, to study the Gemara together after school. At some point, they all got engaged and married. Evyatar didn't seem too anxious about it at first—I think he was still enjoying the benefits his good looks awarded him. After his friends from high school and Bnei Akivah also began marrying, one after the other, he probably started getting nervous. I've no doubt my parents were also pressing him hard about it.

A single, twenty-five-year-old guy is completely normal in secular society. Even in the Religious Zionist community, it's not too old for a man, but it starts to become problematic, especially for a guy like Evyatar who had some experience in the field.

For the last two years, Evyatar had been "wedding-stressed." I thought it was insane for a twenty-five/six year old to be that anxious to find a bride. He was too young, and I secretly hoped that he would join me in the black sheep herd. My parents, on the other hand, were thrilled that Evyatar had finally got his act together.

So now, Evyatar had found his other half… eventually. As I understood from Shira, the young bride's name was Efrat, a sweet twenty-year-old from Tel-Aviv. She was still in her second year of service and her parents were, as Shira managed to point out, "filthy rich."

So, my little brother got himself a rich young chick.

I was exhausted and looked like a wet rag. I decided to go freshen up at home first. I got to Efrat's parents' house about forty-five minutes after the designated hour. Of course, my mother had already called to berate me, but she calmed down when I explained to her that I had to shower and change because I look like someone who had just finished ten hours of interrogation. That convinced her.

The Rosen family lived in a luxurious penthouse apartment in a relatively old building in the Bavli neighborhood in Tel-Aviv.

The elevator door opened straight into the apartment. I stepped in hesitantly. I recognized some familiar faces, but it was hard for me to associate myself with the large, grand living room.

Everyone's eyes turned to me when I walked in. My mother gave me her usual, "That's what you had in your closet?" look. Evyatar approached me with a gleaming smile and pulled me in Efrat's direction.

Efrat was a slim girl, with full red hair and green eyes. Her face was covered by dozens of freckles, which made her appear a bit like a child. Frankly, she was still almost a child at only twenty years old. She was pretty cute, but not the devastating beauty that I expected Evyatar to snatch up. She probably had other characteristics that attracted him. Since I knew the guy, I knew that being up to her neck in money wasn't one of them, although I was sure it made his decision easier.

"Efrati," I had never heard Evyatar speak to a girl so affectionately, "come meet Hadas, my sister." Efrat held her hand out and I shook it.

"Nice to meet you," I said.

"Nice to meet you too," she said, excited. "Evyatar told me so much about you."

"I hope only good things."

"Of course," she giggled. She had a cute laugh. I started to perceive what Evyatar saw in her.

My mother was nearby, talking to Efrat's mother. She stopped their conversation and approached me along with Efrat's mother.

"Geula," she said in a grand tone, "meet Hadas, our second daughter."

"Nice to meet you," I said and shook her hand.

"Nice to meet you," she smiled. "Help yourself to some food." She pointed to a table that was packed with refreshments. To my great joy, the Rosen family hadn't stopped at coffee and cake. As usual, I was starving.

"Our Hadas is a police officer." For a moment, I thought I heard pride in my mother's voice. "She's actually a lawyer, an exceptional one at that," I realized I had something to wait for, "but she decided to make a career change."

"Very nice." Geula smiled politely.

"At this very moment, Hadas is investigating the Danilowitz family case, you know, the guy who killed his wife and kids in Givaat Shmuel a couple of weeks ago." Again, I tried to guess if she was proud of me or just stating a fact.

"Wow," Geula was impressed. "What a shocking story, it must be difficult."

"Yeah," I blurted out and looked longingly at the refreshments table.

"There are rumors going around now that it was a killer from outside the family, maybe their neighbor." She gave me an inquiring look. I tried to understand if she really expected me to answer her question.

I didn't reply and she asked curiously. "Well…is it true?"

"I'm really not at liberty to discuss this investigation." I looked at my mother and Evyatar, hoping they would come to my rescue, but they were silent.

"Oh!" Geula smiled like a satisfied confidant. "So, it's true!"

I smiled to her. I assumed she understood my smile as agreement with her statement. I really can't control other people's thoughts and conclusions and I decided to retire to the buffet.

"I'm starving," I said. "I've hardly eaten anything since this morning."

She grabbed me by the hand and yanked me toward the food. "You should try the mini quiches, especially the sweet potato one." She handed me a plate. "This is from an excellent caterer, they do everything in these cute little bites." The buffet looked delicious.

I filled up a plate and sat down in a corner.

A few minutes later Shira joined me. "What's up?" she asked while she gave me a hug and a kiss on the cheek.

"Excellent," I said with my mouth full.

"This food's amazing," she said and snatched a tiny mushroom quiche off my plate.

"Totally," I nodded, still chewing.

"Our little brother did good," she said, and winked.

"Really good."

"You're super nice today," she said sarcastically.

I rolled my eyes. I couldn't deal with this right now. "I'm just tired."

"Say, are those rumors about Yigal true?" She opened her eyes wide with curiosity.

I rolled my eyes again and she realized the question was inappropriate. "Sorry, sorry." She put her hands up in surrender. "I didn't mean to upset you."

"Where's Ayala?" I changed the subject.

"She's not coming."

"What?" My jaw dropped in amazement and a small piece of quiche fell straight from my mouth onto the lacquered marble floor. I picked it up and shoved it into a paper napkin. "How come Ayala didn't come, but I had to come here half dead?"

"Ayala wasn't feeling well. She had a stomach ache."

"I had a headache, but Mom didn't let me off the hook," I whined.

"When you're pregnant, you can get a pass like that."

"Very funny." I didn't even smile.

"So what do you say about our new sister-in-law?" she inquired.

"She seems nice. What do you know about the family?"

"Besides the fact that they're loaded?"

"Besides that." I smiled.

"Not too much. The father's a businessman. He owns several companies. That's where the money's from. I've no idea what her mother does—I thinks she owns a clothing store. She seems like a serious character. I think our Evyatar is going to hear from her." I smiled and nodded. "She has a brother and a sister, both older than her, both married with children."

"Are they religious?" I asked.

"I think they're like Mom and Dad. They observe, but not fanatically."

"Good."

"I don't think they observe *Negiaa*—I saw Evyatar touch her in their presence."

"What? Do you think they've already done it?"

"Are you serious?" she looked at me, stunned. "Efrat's a religious girl from a good home. She's also only twenty years old. I'll bet my head that she's a virgin."

"So what's with the *Negiaa*?"

She opened her eyes wide. "As if we didn't go to school. The fact that they don't observe *Negiaa* means they don't have a problem holding hands or giving one another a friendly hug. Maybe even a kiss, tops, but nothing beyond that."

Moshe approached us. "Shira, you have to meet Efrat's brother, I told you he looked familiar. It turns out he was in the battalion right after me." Shira left me alone and followed her husband.

I watched Evyatar and Efrat. They stood in the middle of the living room, smiling in every direction. They had already known one another for six months, and it would be a few more months before they got married. That meant they would have known each other for almost a year when they married. It may not be long, but it's not unusual even in secular society.

But, unlike secular couples, they would only know one another, in the biblical sense, on their wedding night. Or the night after, if they spent their first night counting checks, like most couples.

I believed, or wanted to believe, that Evyatar was a guy with a normal libido. I also hoped Efrat would be compatible. But how could they know that for sure if they were going to marry and start a home together without getting to know one another sexually?

If Dina had had a bit more sexual experience and hadn't gotten married a virgin, she wouldn't have married Yigal, a man who didn't desire her and didn't satisfy her. I had no doubt that, for most couples, desire and passion decline with time, but the basis of it existed for everyone. Even if, years later, the fire goes out of it, it was there once. How could a couple that marries with no experience know if this essential part of a relationship, this basic ingredient, even existed?

Did the end justify the means, when the goal was to build a home, have kids and be like everybody else? That kind of pressure existed in secular society too—to get married and have kids, maybe at a later age, but the pressure did still exist. Among secular society, there were those who settled, who just got married so they didn't miss the train—not for love, and sometimes without passion.

The divorce rate among secular couples was higher than for the religious population. Maybe the religious formula was the right one? Statistically, it worked out better for them.

Or maybe religious society was less open to accepting a divorced couple. Dina had spent years living in an emotional prison; almost twenty years with a man who didn't love or desire her, and she did nothing about it because she thought it was like that for everyone.

And the truth was, everyone's the same. None of us invented the wheel.

Most of us wanted family and friends.

Most of us wanted children.

For most couples, desire did wear off with the years.

Dina just got dealt a bad hand.

Because Yigal really wasn't like everybody else.

CHAPTER 17

Wednesday, 6.3.2009

Yigal cracked after two days.

On Wednesday morning, he returned from Abu-Cabir to the station for another day of interrogation. Of course, we could have left him in the station for holding, like other people detained for interrogation, but Alon thought another night in Abu-Cabir would encourage him to start talking.

He looked terrible: unshaven, eyes red from tears, and dark circles around them from lack of sleep. He wore the blue detainee uniform that Abu-Cabir gives to anyone whose relatives don't provide a change of clothes. Usually, only homeless people get the dubious honor of wearing the detainee uniform. Yigal's family hadn't come to visit him and after two days in the same clothes, he showered and wore what he was given.

Against my will, I felt sorry for him. He seemed so defeated and miserable that for a moment his horrible acts were forgotten from my heart.

"Didn't anyone bring you fresh clothes from home?" I asked him.

He shook his head, careful not to speak lest the tears burst from his eyes.

"Do you want me to arrange for someone to bring you some of your own clothes?" I asked.

He thought for a moment and said, almost in a whisper. "If possible."

I left the interrogation room. I had a feeling that Yigal was on the edge and needed a little nudge. I decided not to start the interrogation at all, not to throw accusations and questions at him – to come in peace, as they say. I called Dina. She sounded devastated. In addition to the impossibility of handling the truth about her husband, she had to deal with the rumor mill surrounding his arrest. I asked her why she hasn't visited her husband and told her he had to wear the detainee uniform.

"Good," she muttered. "Let him pay the price."

I told her that Yigal had said nothing for two days and that if she really wanted him to pay, maybe she could help us to get Yigal talking.

It was difficult for her. On the one hand she had the basic need to protect and stand by her husband and the father of her daughters, but on the other hand, she was hurt by him: he had lied to her for years and done horrible things behind her back. She wanted to do the right thing.

A short while after I spoke to her, she arrived at the station with a small bag of clothes and toiletries for Yigal. While one of the officers went through the bag's contents, I took them into the room where the detainees usually meet with their lawyers for privacy.

They were in the room for about an hour. Dina came out puffy with tears. Yigal didn't look any better. He was a mess, too. We transferred him to the holding cell to let him calm down.

At noon, I went to the holding cell to see how he was doing.

"Hadas?" he said.

"Yes?"

"I want to talk."

I set up the recording equipment in the interrogation room. I didn't want anything to go wrong. Yigal sat and watched me in silence.

After confirming his personal information for protocol, I asked, "Yes, Yigal, what would you like to say?"

He didn't speak, arranged his thoughts and then said in a broken voice, "I'm sorry, I'm so sorry." He broke into tears. "I couldn't control myself."

"What did you do, Yigal?" I asked gently.

"But I didn't kill anyone, you have to believe me. I didn't even know it was him."

"Slow down, Yigal," I tried to calm him. "Who is he?"

"Meir Danilowitz, I really didn't know it was him."

"Didn't know what?"

"I didn't know he was the person blackmailing me."

"What do you mean?"

"I always got anonymous letters and sent cash to an unnamed postbox in Tel-Aviv."

"Can you please start at the beginning? How did the extortion begin?"

"Last summer, if I remember correctly, it was in July. I got a brown envelope at work. It said, Personal For Yigal, so no one opened it. When I opened it, my heart sank. It was pictures of me in an embarrassing situation."

"What was in the pictures?"

"Me coming out of the bushes." Meir had, apparently, printed out screenshots from the video he had captured.

"And what's the problem with that?" I played dumb.

"A boy had come out with me…" he looked at me with a meaningful gaze.

I decided to let this go. We would get there eventually. "Was there also a letter?"

"Yes."

"What did it say?" I had to keep him talking.

"It said they were pictures from a video that had no two ways about it and that if I didn't want it to get to the police, I had to place fifty thousand shekels in his postbox."

"And did you?"

Yigal rolled his eyes. "You can understand that... I didn't sleep at night, I didn't know if he was bluffing, if he really had a video, what was in the video? I had nowhere to turn. He didn't leave a name or phone number, I had no one to barter with. I realized that if I didn't pay, I was in trouble, but I didn't want him to think that I was a bottomless pit, so I sent only twenty thousand and told him that's what I had."

"Did the blackmail continue? How much money did he ask for?"

"Yes. Of course it continued. I got several more of these letters and each time I only sent a portion of the money. Overall, to my estimation, he asked for almost half a million shekels and I sent about two hundred thousand. The last two times, I added a letter to the money saying that I couldn't handle it and I didn't have enough money."

"But the extortion went on."

"Right." He nodded woefully, like he was a helpless victim.

"And you didn't think of a way to avoid it?"

"Of course...I spent the last few months trying to find another workplace where I could relocate somewhere."

"And did you find one?" I knew the answer to that.

"Yes, but what good will it do me now..."

"When did you realize you were connected to Meir Danilowitz?"

"Honestly?"

"Nothing but the truth."

"I had a little sting in my heart the morning Meir killed them all and committed suicide. It just seemed strange to me that this horrible story took place in my neighborhood, of all places. I knew it was someone close to me all along."

"How come?"

"The photos were taken in our neighborhood. Whoever took them knew me, that was clear to me."

"Did you know Meir?"

"Very superficially."

"So, after the murder, you thought he was your blackmailer?"

"I had a feeling, but I wasn't sure. When you came to arrest me this week, I was certain."

"Why?"

"Because you were on to me two weeks after the murder."

"Yigal," I stopped for a second, wanting to sound calm. "On to what?"

"You know…" he looked down.

"The pictures? The videos?"

"Yes."

"Is that why you got so defensive?"

He shrugged. It was clear to me that he was hiding much more than we had found.

"We found Meir's video," I told him.

He lifted his gaze and bit his lips; we both knew the videos were only the beginning.

"And what's in it?"

"Enough to convict you of statutory rape," I lied. The video wasn't clear enough.

Tears covered his cheeks once again.

"Who's the boy in the video?" I asked carefully. With the boy's testimony, we could get a solid indictment.

"Tomer Aharonovitz."

"How do you know him?"

"From synagogue. I think he was also with my little girl in kindergarten."

I thought for a moment. "So he's nine years old?"

Yigal nodded.

"And if the video was shot a year ago…" I didn't go on. Yigal looked down.

I had to stop for a moment. It was difficult for me.

"Yigal." He raised only his eyes and looked at me in misery. "What did you do to Tomer Aharonovitz that you were so frightened of?"

He bit his lips again, closed his eyes and shook his head. "I couldn't help myself. I really had no control."

"What did you do?" I asked again.

"He helped me come." He opened his eyes. He had a terrified look.

"How?"

"You know..."

"No, I don't know."

"I pulled down my pants and told him I had a magic trick..." Yigal was a well-known magician in the neighborhood.

"And then?" I needed him to say the words.

"And then he jerked me off," he said very fast.

"Did you reach a climax?"

He nodded.

"I need you to say it."

"Yes, I reached climax."

"And how did the boy react?"

"Like they all do..." He stopped himself for a moment, realizing he had just dug himself deeper.

"How do they all react?" I asked with a quivering voice, understanding how big this story was.

"First they're curious, and then they get scared."

"Why?"

"When I climaxed, it was a little difficult for me to control myself and it alarmed him."

"Were there any more kids?"

He looked at me. I sensed he wanted to talk, but didn't know how to begin. He wanted to put an end to years of living a lie.

"I was born this way," he said eventually. "I've never been attracted to women, and not adult males either, just boys."

"How did it begin?"

"When all my friends in the Yeshiva high school started talking about girls, I sensed that something was different about me. I had no interest in the opposite sex whatsoever. For some time, I thought I was a homosexual because there was someone two grades below me that I had a crush on. I fantasized about him nonstop. Now I know that the reason he aroused me like that was because he was very boyish. He had an almost childlike appearance. At fifteen, he looked like an eleven-year-old. He, unlike me, was a homosexual. When I was in twelfth grade and he was in tenth, we became a couple. I have no way to describe how wonderful those months were for me. It was the most beautiful time of my life—an exciting time full of experiences."

"And then what happened?"

"I went into the army and didn't see him so much. During that time he matured, he had a growth spurt. He got taller, got hair on his body, and when I saw him naked after we hadn't slept together in months, I was really repulsed. I missed the smooth, boyish body he had. At first, I thought I was just over him, but I soon realized I was simply attracted to children. When I was on leave, my neighbor, who was a teacher in elementary school, volunteered me to be a security escort for a class of fourth-grade boys from my settlement."

"What settlement?"

"I'm originally from Elkana. Do you know it?"

"Near Shaarei Tikva, isn't it?" My mother's sister lived in Shaarei Tikva.

He seemed surprised at my familiarity with settlements across the green line and continued. "One day, there was a hike in the morning, and in the afternoon, they went to an amusement park that also had swimming pools. The boys took off their clothes and played in the water and I was aroused like I had never been in my life. I felt amazing and horrified all at the same time. For years, I'd felt horrible with being a homosexual, and now, when I realized that I was actually a full-blown pedophile, I prayed to be just a homosexual."

"And did you do anything?"

"On that trip?"

"Yes."

"No, of course not. I was paralyzed with fear."

"But at some point, did you?"

He looked down. "Yes," he whispered.

"I didn't hear you."

"Yes." He lifted his eyes. "After that trip, I volunteered to stay on the army base as many weekends as I could. I didn't want to go home. I didn't want to be near children and there were no children on the base. Eventually, I finished in the army and I had to see children. Each time I saw a child, I became paralyzed with fear, I didn't know how I would react—I was afraid of myself. Everybody thought I was an introverted person, but, actually, I imprisoned myself at home. I didn't want to face my demons. Things were different then—there was no internet. On the one hand, I didn't know who and what I was, and on the other hand, there was no available pornography for people like me. I'd get aroused by children's magazines and all sorts of pictures I'd find."

"What sort of pictures?"

"Just pictures of kids, nothing that would cause suspicion."

"Why didn't you seek therapy?"

"I didn't know who I could turn to. I was afraid I'd immediately be arrested and thrown into jail or an insane asylum."

"Why did you get married? Didn't you feel like you were misleading Dina?"

"I wanted to be normal so much… for years I felt like I didn't belong to the human race and I thought that if I started a family, then my life would be much simpler, that I'd be busy with routine life. It was very hard for me to approach girls; most of them immediately sensed that something wasn't right with me. Even if I managed to get through the first two or three dates, I couldn't fake enthusiasm, which is necessary at the beginning of a relationship."

"So how did you manage to do it with Dina?"

"When I met Dina, I was already twenty-four and she was barely twenty. She was very young and inexperienced and I felt as if I was a hundred. I think Dina liked me from the start. She was looking for someone quiet, and I practically took a vow of silence. Dina didn't give up on me. She misinterpreted my lack of enthusiasm that distanced other girls so much."

"How could you tie your fate with a girl you didn't even love?"

"I've no idea how many people marry out of love. I can tell you, I'm certain that a considerable number of couples don't marry out of love. Apart from the sexual issue, Dina and I were a great match. We had a good life together. I don't know what you'd call it, love… concern, but I definitely care very much about that woman."

"Weren't you afraid you'd become part of an incest situation?"

He took a deep breath and exhaled loudly. "If you only knew how stressed I was about the pregnancy! I prayed… I just prayed day and night that I would have girls."

"Why?"

"I've never been attracted to girls—not women, and not girls. I was afraid that if I had a little boy in the house, I wouldn't be able to contain myself."

"You have three girls."

"Thank God." Tears came to his eyes again.

"Why? It sounds like you managed to control yourself for years. Did you do anything during that time?"

"Nothing. I never harmed a child."

"And what happened then?"

"The internet—that's what happened. I know it's very superficial to blame the internet for something that was in me, but until I was exposed to child pornography online, I didn't truly release my most secret desires."

"How exactly did the internet free you?"

"Like most people—especially men—who started surfing the net, I immediately looked for pornography. As time went on, the internet became more open and it was easier to find what you were looking for. At first, it was hard to find child porn. I'd make do with pictures and homosexual movies where one of the actors is very young or looks very young. Later, I got pictures and movies of children."

"How did you feel downloading these movies?"

"I can't say I felt great, but I'd be lying if I told you I felt bad. First of all, I wasn't the one who shot these films."

"You didn't feel like an accomplice?"

"No, quite the contrary. The fact that there's so much material and so many views of it encouraged me. For the first time in years, I felt like I wasn't alone in the world—that there were other people who felt like me. The internet encouraged me in that sense. I sometimes went on legitimate gay and straight portals because I was interested to see what other people were watching, and I discovered that movies where one or both of the participants looks like a young boy or girl—I mean, much younger than their real age—were the most watched. I think there's a lot of hypocrisy about it. People denounce pedophilia, but are curious about it."

"And at some point, did you move on from passively watching to actively playing it out?"

"Yes." He answered plainly.

"Will you elaborate on that?"

"The movies I watched online really aroused me. I walked around in a daze. I thought about children all of the time. I felt like I had no life, that my perversion was controlling me. And then I went on a long weekend in Prague with Dina. It was about six months before Noga, our youngest, was born. I was far from home—I felt like I couldn't take it anymore, and if I was going to succumb to the urge, I might as well do it somewhere where it would be harder to find me out. I think I knew I was going to do it as soon as we got on the plane. I was lucky. Dina wasn't feeling well and I had quite a bit of time to walk around alone. My father's father was from Czechoslovakia. All of his family, including a wife and three kids, perished in the Holocaust, so I felt like this was my small revenge."

I was amazed at how Yigal managed to morally justify his horrible actions.

"Anyway, in one of my wanders through the city I passed by a playground. I managed to lure one of the kids there with candy and an electronic game. It was a boy of about eight."

"How did he even understand you?"

"I told you, my grandfather was from there, I knew a bit of Czech from home. I managed to get him to come behind the bushes with me."

"And what did you do?"

"I… raped him." He said in a strangled voice.

"And how did you feel?"

"Amazing… since that romance in twelfth grade, I hadn't experienced that kind of sexual release."

"And didn't you feel for the boy?"

"I managed to distance myself from it, especially because he was Czech and I felt like it was revenge."

"And what happened after this? Did you continue to rape kids?"

He started crying. He couldn't calm down.

After a long while he sobbed and said, "I couldn't do anything else, it was stronger than me."

CHAPTER 18

Thursday, 6.4.2009

Yigal's confession lasted hours. He began it on Wednesday afternoon and finished the next day. A significant part of the time, he was crying and trying to excuse his acts with the fact that his tendency was stronger than him and he had no real control over his actions. He compared himself to homosexuals a number of times, in the sense that they're born with that sexual tendency, like him.

I didn't argue with him. I didn't even try to explain to him that his inherent tendency was hurting children and was missing the element of consent that exists in sexual relations between same sex adults. I didn't tell him that, although he was born with this trait, like any innate tendency that harms a person and his surroundings, he should have gotten treatment and not let it control his life.

After the eventful visit to Czechoslovakia, Yigal began performing indecent acts on children. It started out as small, covert masturbation in playgrounds, moved on to using kids to help him reach climax through masturbation and oral sex, and ended at fully sodomizing children. In the beginning of his life as an active pedophile, he was overcome with guilt and decided to give back to the community to pay for his actions. He began volunteering in children's oncology units as a clown and magician.

What began as a volunteer activity, mostly to ease his conscience, became a paid hobby when he began receiving invitations to entertain at birthday parties. What started off as a salve to ease his conscience quickly became an excellent platform for his perversion. The kids in the neighborhood knew and trusted him.

In those hours, Yigal told me of about twenty-five boys who fell victim to his acts in the past nine years. Some of them were now legally adults. He liked them at about nine years old, although there were a few slightly older boys and even some younger ones. A substantial number of the boys were from his neighborhood and they were repeat victims. Others were random, one-time victims. Horridly, two of the children from the oncology unit were also on the list of victims.

He remembered or knew only some of the children's names, but chillingly, remembered his actions. He testified that he only performed indecent acts on most of the children. Four children, who were repeat victims of his, he sodomized on a routine basis. Since he was experienced in the world of children, he could recognize those who would keep his secret. He selected his victims carefully, buying their trust with gifts and flattery, and even threats.

His testimony was enough to serve an indictment, but we knew that in order to get to a conviction, we would have to get to the victims as well. After Yigal was through with his confession, three teams of youth investigators accompanied by social workers began talking to the victims.

I joined the first team that went to the Katz family in Givaat Shmuel. Their sixteen-year-old son, Boaz, had been a victim of Yigal about six years earlier. Boaz was one of the four kids who were routine victims.

We arrived at the Katz home in the early afternoon. Boaz, a

tenth grade student in the Ramat Gan Yeshiva high school, had not yet come home. Boaz's two younger siblings, boy and girl twins, nine-years-old, were playing a video game when we knocked on their door and turned their world upside down.

Nava Katz opened the door and was shocked to face two police officers and a social worker. After we calmed her by saying that everything was okay and there had not been an accident, we asked to speak to her in private.

Asaf, the youth investigator, and Tzila, the social worker, waited in the living room while Nava and I went into Boaz's room. At first, she had no idea why we had entered her house and life like this. She sat tall and rigid across from me on Boaz's sofa bed, but within seconds lost control of her body, which folded as if I had punched her.

The truth is, she was probably hit much harder than a punch.

I don't, and probably never will, have children, but I can't imagine a pain more terrible than that when a parent discovers their own child has experienced such horrible abuse. A few minutes earlier, Nava Katz had four allegedly happy children, and suddenly she discovered her second child, so introverted and beloved, was the victim of a dangerous pedophile. After crying for a long while, she looked at me with an angry, red glare and demanded to know who this horrible monster was.

I explained to her that right now I couldn't disclose his name and identity, but later on in the investigation his identity would probably be revealed. We went to the living room. Nava drank some water and calmed down. Maybe she was hoping this was all a mistake and that her son was nobody's victim. She sat between the twins and caressed their heads.

Boaz, a slim and handsome young man, a thin mustache over his upper lip, came home about forty-five minutes after we had arrived. He was no longer attractive to Yigal, who admitted he had stopped contacting Boaz about four years earlier. The abuse had gone on for two years.

He stood in the living room, a large backpack on his shoulders, looking bewildered at Tzila, Asaf and me.

His mother got up slowly from the couch, went to him, helped him take the backpack off his back and told him almost in a whisper that there were police officers here who wanted to talk to him.

Tzila and Asaf went into Boaz's room with him, while Nava and I waited anxiously in the living room.

A few moments later, we heard heart-wrenching crying. It was Boaz. Nava immediately jumped to her feet and I stood up beside her, keeping her from going into the room. She put her head on my shoulder and cried hysterically.

Her life had been changed forever in that moment.

Boaz's interrogation was relatively simple and easy. Although he was among the kids who'd experienced more serious abuse, he was already relatively mature and easier to question. He was also not an active victim of Yigal's, so his trauma wasn't as recent and painful as in the case of younger boys who were interrogated.

All of the children we spoke to were brought to the police station and all of them identified Yigal with certainty as the one who had his way with them. At first, we didn't disclose Yigal's identity. Even the outraged parents, who wanted to know his identity, were kept in the dark. We wanted a clean indictment, and releasing Yigal's name and picture before a standard line-up could hurt the chances of conviction. The parents and children were requested not tell anyone the story of the abuse. Some of them realized this was a serial rapist. None of them had any intention of exposing any of it. The wounds were far too personal and painful.

CHAPTER 19

Tuesday, 6.9.2009

Five days later, all the boys Yigal remembered and was able to name, most of them residents of Givaat Shmuel, had been interrogated, and had identified Yigal. We had four rape victims and another ten victims of repeated or one-time sexual abuse. According to Yigal, there were other boys, whose names he didn't recall or know.

At noon, we held a press conference, the objective of which was to release Yigal's identity in order to reach more children. This was not necessarily for the indictment, but so they could then be helped to get over their trauma, and those around them could be made aware that they had gone through such experiences. We knew we would have no choice but to also expose Meir's extortion. Yigal and Meir lived near one another, so it would be too strange a coincidence if, three weeks after Meir killed his entire family and committed suicide, we revealed that another resident of that same neighborhood was a serial sex offender.

This was my first press conference. I decided to play it safe and wore my uniform. That way, my mother wouldn't have anything to say about my outfit. The press room was packed.

They knew they were finally going to get some answers about the Danilowitz case and what their neighbor had to do with the case. They didn't imagine this was only part of what I would be telling them.

I sat in front of the cameras and the dozens of reporters crammed into the small hall. The station's media officer quieted everyone down.

Alon, who was standing beside me, approached the microphones and said that in recent days the Danilowitz family murder case has taken a turn. He presented me and called me to the mic.

I got up from my seat. I was shaking all over, excited by the occasion and what I was about to say.

"Hello everyone," I said in a slightly hoarse voice. I cleared my throat and went on. "Three weeks ago, we found the bodies of the Danilowitz family: Meir, Hanni and their three small children, Ariel, Galit and Noa, shot in their apartment in Givaat Shmuel. All the immediate suspicions led us to the unequivocal conclusion that Meir killed the other family members and then took his own life. The investigation of the case focused on ruling out the possibility of an external killer, and to discover as well as we could, the motive for this extreme act.

"During the investigation, we discovered that the couple was facing financial hardship, which led to Mr. Danilowitz's desperate act. As most of you already know, last week we arrested another resident of the neighborhood, Mr. Yigal Einav. I want to clarify that Mr. Einav has no connection to the horrid murder and that all signs still point to the fact that Mr. Danilowitz is the one who took the lives of his family, and then his own. During our investigation we discovered that due to severe financial problems, Mr. Danilowitz began extorting Mr. Einav, after discovering that he is a sex offender."

I stopped and looked at the crowd of reporters. They were looking at me with shocked gazes.

"This week, Mr. Einav has been interrogated and has admitted his actions. According to his confession, he has raped and performed indecent acts on over twenty children, aged nine to twelve, in the last nine years. Ten of these children have been questioned and have identified the suspect this week."

There was whispering among the crowd of reporters and the media officer had to quiet them down so I could finish.

"In order for us to be able to reach as many of his victims as possible, we have decided to reveal the story and the suspect's identity. In the next few days, psychologists and social workers will visit schools in the appropriate residential areas. The police and social services will do everything in their power to help the victims and their families overcome this trauma."

I nodded in the media officer's direction and the moment he turned to face the crowd of reporters, the room was filled with loud yelling. There were a lot of questions and everyone wanted their voice heard.

I had dropped an atom bomb.

When the press conference was over, I returned to my office and my cellphone rang.

It was Shira.

"What's up?" I asked, trying to sound nonchalant although I still felt the adrenaline pumping through my veins.

"What's up? What's up, she asks me…"

"So, what's up?"

"Apart from the fact that I discovered there was a dangerous pedophile in our neighborhood and that my *own sister* exposed him, everything's fine."

"How was I?" I smiled to myself.

"You were excellent! At first I could see you were very nervous, but all in all, you were pretty cool."

"And what do you say about what we put out today?"

"First of all, good job. I'm really proud of you, you achieved a big thing."

"Thanks," I said bashfully.

"And besides that, this whole story is a giant shock. About Meir and Hanni – there was talk about financial troubles almost from the start, but, actually, you didn't say much about it at the press conference. Everyone in the neighborhood knows Meir's parents are pretty well off, so there was talk about all sorts of entanglements with shady businesses and the black market. Is that true?"

"Shira, as much as I love you, you have to understand that you can't know more than what it says in the paper, but I would also recommend that you don't believe everything that the paper says."

"Okay," I could sense her smile. "But the amazing story is Yigal. It's just horrible."

"Did you know him?"

"Sure. I mean, not well, but I knew him from the neighborhood, from the synagogue. I was even at a birthday party he performed at."

"And what did he seem like to you?"

"Actually, I never gave him more than two seconds of thought. He wasn't a bad clown, I can tell you. That's just the thing; he seemed so ordinary, so normal. You can just never know what's going on with people behind closed doors."

"His wife didn't even know," I said and immediately regretted it. It wasn't really a secret detail of the investigation, but it's not exactly something we publicized.

"Wow." She was amazed.

"But don't tell," I immediately warned her and knew she was happy with the fact she was so close to the information database.

"Of course."

"What's the reaction in Givaat Shmuel?" I was curious.

"No idea. I haven't left the house today yet. I'm going to the playground soon, I'll let you know."

She called me that afternoon to fill me in. Givaat Shmuel was in a flurry. They were in a flurry anyway after the Danilowitz murders, but things were starting to settle down before I threw a tornado into the middle of their neighborhood.

People were starting to get scared. Suspicious. There were no kids in the playgrounds. Fingers were being pointed in every direction, but mostly at Meir, who knew, but hadn't filed a complaint.

Suddenly, there were a lot of good souls who sensed something was wrong with Yigal, that he seemed too strange, even a little creepy. Mothers swore that Yigal offered to perform at their birthday parties for free and they passed it up because they were a little scared of him. Every child who missed school was suspected as one of his victims. Harsh criticisms were also fired at the parents of the victims. "How could they not know?" "How did they fail to notice?" "Why didn't they look after and educate their children?"

The news on TV dedicated half of their airtime to the extortion story that led to the discovery of the dangerous criminal. They interviewed Yigal's neighbors, his coworkers. Most of them described a nice, gentle person, while some admitted they sensed something wasn't right about him.

After describing the horrors, they moved on to magazine stories that are prepared ahead of time for these sorts of cases, with psychologists explaining to parents how to recognize a child who's being abused and a review of previous convicted serial sex offenders.

I sat in front of the television, exhausted. I stared at the newscasters fervently discussing the story I had been investigating so intensively over the last few days. I remembered what Yigal told me himself: that there was a lot of hypocrisy about this issue, and that some of the curiosity surrounding the matter is not so innocent.

I wondered to myself if he was right.

CHAPTER 20

Wednesday, 6.10.2009

The ringing of my cell phone woke me up. I was in front of the TV, which was now showing the morning show. It was discussing, of course, pedophilia. I'd fallen asleep in my uniform in front of the TV in the living room.

It was 9:00am. It was my mother on the line.

Although she was sure that I always screen her calls, I hardly ever do so. I decided to stray from my norm and ignore her call. If she was so certain I always blew off her calls, maybe it was time to justify the bad reputation she'd given me.

I quickly showered and put on the first thing I managed to fish out of the dryer. I was already at the door when Tsumi reminded me that he also has a morning routine. I had a deal with that dog: when I was in a rush he tried to make do with just a pee, but this time he wasn't giving in. He was probably mad at me because I'd neglected him during the last few days. From his usual pee point, he yanked me from tree to tree, searching for the perfect place to lay down his fragrant package.

We eventually reached Bugrashov, so I got a coffee at a small coffee shop I had always passed without checking it out.

"You look familiar." The guy making my coffee tried to make conversation.

"You must be mistaking me for somebody else." I shrugged and shot an angry glare at Tsumi, who was standing outside, tied to the rail and barking.

"Here you go." He handed me the cup of coffee.

"May I?" I tugged at the rolled up newspaper by the cash register.

"Yeah, sure," he smiled. The paper rolled open and I was alarmed to see my face gracing the front page.

"Ha!" he said, surprised "I told you you look familiar! You're the police officer who found that pedophile."

I smiled with exaggerated humility and went out to Tsumi, who was now tangled up in his leash. I sat at one of the tables and stared, dumbfounded, at my picture. I thought I must be the least photogenic person in the world. Why couldn't they have Photoshopped it, for God's sake? Half of the paper was devoted to pedophilia and Yigal.

My cell rang. My mother again. This time I answered. As I thought, she had a lot to say about what was in the paper, especially my photo.

"I don't get it," I said after she was done with her tirade.

"What?" she asked.

"The almost obsessive way this story is being covered."

"But, of course everyone's going to talk about it. It's the biggest news."

"I think the victims would appreciate being left alone. And when I say victims, I'm not only referring to the kids Yigal attacked."

"Who else?" She was curious.

"Yigal's wife and daughters are victims, Meir's family were indirect victims. Meir, and especially Yigal, are presented as monsters, but their relatives had nothing to do with what they did, though it doesn't stop everyone from judging them."

"You're a good soul," she said, and I could hear that she was proud of me.

In the office, a pile of paperwork was waiting for me—all the testimonies collected during the investigation, which I now had to work up into an indictment. Alon buzzed and asked me to come to his room.

He sat at ease in his chair, resting his head on his hands. His table was littered with case files, but it was clear that he was finally satisfied. A big case, covered widely in the media, had reached its end and the indictment would be strong.

"Very nice, Levinger."

I smiled with overt humility.

"I'm pleased with you. Not just me, frankly, the bosses from upstairs are happy too."

"Good."

"Sit down, sit." He let go of his head and pointed to the chair next to him. "Would you like something to drink?"

"No, thank you."

He buzzed Riki's station. "Strong, black, with ten grains of sugar," he dictated his usual request. He was in a good mood.

"I understand that since we came out with the story at the press conference yesterday, there have been quite a few calls."

"Yes," I nodded, "mostly from concerned parents. I assume that most of them are just paranoid, but everyone who turns to us will be referred to youth investigators and social services."

"And what about the Danilowitz family? Did you get a chance to talk to the families?"

"Yesterday I spoke to Meirav, Meir's older sister."

"What did she say?"

"She was very upset. I think she was a bit angry that we didn't fill her in on the results of the investigation before the press conference."

"Did you explain to her that we don't do that?"

"It didn't do much good," I said sadly.

"You sound sad."

"Yeah, I liked her, we got on well. They're a nice family and they're going through a difficult time. They're being judged by the public for Meir's horrible actions."

"They did raise Meir, who blackmailed a sex offender

without turning him in to the police, and eventually murdered his wife and three small kids and then himself."

"I'm not justifying what he did. There's no doubt he committed horrible acts, and if he was alive today, he should have been put in jail for many, many years."

"But?" Alon was curious.

"But I think he reached a dead end and chose to end it all rather than face reality."

"What do you mean?"

"Meir and Hanni were in massive debt, mostly because of Hanni's excessive and wasteful lifestyle. From what I gathered from Iris— Hanni's friend—Meir tried to tone down her spending, but it didn't help. The debt grew and grew, and Meir couldn't control it."

"Until he found someone to extort."

"Not at all."

"What do you mean?"

"The money Meir extorted from Yigal was a drop in the ocean. It's only what kept them afloat. In fact, even with the extortion money, they were facing bankruptcy. And Yigal testified that with his two last extortion payments, he included a letter saying he couldn't pay any more."

"I thought he was a very wealthy man."

"They lived well, but he didn't have unlimited fortune. He was a salaried employee."

"And Meir was scared that his source of extortion was going to disappear."

"Maybe. Maybe he regretted blackmailing him in the first place."

"That's the problem with murder files, especially those where the killer disappears or kills himself. We'll never know all the answers."

"Right." I nodded sadly.

CHAPTER 21

Monday, 7.13.09

I eventually went to London.

I felt like I really deserved it. I was physically and mentally exhausted from the investigation and, to my great joy, I managed to buy a plane ticket before Alon found something else for me to do.

The flurry around the Danilowitz case and Yigal wound down. The newspaper headlines were occupied by new stories, children returned to the playgrounds in Givaat Shmuel, and everyone returned to their daily routines.

My family was up to their neck in preparations for Evyatar's wedding and gave me some rest.

Yinon didn't come back to me, though I hoped he would.

Everyone around me was back to normal, but I couldn't stop thinking about the case, even while I was in London. It never left my mind. Something was missing for me, a lost piece of the puzzle that left the picture incomplete.

The evidence about Meir being the killer was conclusive. Right from the start of the investigation, it was clear that was the story, with the apartment locked from the inside, the way the bodies were lying, the gun with Meir's finger prints on it lying near his body, the computer hard drive that had been erased, and the computer search for how to make a makeshift silencer from mineral wool.

We also found a motive: a financial crisis and a family rift. Meir found someone to extort, but this source didn't have enough money.

As far as the police were concerned, the file was closed and moved on to the state attorney's office. But despite everything being closed, despite the compliments showered on me, there was still something missing for me. I felt as if there was one more secret that I hadn't revealed.

My desk was a bit messier than I had left it before my trip. I skimmed over the papers and files that had been added to the original mess. A small note peeked through all the files: Call Meirav, Meir Danilowitz's sister.

"Meirav?"

"Speaking," she answered in a matter-of-fact voice.

"This is Hadas Levinger from Israel Police."

"Hello," she switched to a softer tone. "I understand you were out of the country for a while."

"Yes. I went to London, and just got back last night."

"Sounds fun. How was it?"

"It was nice. I rested, walked around, saw a couple of good plays. It was fun to get away for a while, especially from Tel-Aviv's intense weather."

"Good, I'm happy for you. You deserve it."

"Thank you."

We were quiet for a moment. Although I had called her, it was clear to me that Meirav had not wanted to ask me how London was.

"Ahh…" she sighed, "I called because I found something important." I felt my heartbeat accelerate. "I have to admit, we found it last week, but on Saturday our whole family sat together and we decided to pass on what we found to you. I'd be happy if it didn't go any further, but I know that's not going to happen."

I nodded my acceptance, not wanting to stop her flow of speech.

"You just have to believe me that we only found this a couple of days ago."

"I believe you."

"Good."

"What did you find?" I asked carefully.

"I found Meir's suicide note," she said simply, and I felt all the blood in my body flow right to my feet.

"What?" I gasped. How the hell did the Danilowitz family just now find Meir's suicide note?

"On that horrible night," Meirav explained, "Meir sat and wrote my parents a letter. He sent it to my email, because my parents don't have an email account, not an active one anyway."

"So how did you only just now get this email?"

"Meir didn't usually send me emails. I have an old Yahoo email address that I hardly use."

"And he didn't know you don't use that email account?"

"I guess not. I think I sent him something from that account not long ago, so I guess that's the address he had. In any case, I hardly open this account and when I do, it's usually full of junk. I usually delete them without even reading anything. By sheer chance, I looked through the mail this time, since we had an unpleasant situation in the office a little while ago where we deleted an important email without checking."

"Can you send me that email?"

"That's why I called."

I dictated my email address to her and waited in front of the computer impatiently. Since Meir had erased the hard disk, unfortunately, that mail had been deleted for good.

About five minutes later, I received a new message. Meirav had forwarded to me the email she received from Meir on May 18th, at two o'clock in the morning:

To my dear family,
Dad, Mom, Meirav, and Michal,

When you read this letter, I will no longer be alive. If my plans play out, my whole family will be gone, too. I am done with my life. There is no point to my life or to my family's life. I am doing all of us a favor. I have wanted to kill myself for a long while, and in the last week I have decided to take my family with me. That will save all of us the shame and hardship. I want you to know I am sorry for everything. For the rift between us, for the dismissive attitude, and mostly for what I am about to do to my children and myself. I should apologize to my father and mother-in-law as well, for taking their daughter away from them, but I admit and confess, I have no bit of sorrow or remorse about what I am about to do to Hanni.

It's almost midnight. The house is peaceful and quiet. I don't know if I'll have the courage to do what I want; I don't know if I want to find the courage or not. I just know I'm fed up with everything. I'm tired of a loveless life, a life of never-ending money chasing. You will discover after we're gone that we have nothing. Everything belongs to the bank, and even if we sold everything, we would still be in debt. I have no tiny hope that anything will change. To my regret, my "beloved" wife manages to shut her eyes and heart from our dire state and, instead of trying to help me get out of the pit we have fallen in, she's only digging it deeper and deeper.

I married out of great love, although, since the very beginning, I had a feeling it was not mutual. I gave everything for my love, and now I'm taking it all back—with interest. Every morning I get up and fantasize that today I'll have the courage to depart from this world, from this endless chase. And each day I have another sliver of hope that everything will be fine, that we'll get by somehow. About a year ago, I discovered that a guy named Yigal—whom I know from synagogue—performed an indecent act on a boy from the neighborhood. For a year, I have been holding in my heart Yigal's horrible secret, and blackmailing this horrible man for my personal purposes. There's not a day I don't tell myself, 'Today's the day I send this video to the police,' but I can't find the strength to destroy this fruitful source of income.

I'm just disgusted with myself. I'm just as bad as he is. I hoped, innocent as I was, that the extortion would prevent him from continuing with his evil deeds. I am so stupid and naïve. In my darkest dreams, I never imagined that reality would knock on my door like that, that the wheel would turn on me. A slightly frightened look from Ariel was all it took for me to understand everything. I didn't want this pervert to come to Galit's birthday, and Hanni thought it was because of the money (actually we couldn't afford a clown, but that's not why I didn't want Yigal). I shuddered at the thought of him touching my children, but that's how I discovered that he already had. I was so intent on manipulating Yigal that I couldn't miss Ariel's reaction. I've prayed with all my might that I'm wrong and misunderstood, but I understood perfectly.

Yesterday at noon, two days after the birthday party, I found the time and place and talked to Ariel. We both went down to the garden when Hanni and the girls fell asleep; I managed to get Ariel to talk. Everything started to connect. For years, we've been told that Ariel needs treatment, because he's difficult, and suddenly he calmed down. Hanni was sure she was right all along, that he just needed some time. She was so wrong. Ariel was getting treatment, but not the right kind. My beloved Ariel had to go through what no child should have to experience.

I almost killed Yigal yesterday. I took my gun and waited for him by his house. I thought I'd kill him and commit suicide, but like everything in life, that went wrong too. When he came home, just one second before I went up to him to shoot him, his two little girls came running to him. Pretty girls, dressed in blue and white with Bnei Akivah blue ties. They hugged him warmly and he was happy. As happy as I haven't been in years. I knew he deserved to die, but I couldn't do it. His daughters didn't deserve me killing their father. If I'd complained about him a year ago, how many kids would I have spared from this nightmare? Surely Ariel.

It's time to take responsibility for my actions. I admit I will be taking Hanni's life with joy. She ruined my life and our children's lives. I take the lives of my beloved children with a heavy heart, but I feel that this way I will spare them the sorrow and pain that they will have to face. Mom and Dad—I love you and ask your forgiveness once more.

Meir

Dear Reader,

I hope you had a pleasant reading experience. If you enjoyed the book, I would be very grateful if you would take another minute of your time and leave a positive review on the book's Amazon page.

I began writing Hill of Secrets in the summer of 2011. That summer, there was a very big social protest in Israel, especially in the city of Tel Aviv. Along Rothschild Boulevard, one of the most prestigious and beautiful boulevards in Tel Aviv, tents were set up by citizens protesting about the cost of living. I didn't join the protest, even though I, too, belong to that sector of unrest - the middle class - which bears the main brunt of the economic burden. Apart from the fact that the protest was of a political nature not aligned with my personal views (and that, ultimately, two of the protest organizers became members of the Knesset after the protest ended) I felt that the protesters were not able to recognize their own failures and preferred to blame their surroundings for their personal failures. I definitely think that the state should support and assist its citizens, especially those who need it, namely the elderly, children, the disabled and the sick. But healthy, young people like those who filled Rothschild Boulevard in the summer of 2011 must understand that every person is responsible for his actions and for his failures. Every person has to understand what his or her economic abilities are and adapt his lifestyle accordingly. I, for example, don't dream of buying an apartment on Rothschild Boulevard - nor does it interest me. But with hard work and a well-defined lifestyle, I'm pleased to have an apartment in a city close to Tel Aviv. I don't live a flamboyant lifestyle, and do not envy my neighbors. I only check my own bank account.

I tried to convey this message and its destructive implications in Hill of Secrets.

I invite you to visit my Facebook page (Michal Hartstein - Israeli writer) to receive updates on new posts, book deals, and, of course, keep up with new books to be published.

I hope I've intrigued you enough to read more of my books!

Yours,
Michal

ABOUT THE AUTHOR

Michal Hartstein was born in 1974 in Israel into a religious family, studied economics and accounting at the University of Tel Aviv and started a career in finance.

In 2006, after becoming a mother, she decided to change direction and began to write. For several years, she has written a popular personal blog, and in 2011 published her first book, *Confession of an Abandoned Wife*. After two years she published her second book, *Hill of Secrets*. In 2014 she participated in the Israeli Nanowrimo contest and wrote *Déjà Vu*. The book was one of the winners and was published in Israel in 2015. Her fourth book, *The Hit*, (the second book in the Hadas Levinger series) is about to be published in 2018.

Ms. Hartstein's books vividly describe the life of the Israeli middle class, focusing on middle class women.

Made in the USA
Middletown, DE
17 November 2020

24287374R00159